Christmas Bizarre

Lizz Lund

DEDICATIONS

For our beloved cockatiel, Chance Marie – she was/is Mina's cockatiel, Marie, and always will be. Her loss on the eve of Hurricane Sandy will always mark a bittersweet anniversary: just one month in our new home, amidst the destruction of homes for many friends. Oct. 29th is a biggie.

For my dad, Robert Lund Sieghardt – his loss on June 16, 2013 keeps Father's Day forever. As did his spiritual hand, guiding our "Vinnie" home that same evening. We've since convinced our fearless feline that being toothless, clawless and senile is not a smart combo in a neighborhood complete with foxes, hawks and the occasional coyote (according to a neighbor). That, and we installed a deadbolt.

And as always, for my chef husband, Mark dear – who convinces me to cope by whipping the virtual egg on my face into some kind of meringue. That, and pouring wine. Lots of wine. And for being my best friend and listening to my whine. Mwah.

ACKNOWLEDGMENTS

I'm excited about this sequel to "Kitchen Addiction!" Special thanks and mentions to friends near and far, physical and virtual, for their assistance and support. In particular, a huge shout out to John Stewart and Maggie Shetz, of Intuitive Consultants (www.IntuitiveConsultants.net) for using their gifts to locate my lost flash drive which was, at the time, the sole device containing this manuscript. I have since learned my lesson and now back-up in triplicate at home, while another six copies are stashed away with a mute Tibetan monk in the Himalayas. That, and we made sure the cat cannot "lovingly play" with the flash drive's clip string, which he fancies a mouse tail. Thanks also to my Twitter bud, @cettedrucks – your zany creation of a Manischewitz Cook-Off Contest complete with "glazed bacon wraps with shrimp" was inspirational. Really.

Much nodding of heads and pats on the back to the Facebook crowd: your earnest anticipation of this sequel propelled me forward. Thank you for your support and please know the third novel is now in final edit mode, while the fourth is in the works. Mina moves on!

Also, sincere acknowledgment to those who took time to post reviews on Amazon. Duly read, and duly noted, positive and negative. One step at a time, and I hope you consider this sequel a good step forward.

And as usual, much gratitude toward the tribe of beta readers for helping me keep it consistent: Carol Kusel, Polly Davis, Kate Achelpohl, Barbara Kurze, Margie Sieghardt, and, forever always – Mark dear.

Last, but not least, sincere thanks to my wonderful new editor, Teresa Kennedy. We've only just begun!

DISCLAIMER

This is a silly story about silly people with silly problems for readers who want a quick laugh fast. There are no metaphors, symbolism, morals or literary goals contained. English majors: keep out.

The story you are about to read is completely fictitious. All of the characters, groups and events were concocted from my own imagination and too much cold pizza for breakfast. Any similarities to actual people are completely coincidental. Some of the geographic locations referenced are actual places. Others are completely make believe. For the purposes of this story, all persons and groups herein are made up from pixie dust.

The recipes at the conclusion of this book are my own, assisted with critical guidance from my chef husband (yes, he's a real chef). If you're inclined to make them, I hope they will bring a smile to your lips as you recall the portions of the story which inspired them.

In the meantime, grab a bag of chips (unless you live in "Pee-Ay" and it's mandatory to consume pretzels), your favorite brewski and put your feet up. You're about to have some fun.

CHAPTER 1

Wednesday

"Help me!"

"What's wrong?"

"I'm desperate!"

"What's the matter?"

"I'm at my wits' end!"

I sat up like a shot. "Do you need an ambulance?"

"Do you have any tape?"

I rubbed my eyes and checked my alarm clock: it was 6:09 a.m. "Not on me."

"I don't know what to do!" Aunt Muriel yelped.

"Did you rip something?"

"No, foolish! I need to get these Christmas presents wrapped before your mother gets here! I've been *everywhere* and can't find any tape!"

I yawned. "Why are you wrapping at dawn?"

"I wanted to wrap last night. I left the house yesterday afternoon for some odds and ends and tape, of course. There's some kind of shortage. Everybody's out. I had no idea. I didn't get home until after ten." Auntie yawned back.

"Can't Ma bring some?"

Aunt Muriel sighed. "I haven't been able to reach her. I keep getting her voice mail. And I certainly can't arrive with the twins' presents unwrapped!"

I considered it. My sister, Ethel, who lives in Northern Virginia, is due to give birth to twins near, or on, Christmas Day. We think. However, I seriously doubted the soon-to-be newborns could spy unwrapped Christmas presents, even in a womb with a view.

Since Ethel hasn't been able to see or tie her shoes since Halloween, Auntie and Ma made plans to descend upon her and Ike, and take care of Christmas and the fixings. This sounded like pandemonium, but a lot of fun, anyhow.

Fate had other plans for me. Or rather, my unemployment status does. Since I'd been let go last summer from EEJIT - Executive Enterprises for Job Intuitive Technologies - I've been working part-time, full time. My mortgage lender thinks it's a good idea for me to pay on a monthly basis. Since my unemployment compensation pays half my former salary, I need to make up the gap somewhere. And playing the lottery hasn't proved to be very reliable.

I'm Mina. Casually, my nickname's pronounced just like the bird's. Formally, the full-length version is Wilhelmina Kitchen. I'm named after a great-grandmother I never met and plan to poke in her spiritual side with a shish kabob skewer slightly post-Rapture. This isn't because I dislike her. I'm just not that keen about our common cooking disorder. Aside from our last name, I also inherited Great-Grandma's catering crazies. Long ago, Bumpa, my great-grandfather, locked the oven door on Grandma Mina cooking for crowds, after she made enough food one evening to feed a large, diverse community - like the Bronx. Her wooden spoon floated down the proverbial genetic cesspool into my hot little oven mitts. To this day, I cannot fathom making potato salad with less than five pounds of potatoes.

"I think the twins will be okay with it."

"Well, I hope so. I mean really – their first Christmas!"

"Don't worry about it."

"I'll try. And don't forget to bring your presents today!"

After assuring Auntie the twins would not need a therapist before their actual birth date, and that I'd arrive with Bounty Noel, I hung up and rolled over. I didn't have to be at my next part-time job until nine o'clock, when I became one of Santa's Sidekicks at Countryside Mall. This has been a steady gig since Black Friday. I get paid minimum wage, with a maximum serving of bruised shins. I also have to sport a lot of "Santa Sparkle" which means I'll get huge employee discounts at all the stores eventually.

3

I've been hopeful the discounts will balance out the crummy paycheck. I'm also hoping this translates to friends and family getting something besides frozen chicken stock for Christmas.

Vinnie, my twenty-plus pound, mini mountain lion-sized tabby yawned and thwacked my head with his tail. Clearly, his breakfast plans did not include my sleeping late. Vinnie was bequeathed to me by Trixie, my BFF who's an ER RN. Trixie's upstairs neighbor made her final visit on Trixie's watch a long time ago. That's when she made Trixie pledge an oath to place her Vincent in a new home. And so Trixie arrived on my doorstep with Vincent, a stuffy name for an even larger stuffed cat. I call him Vinnie, to keep him humble.

I swatted Vinnie's tail away and stared at the clock. Crap. Not quite asleep, with someplace I dreaded to go. I cringed at the thought of another Sidekick shift and slid further under the covers.

I heard the front door bang open, followed by shuffling and grunting. I sat up.

Vito swore softly and continued banging his way through my house and into the basement.

Vito Spaghetti's my retired next door neighbor. He's got a spare key to my place that I haven't had the chutzpah to get returned. He's a good guy mostly, except that he considers himself more of a roommate than a neighbor. And yes, Vito Spaghetti's not his name at all. It's the alias the Feds gave him after he went into a witness protection program that he's kind of strayed from.

His real name is Vladimir Pryzchntchynzski. Gezundheit. He used to be the leader of the Moils, a part of the Jewish Polish mafia out of Bumville, New Jersey. Ever since he got transplanted to Lancaster, "Pee-ay", he's developed a fondness for helping out the crowd at St. Bart's Episcopal and Swiffering. This landed him in a lot of hot water last summer with the St. Bart's crowd, not the Swiffering. That's another story (called *Kitchen Addiction!*)

Vinnie walked over top of me and headed downstairs, greeting Vito and meowing away about how glad he was that someone arose at a sensible hour, and would he mind pouring a heaping bowl of Kitty Cookies, as he was famished?

I took the hint and tumbled into the bathroom, pulling on my robe and tottering downstairs. I found the hallway crammed floor to ceiling with cartons and boxes.

Vito was in the kitchen, giving Vinnie his cookies. Coffee was brewing.

"What's with the boxes?"

"Sorry, sorry, sorry Toots," Vito answered in his usual triple-speak. "I ran outta room at my place. These are for the Christmas Bizarre."

"Don't you mean bazaar?"

"Whatever."

"These are legitimate, right?"

"Absolutely!"

Ever since last summer, when my basement became the unsuspecting cache for a not-too-legitimate enterprise, I've been on the nervy side where Vito and cartons are concerned.

I shook my head and poured myself some coffee. Some things are better left unsaid. Especially before a cup O'Joe.

The phone rang. "Whaddaya got for tape?" It was Trixie.

"Where are you?"

"On my way home from night shift."

"Night shift? I thought you got put on days?"

Trixie grunted. "I was, until everyone came down with Crew Flu."

"Crew Flu?"

"Yeah, the flu the whole staff gets right before Christmas – especially when they're spazzing about a tape shortage."

"Tape shortage?"

"Good grief, don't you watch the news?"

The truth is, I do. But since I couldn't afford to buy anything to wrap yet, I really hadn't made the connection. Then I remembered Aunt Muriel.

"Is it really that much of a crisis?"

"Are you kidding? You and K. were my last hope. Guess I'll end up using Band-Aids after all. Hope Mike doesn't think it's a nursing fetish."

Mike Green is Trixie's somewhat new-ish SO. She hooked up with him sometime after Vito gave up his protected status, just before Mike, a US Marshal, was able to fully investigate why. Apparently their relationship is still on the horizon for the holidays.

"You're wrapping boyfriend presents! I'm happy for you!"

Trixie sighed. "Yes. No. Sort of. We're unofficially official."

6

"What the heck does that mean?"

"We talk every night on the telephone, and see each other just about every weekend. So we're kind of assuming the exclusive relationship thing but we're both too chicken to bring it up."

"Wow." Dating sure got complicated since I last ventured out, sometime around the Ice Age.

"So I'm hoping our Christmas presents do the talking."

"What'd you get him?"

"Silk boxers and a mask!"

That should speak volumes. At least she hadn't bought him the complete costume. Trixie's always had a thing for a guy in uniform. Prior to her current beaux, this inclination took some odd twists.

"That sounds... convincing. Do you think you'll get a ring?"

"God no!"

"Oh. Well, what do you want?"

"Plastic. I've seen his tastes. A Visa gift card would be excellent."

Ah, young love.

"Are you still working at the mall?"

"Yeah, I've gotta be there this morning."

"Great! Can you look around for tape?"

"Sure."

"Thanks. Maybe as a mall employee you'll get a deal?"

I shrugged. "It's worth a shot."

Vito lumbered back down the basement stairs with more cartons.

I glanced up at the clock. I was becoming a quarter-till late. "Gotta go! Later!" I hung up and dashed upstairs, whirling myself in and out of the shower and into my garb.

Luckily, Vinnie was occupied with tripping Vito's travels up and down the basement steps. This was helpful, since I found out the hard way that Vinnie has a definite thing against my Sidekick shoe covers. Which is odd, even for him. I mean, they're just a kind of slip-on cover that "converts" your shoe into a pointy elf boot, complete with a jingle bell toe. Unfortunately, my right jingle bell is dented and the fabric's a bit frayed since Vinnie's last encounter.

I returned downstairs, bedecked. Vito sat in the kitchen sipping coffee, petting Vinnie on the counter, while they read the paper together. "Hey, you look cute, kid. You made sure you got all your Sparkle this time, right?"

I nodded. The first time I arrived for my shift I was missing my hat which I immediately discovered was a big no-no. They made me drive all the way back home to get it, or I'd miss my shift. With gas prices the way they are, I've been very careful ever since.

However, I'd also learned I had to hide specific costume bits from Vinnie. Oddly enough, his antipathy toward the booties is dysfunctionally proportionate to his fondness for the hat. After a daylong frantic search, I finally found it wadded up and stashed as one of his coveted possessions. No hat, no job, see? Now I hide it in the bread drawer. It also keeps Ma and Auntie's paint swatch samples from getting lonesome. And what the hell, it's festive, no?

The rest of my costume consists of a wide, fake plastic leather belt, and a red felt vest that sports Sparkle buttons and pins from each of the participating stores in the mall, in case the little tikes don't know where to shop after they tell Santa about their lists.

Vinnie recognized his bootie prey and came racing down the hall. I grabbed my coat and shut the door to the garage with a bang.

I jumped into the Doo-doo – my poop brown mini-van – and turned the key in the ignition. Bupkis. I banged my head against the steering wheel, reprimanding myself about forgetting her bent toward religious stations.

I turned on the radio, and Christmas carols filled the air. Luckily, this being Lancaster, every local radio station began playing Christmas carols post-Halloween. I'd listened to nine-thousand plays of "Dominique the Donkey" and can now sing it in Pig Latin, backwards.

However, Christmas carols are a lot easier religious-esque listening than Reverend Hollers-a-lot. I turned up the radio's volume and re-started the van. She purred and we backed quickly down my steep driveway. Which is why I almost ran over my neighbor Bruce, and his Goliath-sized Great Dane, David.

"Sorry!" I called out the window. Bruce was brushing the snow off his jeans and his dog from where they'd rolled sideways to avoid getting flattened.

"Geez, Mina! Careful, huh?"

"I know, I know. I'm late."

"Oh great! You're working?"

I shook my head. "My other part time job."

"You're cooking at Squirrel Run Acres? Fabulous."

"Nope. Santa's Sidekick."

"Oh! At the mall? Hey, can you pick me up some tape?"

"I'll try..." I shook my head. This was the third request for tape in one morning. I made a mental note to pick up gift bags for my presents while I was locating tape for everyone else. I'm not that good a wrapper, and figured bags are better for frozen chicken stock, anyway. I chugged the Doo-doo down the block and toward Countryside Mall.

I pulled into the lot and parked way, way back as instructed. After all, I was at the mall as an employee, not a shopper. I had ignored this rule for my first couple of shifts (how would they know it was my van?) and got a written warning, along with a demerit from my upcoming coupon cache. Since they already had a fix on the Doo-doo, I didn't want to risk losing anymore coupons.

Tiny flakes of snow began to flutter down from a dreary, grey sky, as I walked across the parking lot. It wasn't exactly Christmas-type snow, but at least it wasn't rain. The bland day matched my plain-vanilla mood.

Inside Christmas carols blasted more or less merrily. The mall was already open for business with expanded store hours, welcoming stouthearted early birds. I made my way toward the Santa kiosk. As usual, I walked smack dab into the middle of a fight.

"I did not!"

"You did TOO!"

"NOT!"

"TOO!"

Santa sat on top of his St. Nick throne with his head in his hands. The kid standing next to him, who was supposed to be in his lap, was wailing to beat the band.

"I want my picture with Santy!"

I looked around for the kid's mother. She was yakking on her smartphone nearby. I rolled my eyes back toward the kiosk and attempted to referee Sheree and Barry.

"Wazzup?" I took off my jacket and tucked it under the employee table, behind the computer picture taking setup.

Barry harrumphed and shoved his hands on his hips. "She's deleted all the photos off the hard drive!"

"I did not!" Sheree whined.

I held up a hand. The boy next to Santa cried some more. "Look, go give the kid a cookie while we fix this." I shoved a Santa's Snack at Sheree.

"Are you kidding? We can't give him this – they cost seven-fifty!"

"Just give it to him! I'll pay for it!" Santa hollered back.

Sheree shrugged, took the cookie and left.

"So what happened?"

Barry sighed and threw his hands up in the air melodramatically. "I don't know. I think she did a reboot in the middle of starting up. I can't find any of the photos from last night! All those families are allowed to email us for the next *year* for more prints! I'm afraid to take the kid's picture in case it permanently erases the previous ones!"

"Wow. That's a problem."

"Thanks."

"Did you call Nelson?"

Barry shook his head. "No. I guess I have to. I hate calling Nelson."

I nodded in agreement. Nelson is a real SHIT. Don't get me wrong. I'm not cussing or making judgments. It's just that Nelson is Santa's Helpful Information Technology - SHIT. It even says so on his badge. The fact that he acts like his acronym makes the computer phobic among us a bit tense when we need his help. Which is ramping up to a daily basis, since our motley crew is a tad techno challenged. My team usually reserves calling Nelson toward the end of our shift, so the next crew can deal with him.

"Who called last time?"

"I did."

"Okay, I'll call Nelson. Why don't you give the kid's mom some coupons and send her shopping?"

"What will we do about the line?"

I looked around. A line had already formed. A dozen parents and their charming offspring wriggled in agitation, waiting to get their magical moment with Santa over and done with.

"Give me some coupons. I'll handle this."

I took the coupons and shoved them in my vest pockets. Then I called Nelson on one of the mall's walkie-talkies.

"What is it?" he barked.

"We can't take any pictures and there's already a line."

He grunted. "She rebooted the system again, right?"

"Dunno," I lied. "When can you be here?"

"Right behind you."

I whirled around to see Nelson slinging his walkie-talkie onto the seat next to him as he whirred past me on a golf cart. Which he really didn't need. He could have used the exercise. Nelson is quite talented, computer-wise. Unfortunately, all those years sitting in front of a computer hasn't really helped his physique. He rolled off the cart and huffed toward me, and immediately began tapping away on the keyboard to save the day.

"How long do you think it will take?" I gazed nervously at the growing line.

"How do I know?" he snapped.

I held my breath, counted to ten, and began again. "How long do you think I should advise these families that they're going to wait?"

"Forever."

I bit my lip, turned around and headed toward the frustrated mob. While the crowd was comprised of exhausted parents scouring the Earth for bargains, even they had to be less hostile than Nelson.

"Hi! Look folks, Santa's run into a teensy-weensy technical glitch, so we'll be a little while longer before we start taking pictures."

A collective groan and various uncomplimentary comments hurtled forth.

"In the meantime," I yelled above the din, "here are some advance store discount coupons, so you can take a jump on your holiday shopping, and not have to wait in line!"

"I stood on line for two hours last night and you closed up on us! I had to take a vacation day just to get my kid onto Santa's lap this morning!"

"Hey, me too!"

"Yeah, I thought I recognized you."

I sighed. I was wondering how I could get assigned to another shift sans Sheree. "I'm very, very sorry. We're doing the best we can." It was lame, but truthful.

An older lady with her Shirley Temple cloned granddaughter trotted up to me, as I moved down the line doling out coupons. "Excuse me, but you wouldn't happen to have any coupons for Carols Cards 'n Wraps?"

I rummaged around and shuffled my discount deck. "Umm... yes, actually I do." I held out the coupon. She snatched it from my fingers and hustled away as her grandkid stomped her patent-leather feet. "No, no, no! Grammy's coming back here with you later, after we find some tape!" she shouted, hustling the tapping child away.

"Tape?" someone in the line called out. Immediately, several families followed behind, noses toward the ground in search of the scarce commodity.

I put the Cookie Break sign up, to keep the line from expanding farther while Nelson fixed his sights on keeping us from computer doomsday.

A kid at the back scowled at me. "I wanna see Santa NOW!"

"Very soon. Santa's special computer helper is working on it now." Even I couldn't bring myself to call Nelson a SHIT out loud.

The kid snorted. "That loser couldn't install a Wii."

I thought about it. "Luckily, it's just a camera setup on a desktop."

"Loser."

I stared at the kid, and then looked at his father. The dad was engrossed with texting someone. Hadn't heard a word. I reciprocated by sticking my tongue out at the brat, and stalked away.

While I usually try to fit in with the Lancaster folk and they're being so nice and all, there are some things that just irk the Jersey out of me.

Nelson was right. After what felt like forever, we were back in business. After Sheree's technical gaff, we figured it was best if Barry did the picture taking, while she worked the line. I got the happy chore of settling the tots on and off Santa's lap. Another serving of bruised knees, please.

Eventually the rotten kid's turn came. He hopped up onto Santa's lap and immediately pulled his beard.

"Ow!"

"Hey, it's real!"

"Of course it's real, you little punk! I'm Santa, dammit!"

After the kid recited an expansive list of high-end computer games and gadgets, he hopped off, stuck his tongue out at me, and kicked me in the shin for emphasis.

"Another name for the lump of coal list!" I shouted after him nastily, rubbing my leg. It was all I could do since his father had detached from the Borg and stood patting his offspring's head.

After most of Central Pennsylvania's children kicked, puked and peed on me, my shift was done. And so was I. The next shift arrived; we traded places and I limped toward Chi-Chi's department store.

Shopping while wearing Sparkle was a no brainer, even if I did smell like slightly used diapers. The store clerks were instructed to add a thirty percent discount toward Sparkle purchases, even on top of sales and coupons. I clutched the precious fifty percent employee coupon I'd received with my last paycheck, and wandered in, holding my breath and hoping my purchases would amount to free – or maybe even cash back?

After a quick sprint of selective looting and pillaging from Kids Wear to Housewares, I stood in line with my arms aching and full. Package handles and hangers sliced into my fingers like cheese. I was happy.

I made it to the register and dumped my stash on the counter. "Do you have any coupons?" the clerk asked.

"Yes!" I produced my crumpled half-off coupon from behind the mountain of merchandise. She took it, then looked at me sympathetically. "Oh, I didn't see your Santa Sparkle from behind your pile," she said. "You're wearing a Chi-Chi button somewhere, right?"

I panicked and fumbled around my vest front at the fifty or so store buttons pinned to it. It stuck me in the finger and I began to bleed. "Here!" I shoved the button at her with my un-pricked hand, while sucking my thumb.

"Thank you, and here – you wouldn't want to bleed on your purchases," she said nicely, handing me a paper towel.

Well, I guess she has to be nice. She's probably a Lancaster native. It still makes me uneasy, especially around the holidays. I mean, who's nice to you at Christmas? Especially when you're bleeding.

She rang everything up. The total came to a little over four hundred dollars. I felt my credit card wilt inside my wallet.

"Now, let's add your mall employee coupon, along with your Sparkle discount!" she added brightly.

My heart began to beat again and I exhaled.

"That will be $138.80."

"That's great!"

"But wait, there was a fifty percent coupon in the paper."

17

I sighed. "Sorry, I don't get the paper. I don't have that coupon."

"No worries, we have one here." She held up a pristinely cut-out coupon, complete with bar code. "Lots of people forget them. The store wants you to come back, see? Now, it probably won't take because of your other discounts. But let's try."

She scanned the coupon and we heard a beep. She smiled at me. "Your total is $69.40."

Yippee!

She handed me several miles of receipts along with my bags.

"Oh! Wait! Do you have any boxes?" I asked.

She shook her head. "Not here, but if you go upstairs to customer service they do. And, if you're willing to wait in line, just show them your receipt and they'll wrap everything for free.'"

Free? Wow. You can't beat that. I wondered if they'd wrap frozen soup. Maybe if I gave them some? With the money I'd saved, I could splurge and make beef bourguignon for all of Chi-Chi's staff – it's to die for.

I took my stuff and made my way toward the escalator. From there, I schlepped toward the back of the store, and joined the end of a line I sensed was waiting for their free gift wrapping, too. I took my place behind a determined Grandma and her BFF.

"You bet! Why should we buy wrap when they'll wrap for free?"

"You don't have to tell me twice. Besides, how's anyone supposed to wrap with no tape? I can't find tape anywhere."

I winced, remembering my mission for Aunt Muriel. And Trixie. And Bruce. And probably K. Yeeshkabiddle.

We shuffled our way toward the counter. I was just about four persons in, when a clerk came to the front and shut down the works.

"Hey, what gives?" the grandma in front of me shouted.

"We've been waiting in line for an hour!" her buddy added.

A short, pudgy sales manager sporting a mayonnaise-spotted tie spun around. He cringed and bore it. "Ladies and gentlemen, our apologies. But our gift wrapping services are closed for the day."

"You're supposed to stay open as long as Chi-Chi's stays open!"

He nodded sadly. "Yes, I know. But we've run out of tape."

A resounding groan ensued.

"Now, if you don't mind coming back with your merchandise tomorrow, and of course your receipts; we're expecting a shipment from our Connecticut store in the morning."

"Got any boxes?" a man in back of me shouted.

"Boxes, we can do!" He leapt behind the counter to dole some out.

About an hour later, I was waddling back through the mall, grasping my bags and clasping folded gift boxes under my armpits. They were free, right? I figured the best thing to do was load up the van, then return to my tape mission. Which was a shame, since I was literally walking past Carol's

Cards 'n Wraps. But I figured carrying all my purchases into the tiny store would cause a lot of breakage I couldn't afford.

As soon as I reached the entrance of the store, I realized the detour might be well-timed. A line extended all the way to the mall entrance.

"What's the line for?" I asked out of curiosity.

"Tape," a man replied glumly.

I looked at him. He shrugged. "My wife said I had to get tape. Everyone's out. I just happened to see an office supply truck pull into the mall, so I'm hoping. I guess a lot of other people had the same idea."

"Wow. I better get in line right after I put my gifts in my van."

"Lady, if I were you, I wouldn't wait. I've been to every grocery store, drug store, box store and gift store in the county. If I can't get tape here, I'm telling my wife to fold everything up in grocery bags and tell the kids Santa's gone green."

I hurried out to the Doo-doo, threw my stash inside and hurried back. The line now extended out into the parking lot, stretching toward Hellum and back.

After I'd grown visibly older, I'd made my way up to where I could at least glimpse the counter. I saw the sales clerk ring up another sale, and handed a bag with several containers of tape to a relieved patron.

He turned to leave when the man behind him grabbed the bag.

"You can't do that! That's stealing!"

"Here! Here's your money!"

"Gentlemen, please, if you can't resolve this peaceably I'll be forced to call Security. Next," the clerk went on about his business.

The two men came wrestling out of the store, grabbing at each other and clutching the bag of tape. This escalated into shoving, some punches and the arrival of Security. The rest of us stood in line watching calmly. 'Tis the season, right?

"What was that all about?" I wondered aloud.

A disheartened customer walking past me answered. "They ran out of tape. That guy bought the last few rolls."

The rest of us threw our collective arms up in the air and disbanded.

I wandered along the mall, mulling about tape alternatives. I ruled out glue. I headed toward Dollar Daze, considering staples and safety-pins. That was when I ran into James and his Stressed Shoppers station.

James is my godmother's massage therapist. Formerly a Wall Street type, he traded in his ticker tape for New Age tapes at the suggestion of his former lingerie model girlfriend. That was when she was his girlfriend and just before she moved in with her girlfriend. It proved to be a little startling, especially to James. But it worked out in the end and everyone, especially James' clientele, are a lot less stressed.

"How's business?" I asked.

"Excellent! There is never a shortage of aching backs, feet or shoulders around the holidays!"

James also hires me occasionally, to cater for some of his clients. It's been exorcising my catering disorder, and gives me cash on the side. It's a pretty good setup actually, even if it isn't steady. He offers his clientele menu options via me for anniversaries, parties and the like.

And I mostly like. That is, I mostly like James. But I keep getting tingly feet around Chef Jacques – Jack – at Squirrel Run Acres. It's complicated. Especially since these are working relationships. I'm betting that once I have an actual date with an actual guy, I'll get over it. Them. Whatever.

I nodded and left. The line to Stressed Shopper's was almost as long as the one I'd been standing on for tape. Clearly, James' bottom line would have a happy holiday.

I stepped into Dollar Daze and headed over to the aisle with the gift wrapping stuff. Boxes, bows, paper, and tissue paper abounded. Everything except tape. I looked down and saw a clerk on her knees, unpacking a carton of puppy wee-wee pads.

"Excuse me, but do you have any tape?"

She sat up and shook her head emphatically. "Boy, if I had a nickel for every time someone's asked me that today..."

"Gotcha. Ideas?"

"We got a whole bunch of duct tape, and some masking tape," she said, pointing toward the rear of the store. It wouldn't be elegant. But it was better than glue.

About twenty bucks later, I walked back with a couple dozen rolls of duct tape. I was lucky though, because Dollar Daze branched out past the usual silver variety and carried red and green colored ones. That was Christmassy, right?

I weaved back across town toward home. Bing Crosby sang out "There's No Place Like Home for the Holidays" just as we scaled Mt. Driveway, which was now covered by a fine film of ice. We slid back a bit as I pressed the garage opener. I backed up, got some momentum, then skittered inside.

After bringing in all the bags and boxes, and pulling Vinnie's head out from all the bags and boxes, I plugged in our fake Christmas tree. I'd bought the pre-lit tree last year when I was gainfully employed. This year, only half the lights worked. But they were all on one side of the tree. So I faced the dark half into the corner. Unfortunately, Vinnie loves to play spin the tree. In effect, it's the world's largest cat toy.

I called Auntie, hoping she hadn't had another nervous breakdown about the tape.

"Hi. I got your tape. Sort of. "

"Oh, thank you anyway! Luckily, I remembered Vito's on the bazaar committee, and he was able to bring over several roles! Phew!"

"Oh. That's great." I wondered what K., Trixie and Bruce would make of colored duct tape, but I figured they'd get creative.

"Is Ma there yet?"

"She had a last minute meeting. She rescheduled for tomorrow."

This was typical. While I exhibit various forms of techno-phobia, Ma is the VP for SUZ – a top notch

IT company back in Jersey. Ma's test-driven or owns more gadgets than Brookstone. It figured she'd be wrapping up loose ends just before she took time off to be with Ethel and her soon-to-be grandkids.

I poured a mug o'Merlot and sat down on the sofa and turned on the news. A plump gal with short, platinum-blonde spiked hair, tipped jet black, grinned wildly at the camera. She looked like a deranged hedgehog. "Now, of course, as everyone's finding out, Central Pennsylvania's experiencing a tape shortage," she began. "Here's some helpful tips to help you with some gift wrapping alternatives." I raised my eyebrows and glanced warily at the rolls of duct tape. Should I hide them? More practically, should I sell them?

CHAPTER 2

Thursday

My alarm went off at 6:00 a.m. Outside, it was black as night. I rolled over and slapped the snooze button. Vinnie rolled over and slapped my face with his paw. Polish curses wafted up from my kitchen. I turned on the light, shrugged into my bathrobe and went downstairs.

Vito stood at the top of the basement steps, holding a large cardboard box while attempting to shake off Stanley, his terrible terrier, from his trouser ankle. "C'mon Stanley, a fella could get hurt on the steps like this."

Stanley growled.

I yawned. Another confused morning in my confusing household. Some of my married friends feel sorry for me, living alone. I still wonder what that's like.

I dug around a cabinet and found some crackers. I crinkled the wrapper at Stanley. He did a one-eighty, nipped the cracker from my hand and trotted down the hall to crunch on the rug.

Vito inspected the slobbery damage to his once-creased trouser leg. "I don't know what gets into him. I just fed him," he wondered aloud.

"Maybe he's just lonely and didn't want to see you leave your house." I crossed my virtual fingers that the polite hint would be taken. Especially at this o'clock.

"Nah, that's not it. I'm here all the time and he doesn't act like that." The arrow flew, missed its mark, and fell with a dull thud. I sighed and moved on.

"Maybe it's what's in the boxes. Do you have Christmas cookies or cakes in there?" I moved forward to inspect the loose end of Vito's carton.

He clutched the box fervently. "NO! No! I don't have any food! It's for the bizaaa..." Vito's voice trailed away as he fell carton over tea kettle down the basement stairs, landing with a thud.

"Vito! Are you all right?"

"Ugh."

I flew down the steps to find him with his head planted firmly in the middle of the cardboard box he'd been holding. Which was a good thing. Otherwise it would have been planted firmly in the middle of the basement wall.

I helped him sit up. "How many fingers am I holding up?" I asked, showing one finger.

"Yes."

Well, that was good enough for me.

I picked up the crushed box. It didn't feel very heavy. I looked around to put it near my usual piles. But didn't see my usual piles. Instead, I saw row upon row of boxes stacked floor to ceiling.

Ever since Vito used my basement as storage for a not-too-kosher sideline last summer, I get a little suspicious where large volumes of anything and Vito are involved. This smelled a lot like deja vu.

"Vito..." I began warningly.

"No, no, no, Toots! It's legit! Pretty much... I mean, it's for St. Bart's!"

I stared at him levelly.

"I mean it! Honest! I swear! Hey, my ankle kinda hurts a little."

I helped him back upstairs and had him munching on some Tylenol in no time. Meanwhile, I wondered how many Federal offenses I was committing as the owner of a basement full of who-knows-what?

As usual, I was running half past late. I was supposed to be at Squirrel Run Acres at seven o'clock, and it was almost six-fifteen. To be on time, I had to leave in fifteen minutes.

Vito sat on the kitchen stool, rubbing his ankle and petting Vinnie. Stanley yipped happily from the hallway.

"Vito, sorry, I gotta run!"

Vito held up his hand. "No problemo, Toots. Sorry about the tumble."

I dashed upstairs and in and out of the shower quicker than a Christmas shopper through revolving doors. I threw on my now standard foodie service wear: black pants, white shirt and orange crocs. I sprinted downstairs and threw on my coat. Vinnie sat next to his cookie bowl, staring at me accusingly.

I'd forgotten his breakfast.

"Oh jeez," I said, and started down the hallway. Then Marie, my cockatiel, shrieked from upstairs. I'd forgotten her, too.

"No problemo Toots. I'll give Vinnie and Marie some breakfast."

"Are you sure?" I had my doubts.

"Sure. Vinnie gets Kitty Cookies. Marie gets Cockatiel Clusters. Besides, it's the least I can do after complicating your morning and all."

Sometimes I wish Vito was a figment of my imagination. This morning I was glad he could feed my real – and hungry – pets. "Thanks, Vito. Bye!"

I slid the van into the parking lot at two minutes past seven, thankful that the early morning radio jockeys favored retro hymnal selections, specifically the Kingston Trio's rendition of, "God Rest Ye Merry Gentlemen." Then I got out and slid on my butt.

"Whoa, careful there! Can I help you?"

It was Chef. Great. Lying on my keester in the middle of the parking lot sure wouldn't help my case for being competent enough for full-time work in his kitchen. I scrambled to my feet.

Chef helped me up as I dusted myself off. "Glad you could get here this morning. We've got a ton of deliveries."

"Deliveries?"

"Sure. For Christmas parties and lunches and such. You're okay with that, right?"

"Sure," I fibbed. I had no idea what he was talking about. I thought he wanted my help in the kitchen, you know?

"Great. If you don't mind, it'd be helpful if you could use your own van. The others are out. Just keep track of your mileage so you get reimbursed. Hilda will help you with that."

Once again, I was grateful Christmas Carols abounded in Lancaster. Otherwise, there would be a lot of spoiled platters.

I nodded and followed him into the kitchen. Chef is tall, dark and blue-eyed with black curly hair – and he smells like sugar cookies. When he's not barking culinary instructions at me, my feet get tingly around him. Or when I think about him. My feet got tingly again and I stomped them to stop. Business was business, right?

I looked around, and saw a few dozen trays of cookies cooling on racks. Oh. So maybe that's why he smells like cookies. Huh.

"Thank goodness you're here!" Hilda hustled toward me. She's the manager. I like her, she's a good egg. I also like that she signs my paychecks. "C'mon! I need your help setting up fruit platters!"

I hung up my coat, washed and went to work.

We got the platters arranged, and Hilda finished her delivery instructions. "Now, I've got these all labeled, with the addresses on and everything. If you get lost, just use this cell phone. The customers' phone numbers are on all the orders, see?"

I gulped. Cell phone? I still don't own one. And haven't the vaguest idea how to use one. But I can claim bragging rights for no brain cancer, right?

"Sure."

She scurried away.

Chef looked at me. "You know how to use a cell phone, right?"

"Yep."

He shook his head. "Well, umm... they're all different. Here's how this one works."

After he gave me my tutorial, I was all set. Arnie and I loaded up the Doo-doo – which conveniently acted like a refrigerated van since her heater's sporadic at best – and I followed my marching orders toward Penn Square.

I reached the traffic circle, and waited at a decades-long traffic light at the intersection of King and Queen. There, Lancaster City's Christmas tree lay half prone. It was a shame. Trixie and K. and I always attend the tree lighting ceremony. It's a lot of fun, with lots of kids' choirs. But the ceremony's true claim to fame is *A Tuba Christmas*. Where else can you go to hear Christmas carols from a band of tubas? It certainly was different. When it's cold enough, the lack of ambature makes them sound like a pod of dirgeful whales.

A week after the tree went up, several storms blew in, bringing high gusts of wind. The Christmas tree toppled out onto King Street not once, but thrice. It was after the thrice that the Fire Department wired it up to a nearby streetlight, to bypass the Russian roulette of it falling on passing vehicles. Apparently the wire had loosened a bit. It pointed sideways like an evergreen missile.

I continued down King Street, turning right at Duke Street, where I pulled into a side alley that led to a private parking lot. It served several professional buildings and a church. I pulled up to the gate, and used the parking pass Hilda had given me, remembering her stern warning that it was my only way in – and out – of the parking lot.

I double-checked the building address and my order, and proceeded to take out two very large pastry platters. I hoofed them toward a rear entrance and was lucky to find some smokers on break, who were nice enough to hold the doors open for me. Then again, they were probably all Lancaster natives.

I took the elevator up to the second floor, and laid my bounty on top of the receptionist's counter.

"Did you try Buy-A-Lots?" a frazzled receptionist hissed into the phone.

"Excuse me..."

"How about the grocery store?!"

"I've got your breakfast trays."

"Wagon Wonders?"

"Ummm...holiday pastries are here, right?"

"Mom, I don't care! You're retired! You have time to look for tape! How am I supposed to look for tape tethered to this desk?"

The penny dropped. "Oh, are you looking for tape?"

That got her attention.

"Wait a minute!" she held her hand over the receiver. "You have tape?"

"Not on me. But I picked up some red and green colored duct tape at Dollar Daze, at the mall."

"Huh. Duct tape. You hear that?" she barked back into the receiver. She grunted some more instructions at her poor mother and hung up. "Thanks." She hung her head in exhaustion.

"No biggie."

"You have no idea. I'm divorced with three kids and we moved in with my mom last summer. It's hard enough getting Christmas together without being able to wrap any presents. I can't hide a thing! My eight-year-old's becoming agnostic. And most of the stores have run out of gift bags, too, ever since they ran out of tape. It's a mess. I'm not usually this mean. My mother hates me."

I assured her that her mother didn't hate her and discussed the intellectual plusses of agnostism. She obviously wasn't usually mean, since she lived in Lancaster. It was consoling to know that the holiday crazies made even a long- time resident a little looney.

"Oh, are these our holiday trays?" she asked, finally acknowledging the covered platters on her counter.

I nodded. "Here, follow me." She took one of the trays while I followed with the other.

She led me into a somber conference room that was supposedly set up for the holidays. "Just put them down here." She set her tray on a long, empty conference table.

I looked around. I imagined a line of sad, numb office workers standing single-file to partake of the bounty, carrying their individual portions to eat silently at their desks. Feh. I performed an invisible genuflect regarding working in an office environment.

After the delivery, I made my way back to the van for the rest: a bagel platter for a gift shop, some sandwich trays for an investment firm and deli trays for some government offices.

I walked across the street with the bagel order. The door was locked. Which stood to reason since the hours posted on the door stated they opened at 10:00 a.m.

I banged my head softly against the door, hoping it would help me think. I was re-shuffling the delivery deck in my head when suddenly the door opened. A fraught, middle-aged woman stared quizzically at me.

I slapped my smiley face on. "Delivery from Squirrel Run Acres!"

A jolt of recognition shot across her face. "Of course! Sorry! I placed the order long ago, so I wouldn't forget. And then I forgot! Come in!"

I followed her inside a small gift shop chockfull of knick-knacks and bric-a-brac. She led me toward a miniscule office where two workers sat resolutely, tying ribbons around gift boxes. The wrapping looked more than a bit absurd.

"I just can't get this to stay!" the dark-haired girl cried. "This is useless!"

"I think we need to make a statement. If we can't wrap correctly, let's wrap creatively!" A short-haired girl with glasses showed off her project: a box wadded in a few thousand yards of wrapping paper, wrapped sloppily across the center with another few miles of twine.

The owner stood in the doorway shaking her head. "We may just have to forego offering gift wrapping this year."

"Would that be so bad?" the dark-haired girl asked hopefully.

The owner nodded. "Yes, service like that is what puts a store like ours above the big box stores."

I bit my lips and made a note not to spill the beans about Chi-Chi's.

Suddenly, the girl with the glasses pointed at my tray and barked. "*What's that?*"

"Why, it's our holiday breakfast platter, bagels and sides, like you girls asked for," the owner answered.

"No! THAT!" the girl screamed, jumping up and pointing toward the address slip that Hilda had on top of the platter. "TAPE!!"

I suddenly felt like I'd wandered into a room full of zombies and I was the only one with brains.

"Umm... well, here you go, Happy Holidays," I said, setting the platter down in the midst of the wrapping mess and backing toward the door. I felt the owner's hand on my back. Both girls stood up, directly in front of me.

"I hope you don't mind," she began.

After several misguided attempts to call Hilda on the cell phone, we got connected. Hilda insisted that we didn't sell office supplies. But given the situation, they would make an exception – for an exorbitant fee. After what seemed like a couple hours later, I was finally released.

I rubbed my neck a bit. "I have other deliveries to make before I can come back with your tape."

"Don't bother! I'm on it!" the girl with the glasses said, hurrying out with a bagel in one hand, and her keys in the other.

"You're a lifesaver!" the owner cried, pumping my hand up and down.

"Huh?" I replied brightly.

"Just wait until you see the traffic we get from this!" the dark-haired girl displayed a newly scribbled blackboard sign: "GIFT WRAPPING with every purchase! WE HAVE TAPE!"

The owner jumped up and down. "This is going to be the best Christmas ever!"

After extending my congratulations, I made my way back to the van, hoping that the winter sunlight pounding down on it hadn't heated up the remaining trays. Luckily, it was still bitingly cold. I began to gather up the food, then stopped. I quickly removed the taped delivery notes and transcribed the address information with a Sharpie onto each platter's lid. I was already late; I couldn't afford the risk of becoming a hostage again.

I made my way across the street and into the lobby of an investment firm. Instead of a large reception desk, there was an inlaid round wooden table, with an extravagantly-sized bouquet of fresh lilies and Christmas greens. I knew they were fresh because their scent filled the lobby. Heaven. Clearly, even in this economy, the investments of the rich don't stink.

I looked around. There were a few hallways leading into the lobby. I wandered down one, and called out. "Hello?" No answer.

I came back and repeated down another. Nothing. The sandwich trays were starting to get heavy. I looked around and the only place to set them, other than the floor, was on an expensively upholstered pair of side chairs. I lay the trays down and hoped the hungry masses wouldn't enter and depart with the largesse. Or more importantly, spill on the upholstery.

I wandered down another hallway and heard voices. A door stood ajar.

"You'll get fired for this!"

"Just try to stop me!"

"You can't do this!"

"Get out of my way!"

Fools rush in. Caterers deliver. "Excuse me..."

The door opened and two red-faced women peered out. One of whom clutched a cardboard carton. "Who are you?" she asked.

I parroted my automatic response: "I have your holiday delivery from Squirrel Run Acres."

The red-head (who was really more magenta) smacked her hand to her forehead. "Gosh, I completely forgot."

"Well, I won't keep you," the closely-cropped grey-haired woman responded, hugging her carton.

"Just a minute! No you don't!" Magenta cried, shoving Grey back into the supply closet. Scuffling ensued, with a lot of paper clips and paper hit the floor. And tape. Lots and lots of tape.

"Wow. You sure are lucky with all this tape you've got. Hey, you could probably sell it for a profit. Ha, ha." I hoped the joke would clear the air.

Magenta and Grey stopped mid-scuffle. They stared at me. Then, at each other. "Just a minute," Magenta instructed me, and closed the door.

A little while later, the door opened and Grey traipsed happily down the hallway hugging several cartons. Magenta came out carrying a very large cardboard box. She locked the door. "I'm the Office Manager. I'm in charge of supplies." She smiled weakly.

I looked at her box.

"Christmas, you know?"

After she'd hidden her stash under her desk, she helped me bring the sandwich platters back from the lobby. After all this time, I hoped the mayonnaise hadn't gone bad. We carried them into another large area, complete with a receptionist's desk and a designer Christmas tree. A small, unadorned fold-up table stood nearby.

"Just put these here."

A few heads popped up from their cubicles. "Is it lunch?"

"Yes! Come and get it!" Magenta cried. I was confused. It was still late morning. But hey, maybe they started their day early.

Dozens of workers and smiles ambled forth, many of whom carried covered bowls and trays of homemade goodies. Someone turned on a boom box. Someone else brought in a case of beer.

"Wow, this is the nicest party I've delivered today," I said honestly.

Magenta shrugged. "The partners are all out of town. They take off the week before Christmas through New Year's. We put our pennies together and put up a party."

"Your office doesn't pay for this?"

Magenta grunted. "Are you kidding? The only reason we get Christmas off is because the stock market's closed."

I made my way back to the parking lot just as the sky opened up and another fine, powdery snow fell on the streets, like a giant salt cellar. You know what they say about the weather in Pee-Ay, if you don't like it just wait five minutes and it will change. I brushed myself off and hopped in the van. I had a moment of panic when I couldn't find the card pass (oh good Lord, please don't make me go back to the bric-a-brac shop!) but finally found it and let myself out of the lot.

I came to the corner of Orange and Queen, and was about to turn right, when the traffic light turned red, of course. I sat and waited, staring at the long line of people wrapped around the corner drugstore. Then I read the sign in the window, "WE HAVE TAPE!"

A tired, disheveled store manager appeared next to the sign, and whipped it off. The crowd emitted a loud groan, and dispersed. The light turned green, and off I went.

I finished up the rest of the deliveries and pulled into the back of the lot, near the smoker. I hurried through the cold and into the kitchen and found Hilda sitting at her desk, grumbling at her calculator. She looked up. "I was wondering if we'd ever see you again."

"I'm really glad you had spare tape."

"For a five hundred percent markup, I'd have a spare leg."

I handed Hilda the parking pass. "Anything else?"

She shook her head. "Better check with Chef."

I looked around the kitchen, and saw him leaning over a steel counter, staring at a clipboard. I cleared my throat. He looked up.

"Hilda wanted me to check with you, to see if you need any more help."

Chef checked another clipboard, then looked at the clock. "We're good for today. But I was wondering what kept you. You hit a lot of traffic?"

"I got kidnapped."

"What?"

"Really."

Chef looked at me oddly. Then, he turned back toward his lists. "By the way, what are you doing about Christmas?"

"I'm using red and green duct tape."

He stared at me again. "No, not what are you doing for wrapping. I mean, what are your plans for Christmas?"

I shrugged. "I guess I'll be a Sidekick up until the eleventh hour."

He stared at me. "Mina - are you spending Christmas with anyone?"

Part of me began to blush, while the other part of me told me to quit it. Was he asking me out? For Christmas? I virtually pinched myself. Chef? Naw. He probably has a breakfast to deliver, and no one with family would be too keen on working Christmas morning.

"I've got Vinnie. And I'll probably wind up with Vito and Miriam, too."

Chef shook his head and smiled. "Sounds like fun."

I nodded mutely. Was he going to ask me to deliver something, or what?

"How about we go over next week's schedule?"

My next shift got scheduled. By now, I completely understood the concept of living paycheck to paycheck. Luckily, I have several of them.

I headed off, and pulled up to my garage with an abrupt stop. That was because I didn't want to run over Vito and his new buddy, having a shoving contest in the middle of our driveways.

Vito, and a guy who looked a lot like someone Vito might have gone to school with, took turns pushing each other. I parked at the bottom, hoping the van wouldn't slide backward. I stared up the hill toward them.

"I know you underbid them!" Vito's pal screamed at him.

"No, I didn't!" Vito poked back.

"Did too!"

"Did NOT!"

"You did! And it was my idea in the first place! You're not beating me to the punch!"

Vito threw his hands up in the air and sighed, exhaling a Yiddish expletive. The other guy got bug-eyed and purple. Then he grabbed Vito by the neck and tried to bite him.

"Hey, cut that out!"

"I'm gonna suck your blood!"

"You put your lips on me again, you'll be sucking teeth."

"Shut up! I'm a vampire and I'm gonna feed on you!"

"You ain't no vampire! You're out in broad daylight!"

"I'm in transition!"

The weird guy grabbed Vito by the neck again. Vito shoved him down on the lawn. They rolled down the hill together and landed at my feet.

"Hey, you can't do that!' I screamed.

"Why not?"

"This is my driveway!"

The guy nodded, then helped Vito up. They shook hands.

Then he socked poor Vito in the bread basket. Vito fell over like a deflated lawn ornament.

The senior perp held up both hands and backed away, slipping a bit. "Sorry, sorry, sorry, kid. This is family business. Nothing personal."

"Who are you?"

"Umm... Buddy. Buddy Burgers."

"Are you kidding?"

"Nope."

"You own *Buddy Burgers*? The fast food chain?"

He shook his head. "It's an unfortunate coincidence."

Vito stood up and waved him off. "See you around, Bernie," Vito said knowingly.

"Sorry. Hey, no hard feelings, huh?"

"Next time, pal." Then Buddy – Bernie? took off.

"What was all that about?"

"Bernie is an old-time buddy of mine. Which umm... is why he calls hisself Buddy. But sometimes he gets wrong ideas in his head."

"Great. I hope he's just visiting from out of town."

"Actually, he relocated."

I stared firmly at Vito. "Not like you, right?"

Vito shrugged. "Truth is stranger than fiction."

I gave myself a virtual spatula slap to my noggin. I wanted to flip my brains over and start again.

"Are you okay?" I asked. It looked like Vito really got the wind knocked out of him. It would have been hard on anyone, but especially for someone old enough to be my uncle.

"I could use a little sit down, actually."

I got us inside my townhouse, and Vito comfy on the sofa. I handed him a glass of water, and the doorbell rang. It was Miriam.

"My sweetie isn't at his home. I waited *forever* out in the cold, waiting for him to answer his bell. Of course, I could have found out easier if I'd have my own key..." Miriam chastised Vito from the foyer, inspecting my living room while glaring at him, hands on hips.

Vito shrugged. "Sorry, Sweetie. Keep meaning to get around to it."

I looked at Vito. Vito stared at his shoes. Miriam kept her hands on her hips.

"Do you mean to tell me you forgot?"

"Sorry, sorry, sorry. Had a few more events than usual today." He rubbed his tummy.

"Not about the key! About the..."

Vito looked up.

"About the... WATER! With all this precipitation, I was worried WATER might be in your basement!" Miriam nodded brightly at Vito.

I shrugged and hung up my coat, glad to move out of bickering range.

"No, there's no more WATER in my basement. But I think there might be some WATER in Mina's basement," Vito answered.

I spun around from the closet. "Water in MY basement? What the?" I hurried toward the basement steps.

"NO! NO! You just wait here! I'll check it for you!" Miriam screamed, chucking me out of the way and running down the steps.

Well. The idea of water in my basement got me more than a tad upset. I needed to calm down. I mentally recited the necessary ingredients for a turkey dinner with all the trimmings.

After some scuffling and sounds of boxes falling, Miriam came up from the basement, preceded by Vinnie, who was chattering away and looking severely disgruntled. Apparently, she'd woken him in his kitty kingdom. But Miriam was beaming as she clutched a large, dented box. It looked like the box Vito had fallen into this morning. Huh.

"Nope! Not a shred of moisture! Thank goodness!"

"Well, that's a relief," I said. I scaled back the turkey dinner and thought about whipping up a soufflé.

Miriam lugged her box into the living room. "Thanks, Honey Pie. Would you mind helping me to my car with this?" Miriam tossed the box on Vito's lap.

He responded with a wince as the box plunked against his middle. "Sure, Sweetie." He got up and toddled out the door, with Miriam giving me bye-bye finger waves.

The phone rang. "You're mother's here. When are you going to drop off your presents?" It was Auntie. I had yet to make my way to Aunties' with my Christmas presents for her, Ma, Ethel, Ike and the unborn. I sighed. Was it too early for a glass of wine? Wasn't it five o'clock somewhere?

"I don't have them wrapped yet, exactly."

"Don't worry. Just label them and we'll take care of it at your sister's. Your mother's brought scads of tape."

"When are you leaving?"

"Now! We wanted to leave an hour ago. We've tried to reach you, but you weren't at home. Can your mother get you a smartphone for Christmas?"

I groaned inwardly and made arrangements to bring the unwrapped presents ASAP.

I finally got the presents stashed inside garbage bags, which took a bit longer because Vinnie kept insisting on getting stashed inside the bags, too. I sped toward Auntie's.

As I pulled up the long driveway, Ma and Aunt Muriel met me outside. We made a chain gang to repack the goods inside Auntie's Lexus.

"You're not taking Ma's car?" I asked.

"Both," Ma huffed as she threw another garbage bag full of goodies to Auntie.

"We're packed to the gunnels!" Auntie chimed in.

I was going to miss a really good time. Rats.

We hugged quickly, just before they handed me presents for me and Vinnie. Their presents were wrapped beautifully. They certainly looked a lot more festive than my black trash bags.

Auntie pulled out, followed by Ma. I waved at Ma as she got a new-fangled looking GPS up to speed. Once again, I wondered about my mother skating on the bleeding edge of technology, while I clung fervently to LPs.

I got back to the house just as the snow turned to drizzly frozen rain. But my neighborhood looked pretty - everyone had their Christmas lights up. And a few houses sported inflatable lawn ornaments, too, which were luckily puffed up and not lying like inert puddles on the ground. After I gave the tree a spin, I got the presents and placed them underneath. Vinnie made sure to sit on top of the boxes to guard them. I hoped my new clothes wouldn't get too wrinkled as he sprawled his girth across, smashing each box.

I'd had enough stress for one day. So I rummaged around the freezer and found a thick chuck steak to double as a pot roast. I set it in the microwave to defrost, then checked around for the rest of the fixings and lucked out: yes, we have carrots, onions, potatoes and more importantly, ginger snaps for the gravy. I even had a jar of pickled red cabbage. Woot!

The microwave binged just as I was hauling out a large pot from beneath the cupboard. The phone rang.

"I'm bored and hungry. Let's go out." It was K. K.'s been in my best-bud club since I moved to Lancaster. And yes, K. is his legal name – after he paid an exorbitant sum to make it official. At the time he shrugged it off as a business expense; part of the trappings for his interior design firm. Since he's the sole proprietor, there wasn't much argument.

"I'm making pot roast."

"Good grief. Was your day that bad?"

I clattered around the utensil drawer, digging with one hand. "It got a little better after I got ransomed."

"Ransomed? Why, were you kidnapped?"

"Yes."

He took a breath. "You're kidding right?"

"Nope."

"All right, when can I come over for pot roast and this story?"

"Anytime."

K. soon arrived with a large, wrapped gift basket.

I frowned. "I haven't wrapped your Christmas present yet. I didn't know you wanted to exchange this early."

"Heavens, no. One of my clients gave me this. I brought it over to divvy up. Do you think Bauser would actually drink good beer for a change?"

"Nope. He's a Krumpthfs die-hard."

"That's too bad. There's a bottle of a very good artisanal ale in here."

K. set the basket on the counter and began divvying, while I fiddled with the pot roast creation and filled him in.

"Really, dearie, you don't need a cell phone. You need a panic button. The idea!"

"Holidays can be very stressful."

"Especially with no tape! By the way, were you successful?"

"Sort of. Here." I held out the bag full of red and green duct tape.

"My." K. looked at it like I'd handed him the contents of Vinnie's litter box.

"Look, it will hold paper together, right? And they're red and green. That's Christmas-y, right?"

K. tried not to make a face. "Actually, my theme this year is 'Sugar Plum,' so all my presents are hues of silver and eggplant."

"Theme?"

"Of course, dear. I vary my wrapping theme each year. Clients expect it." K.'s design clients ranged the gamut, from top notch developers to local celebrities.

I looked at him and thought about the red and green duct tape sticking bits of grey and purple paper together. Maybe he could alter his theme a little. How would they feel about 'recession'?

K. patted my hand. "It was very nice of you. Actually, I do have a stash of double-sided tape. I'll make do with that."

I put the bag aside and stirred my pot roast. I was a little ticked. I didn't think K. should look gift duct tape in the mouth. I flipped the roast, and thunked the lid on the pot.

"Here, look – peace!" K. said. He held up a nice Syrah, and two bonafide wine glasses. "Where's your wine opener?"

I hadn't used a wine opener since Ma visited last summer, since my budget allows for only mugs o'Merlot, varied by the occasional box o'Burgundy. After some confused inspections, we dug out the wine opener from inside a crock pot.

"I don't understand what the big deal is about stores being out of tape. I mean, why don't people just order online?"

K. swallowed. "Oh, I tried that. Of course, you can get everything under the sun. But only with a steep delivery fee."

"You mean there's a huge profit margin for tape?"

"No, the costs are reasonable. The delivery fees, not so much. Especially with just a couple weeks before Christmas."

"Huh?"

K. shook his head. "Lancaster. Frugal. Remember?"

I nodded. "Got it. Want to catch the early news?"

"Of course," K. answered nicely, pouring the wine.

We sat and sipped. A male anchor sat grinning wildly, direct from TV Land. "And now, some good news for our anxious gift-wrapping viewers! A new gift-wrapping service opens tonight in Countryside Mall, just in time for the holidays." The camera cut to live coverage inside the mall.

A long-haired blonde woman stood by a mall kiosk, holding a microphone. "That's right, Glenn. The 'Mail-It-2' kiosk opened today here at Countryside Mall. And not a moment too soon, given the tape shortage in Lancaster County. Any shortage of tape here, Mr. Bergers?"

"Heck no! We've got plenty of tape here! We've got all your gift-wrapping and holiday needs! We even got stamps!"

I stared at the screen and tried not to blow wine through my nose. Buddy – Bernie? - Burgers stood smiling and waving his arms in front of the kiosk.

"Well, you're timing couldn't be better this holiday season, right, Mr. Burgers?"

He nodded enthusiastically. "I had a hunch last winter. So I built my business model around it. Bought boat loads of tape! And postage! Bring your presents – any size, any amount – we'll wrap 'em! And mail 'em!"

I choked a bit.

"Problem?" K. asked, patting me on the back.

"That's Vito's friend."

"Oh, that's nice. When did you meet him?"

"Right after he punched Vito in the stomach."

CHAPTER 3

Late Thursday into Friday

Long after I explained to K. about the driveway drama, I hit the hay. Later, I awoke to claps of thunder. A brilliant flash of lightning lit up my bedroom. Vinnie put his paws over both ears, and mumbled in his sleep. Another clap of thunder got me up and in my slippers. That, and the phone was ringing.

It was Bauser. Known only to his mom as Ralph Bausman, he was my ex coworker buddy from our EEJIT days, and remains on my roster of friends. Especially while we compared our unemployment stipends. He's destined for a creative technology job soon. Seriously, he's genius wherever IT is concerned. Just not so much regarding a clock and the telling of time.

"Seriously, Mina, look outside! You'll never see this again!"

I yawned. "You woke me up for a thunderstorm?"

"A snow thunderstorm!"

I reached over Vinnie and pulled the curtain aside. Snow was swirling in the backyard at a dizzying pace. Another flash of lightning lit up the spirals of flakes. More thunder growled in the distance.

"What the--"

"I've heard about these! But never believed it! This is so cool, right?"

I considered it. "Is this another odd-ball Lancaster thing?"

"Nope. More like oddball Central PA. Because when the lower troposphere becomes unstable, along with a net flow of air, it increases lift."

"Huh?"

Bauser sighed. "The weather here is conducive to small thunderstorms."

"Got it. Thanks." I yawned.

"Don't mention it!"

"Do you and Norman want tape?"

"You got tape?"

I explained.

"Actually, Norman headed off to the mall to that new gift wrap place right after the news."

I hung my head.

"But I could use some. I mean, not a lot. Most of my presents are 6-packs. I'm mostly going with bows."

I hung up and sighed, fervently hoping my Christmas present from Bauser wasn't a 6-pack of Krumpfths.

It was about three in the morning, and I was wide awake and fretting—about lousy beer, my mortgage, gas money—not to mention the impending Sidekick gig. So I decided to make some breakfast breads to take the edge off. Yawning and stretching, Vinnie escorted me to assist. He eventually settled on more stomping of the presents under the tree, mashing them into something suitable for a nap. I hoped none of the stuff was breakable.

A few cranberry orange, banana nut and cinnamon swirl loafs later, I finally felt sleepy enough to head back to bed. I looked out the French door onto the deck at the newly fallen snow, which shone glittery white and undisturbed,with the exception of the footprints that went from around the corner of my townhouse, through my backyard and up to Vito's deck. The tracks retraced themselves, straight back toward my deck: someone had been standing out there, looking in. Since the snowstorm. Someone was watching me cook? It couldn't have been Vito. He'd have let himself in and made a pot of coffee.

Somewhat shaken, I went upstairs and lay down on my bed, feeling a little lonesome and a bit colder, since Vinnie was still snoring on top of his stash. I threw a sweatshirt on over my jammies and some socks. Before I knew it, I was fast asleep.

A nano-second later, the phone rang. Well, actually it was more like four hours later: it was after eight.

"Hey, can you be here at five this afternoon? We've got a huge off-premise dinner party and Arnie's called in sick." Hilda sounded frazzled.

"Sure!" I brightened. I momentarily wondered if that could translate into calling off this morning's Sidekick stint in order to spare what remained of my shins. I rolled over, face-to-face with a neglected stack of bills on my nightstand, and thought better of it.

"Should I wear the usual?"

"That'd be great." Hilda gave me the gist of the menu, how many guests and what she'd need help with.

I rolled out of bed and downstairs and finally into Vito, who was already making coffee.

"What's up I should know about?"

I yawned. "Nothing. Yet."

Vito stared at the breakfast breads. "You sure?"

"Oh. That. Bauser got me up for Snowmageddon and that led to a little insomnomania."

Vito shook his head. "You need a large family. With lots of cousins and in-laws and such."

"Have you been talking with Aunt Muriel?"

Vito held up a hand. "But, hey, since you was up, did you see anyone outside last night?"

I yawned again. "Nope. But I did see footprints."

"Me too."

We peered out the window at the tracks that led to Vito's deck.

"Yep. I'm not liking it."

"What are you hiding in my basement?"

"Nothing! I swear it! Just stuff for the bazaar. But those prints make me think it could be some punks out to rob us, on account of Christmas and all."

I wondered sleepily who would consider my home full of Christmas bounty? I had nary a wreath on the door. But maybe the footprint people had watched me freeze all that chicken stock last week. "You think I should take my tree down?"

"Don't be such a Grinch."

"So what then?"

"A security system might be a good thing."

I looked at him. While he was probably correct, what with my being a single gal and all, I had him, right? If the theory that nosey neighbors make good security, then a live-in neighbor has to be better. Besides, there wasn't any room in my budget for another budget.

"I'll think about it."

"Okay. So what are you doing for dinner tonight?"

"An extra shift at Squirrel Run Acres. Hilda called this morning."

"Hey, I was wondering who was intruding on you this early in the morning." Vito helped himself to the creamer in my fridge, and poured himself some more coffee.

Well.

"So you won't be home for dinner?"

"I'll probably be home late-ish. Depending."

Vito shook his head. "That's a shame. Miriam and me are gonna test out a new recipe. Straight from Julia Child!"

I shuddered inwardly and grimaced at the vision of my icon spinning in her grave. "Yeah, that is too bad. What are you making?" I had to ask, yes? I mean, someone has to tell the paramedics, right?

"Choucroute Garnie."

I knew I was going to regret asking. But I had to verify Vito's translation. "Come again?"

Vito held up a hand. "I know, it sounds pretty hoity-toity. But Miriam says it's a classic!"

"What is it?"

"A supped-up pork and sauerkraut dinner! With sausages and everything!"

"Gee, I'm sorry I'll be working and have to miss it." Thank-you-baby-Jesus.

"No problemo, Toots. I'll leave a plate for you on the counter. That way, you can look forward to a home-cooked meal when you get home."

I could also look forward to a large bottle of Tums and some solitude – neither of which I had.

Vito went on with his usual kitchen puttering. "So what's the drill for today?"

"The usual. Sidekick, then Squirrel Run. Why?"

"No more catering gigs with that massage guy, huh?"

I shook my head. "Not yet. But I'm hoping things will pick up after Christmas."

Vito grinned at me: as usual, his bridge was not where his bridge was supposed to be. "Hey, that would be great!"

"I hope so." Well, at least I hoped so for my bank account's sake. My shins will certainly be relieved after the holiday.

"So what time will you be back from the mall?"

"Why?"

Vito blushed. "I was kinda hoping to get a Swiffering in for you this morning. It's been awhile. And what with Miriam coming over tonight and all... I might not get around to it over the weekend."

OMG Miriam and Vito are serious! Miriam is a weekend wife!

I choked back some coffee. "I get off my shift after three. Then I'll have to dash home and change for the off-premise party."

"Great! So you're leaving soon?"

I looked at the clock. For once, I was ahead of schedule. "I'll leave here about nine-thirty."

Vito nodded. "That's great! I'll get ready so I can get on it as soon as you head out the door. I picked up a brand new style Swiffer! Did you know they made a new model? It's a beaut! Wait until I show you!" Vito huffed out the door in a hurry, with his kitchen towel slung over his shoulder.

"Where are you going?"

"I bought it last night! Still got it in my car!"

I closed the front door after him to keep out the cold. I worried about Vito and his enthusiasm regarding Swiffer products. I worried a lot more about him after a loud explosion shook the house.

"Vito!" I ran out the door and saw the remnants of the Towncar smoldering near the garden island in the middle of the cul-de-sac. I hopped into the snow covering the front walk, and someone grabbed my elbow.

"It's okay Toots. I'm here. Good thing I didn't make it to the car. Shame about my new Swiffer, though."

I stared at the flaming vehicle. "How come you didn't park inside your garage? Or your driveway, like you always do?"

Vito got a little red in the face. "Well, you see, I came home from Miriam's kinda late and all... and Miriam has the beeper. And the driveway wasn't plowed out yet – so I parked it on the street. I figured we'd get dug out today."

"You're lucky we're not digging you out." Miriam has his beeper?

"You could say that again."

"What do you suppose happened?"

Sirens wailed toward us, coming up from Millersville Pike. Obviously, we had concerned neighbors who called in the explosion. That, and they didn't want their own cars charcoal broiled.

"Tell you in a minute." Vito hustled toward his car, sliding down the driveway. He made his way to the burning vehicle, and carefully picked something off the flaming windshield. He came back and deposited what looked like a charred turd onto my porch.

"Yuck! More flaming feces?" I was wondering what scatological karma I'd deserved from a past lifetime. Or novel. Whatever. Last summer had more than its share of flaming feces, thanks in part to the St. Bart's crew. And the Doo-doo's moniker really stuck after the discovery of a vast amount of doggie poop stashed inside her. But I digress.

Vito grimaced. "I wish. It's a kosher dill."

"Someone garnished your windshield?"

He shook his head. "Nope. It's a sign."

"Of?"

Several police cars screeched to a halt, with a few fire trucks tagging behind. After the policeman assured themselves the explosion wasn't Homeland Security related, the fire guys doused the car with a zillion gallons of foamy gunk. I hoped Vito had insurance. Lots of it.

A policeman made his way up to us. "You own this vehicle?"

Vito shrugged. "Used to."

"What happened?"

"Honestly Officer, I have no idea. I'm going to ask my insurance company to investigate first thing. Gosh, I hope it wasn't something electrical. Sure glad I didn't park in my garage."

The officer looked at Vito's garage, attached to mine. "Darn straight!"

"So what happens now?" I asked.

"The insurance folks will look into it."

"After the police impound my vehicle, just to make sure it wasn't done on purpose," Vito added.

The cop looked at Vito funny. "Been through this a time or two?"

Vito shrugged. "Lucky in love, unlucky in..."

"Right."

Suddenly the clouds opened up, and bright sunlight bounced off the snow and the charred remains of the Towncar. I suddenly realized it was much later than I thought – so much for my lead time. I dashed inside to change.

The policeman retreated to his car. Vito tossed the burnt pickle inside my front door. Vinnie ran toward it, and did an immediate about-face.

"What the?"

"I didn't want the nice officer to think you had a dirty porch."

"Huh?"

"He's single ain't he? He's not wearing a ring. And he's got a reliable job."

Yikes! Vito was setting me up? Did he actually blow up his car to find me a date? Stranger things have happened. It was too bad. The Towncar was the only vehicle I had access to with AC. And heat. And didn't have a weird religious radio compulsion. Although it preferred Polkas.

I raced around my bedroom like an idiot, donning my Sparkle at the last minute. Vinnie raced toward me as I slid out the back door. The engine finally turned over after I was forced to sit through the first chorus of that horrible Country Western song about the Christmas shoes, yada-yada. Excellent – very uplifting.

I started down the driveway and got stopped by the cop. "Whoa, Missy, where are you headed in that outfit?"

Missy? I haven't been called Missy since kindergarten. "Countryside Mall."

"What for?"

"Santa's Sidekick."

"Come again?"

I explained about the merits of a part-time job with full-time injuries.

He shook his head. "Too bad you can't carry a gun."

"Yes."

"Hey, since you work at the mall, you wouldn't have a lead on tape, would you?"

I sighed and explained about duct tape Noel.

"Hey, that's great! Think they still have some?"

"It's a possibility."

"Thanks a lot! Hey you're late, right? Follow me!" He took off like a shot, lights and sirens wailing, and me in tow. For once, I might actually get to work on time.

The patrol car cut its lights as it turned into the parking lot, parking in a rock star space just next to the main entrance. I parked in East Jabib and hoofed it back across several counties. The sky had changed back to being bleak as dishwater, and threatened to dump something else down on us. It did not promise a White Christmas.

Inside the mall it was very Christmas-y -- that is, if you like hot pink and turquoise. Apparently the mall execs had taken a cue from a competing mall in south Florida. I walked past the new 'Mail-It-2' kiosk, which was doing a brisk business: the line stretched back to Blue Ball. I trudged toward Santa's Station with all the enthusiasm of a condemned prisoner.

"I can do whatever I want!"

"I'm sorry ma'am, but you have to buy the package first."

"But she's already on his lap!"

The little girl on Santa's lap immediately began to bawl.

"See! Look what you did! Now she's crying! We haven't had a picture of her not crying on Santa's lap for four years now!"

The six-year old concurred and immediately whipped up a fresh batch of tears, along with a side of screams.

I pulled off my coat and shoved it under the table. "What's the problem?" I had to ask. I was wearing official Sparkle, right?

The red-faced woman fumed at me. "This idiot won't let me take a picture of my own kid, with my own phone!"

I looked at the woman blankly and sighed. "Yes, I'm afraid that's one of Santa's rules."

"Where? Where does it say that? What rules?"

I pointed to the enormous sign on which she was leaning.

She stared. "Oh. You mean you have to buy a package for a picture with Santa?"

"I'm afraid so."

"Oh, all right. What's the cheapest one?"

I handed her a pamphlet with the various descriptions of how to part easily with one's hard earned cash.

"$29.99?! That's the cheapest one?"

I nodded and repeated the jargon we were instructed to relay. "Yes, it's quite a bargain for the memory of a lifetime."

The little girl now escalated from sobbing to an all-out conniption fit, complete with stomping of feet. Groups of shoppers turned to stare but once they saw it was just a kid with Santa, they continued on their way.

"Fine! Here, do you take plastic?"

Barry stepped in. "Indeed we do. Please step right over here…" Barry led the malicious mommy to the register, mouthing *thank you* at me.

You owe me, I mouthed back.

Soon the little girl's screams were drowned out by her mother's--Genetics work. She was begrudgingly seated on Santa's lap. Santa was rubbing his temples vigorously as the kid mugged a cherubic smile for the camera. Sheree clicked away.

Then the lights went out.

Barry threw his hands up in the air. "Oh, for goodness' sakes, what did you do this time?"

"I didn't do anything! I just snapped the pictures!"

Everyone in line groaned.

I looked around. All the stores were dark, with the exception of Chi-Chi's and another big box store. Since they were anchors, they probably had their own backup generators.

Barry shook his head. "I can't bear the thought of calling Nelson again." He sighed and reached for the mall walkie talky.

"Me neither." Nelson whirred from behind, squealing to a stop.

Sheree flinched. "I'm really sorry Nelson, I really didn't do anything wrong this time, honest."

Nelson smirked. "I'd love to blame you, but this time you're right."

"What's going on?" I asked.

"Power outage."

"When will the lights come back on? Have we lost our pictures?" The maniacal mommy had a point.

Nelson shrugged. "Dunno. Could be a few hours."

Another chorus of groans spewed forth from the line.

"Oh no! Not again! Here – Petunia, smile again for Mommy!"

"I want a Santa Snack!"

Mommy gritted her teeth. "After you smile for Mommy, precious!"

Petunia complied and did a repeat mugging as Mommy snapped away with her smartphone.

"Hey, you can't do that! It says so right there!" Barry pointed at the billboard like sign.

"Listen pal, I paid thirty bucks for a picture of my kid smiling with Santa, and that's what I'm gonna get."

"Yes, I know, we just took them. If you'll just be a little patient, we'll have them to you as soon as we get power back."

The woman snorted. "How do I even know you still got them and they're not whacked? Did you save them?"

Sheree stared down at the floor.

Nelson chewed on a candy bar. "She's got a point."

The kid pointed at Nelson and wailed. "I'm hungry! I want a Santa Snack!"

"Are you kidding? $7.50 for a cookie? C'mon," she grabbed her kid by the armpit and led her screaming down the aisle.

"I WANT A SANTA SNACK!"

"Shhh! I'll take you to Buddy Burgers for a Buddy Pie."

"AAAAHHH!!"

I looked after the kid and completely agreed. Fried frozen pie wasn't my idea of a treat, either.

A harassed-looking father stepped out of line, clutching his toddler. "Excuse me, but how much longer do you think we're going to have to wait?"

Nelson's walky talkie jumped to life. He held up a hand, and grunted into it. Then he hung up.

"Well, that's it."

Barry looked nervously at the line that stretched back toward the dawn of time. "Oh, you mean we'll be up and running in no time?"

Nelson smiled. "Nope, we've got a snow day. The mall's shutting down."

A collective wail crashed over us from the masses.

Barry looked like he was about to lose his Santa Snack. "You're joking, right? Aren't there any backup generators?"

Nelson nodded. "Sure. They're just not working. They gotta have the power company come out here and everything."

The nervous father piped up again. "I'm sorry, but isn't there anything you can do? My wife told me I had to get this done today, or else!"

We all looked at the man sympathetically. "We'll put a notice on the mall's website, once we're up and running again," Barry said nicely.

The man shook his head vehemently. "No! You don't understand! I completely botched last year! I put it off until the last minute, and then Caesar here came down with strep – and bam! No picture with Santy! My mother-in-law hasn't let me hear the end of it!"

Barry looked beaten. "I'm sorry, there's really not much we can do."

"Oh, yes there is!" A formidable grandma marched out of line with a pair of wriggling twins. "We're gonna do what that gal just did! We'll take our own pictures!"

Barry looked pale again. "I'm sorry, you really can't do that. Besides, we have no way to process your payments now."

"Payment? You think I'm gonna pay you to take my own pictures?"

Barry gulped. "Well, you see, Santa is also one of Santa's Sidekicks, and Santa cannot pose without being reimbursed for being a special helper."

The grandma waved him off, and shouted at Santa. "How's cash?"

"How much?"

"I'll give you twenty bucks."

"Done!"

The frightened father brightened a bit. "Me, too!"

In a matter of moments, Santa had made a few hundred dollars. The rest of us were without a shift.

"Well, that's that," Sheree said, grabbing her coat and wrestling away from the mob.

Barry nodded sadly. "Next year, I'm applying to be Santa."

"You'll get a wet lap."

"But I'll get cold cash."

Nelson snorted. "I wouldn't count on this happening again in your lifetime. I've been here for eight years, and the longest outage we ever had before this one was two hours. This is really something."

I imagined shoppers and store owners alike were none too happy about a missed morning of material gain. Judging by the orange that sailed out of the crowd and into Nelson's back, I was correct.

"What the?" Nelson grabbed the orange off the floor and hurled it back.

Someone yelped. "Ow!"

"Oh, great." Nelson jumped back and sped off on his scooter.

Sheree and Barry looked at me. "This would be a good time to not be here."

We turned to leave just as Myron Stumpfs strode angrily toward us. I mean, me. Which made good sense. I also used to work with Myron during my EEJIT days. Or, to Myron's way of thinking, I worked for him. At least, that's what his daily dose of verbal vomit intimated. That ran, until he got arrested for stealing company data and re-selling it through a hacking outfit dealing somewhere outside of Bangladesh. Miracles of the internet, yes? He'd been picked up easily after leaving a boat load of clues. But apparently he'd moved onto other waters. I had hoped he remained in jail. I was wrong.

"Of course, it would be you, wouldn't it?"

"But I…"

"Don't think you'll get away with this. I'm going to call Security!"

"Myron, I…"

Barry stepped in. "I realize you're upset, you probably just got pelted with a nasty old orange, didn't you?"

"Yes!"

Barry nodded sympathetically. "Yes, they really do get out of hand when they can't have their Santy pictures."

Myron swung around. The masses of devices snapping pictures looked like a sea of paparazzi surrounding Santa.

"Aren't they getting their pictures?"

Barry shook his head. "Our equipment is down because of the outage. Those are black market pictures – not of our doing, of course."

A glimmer of understanding came over Myron.

"Are you saying one of those families hurled an orange at me?"

"Well, probably not specifically at you. And not one of those families. Specifically, it was probably her." Barry pointed at the mean mommy returning back down the mall with Petunia and her pie.

Myron huffed. "Yes, well, of course. I suppose it goes with the territory."

"Exactly."

"As for you, Mina. Unless you are dressed for trick-or-treat I can only assume you work here as well."

"You work here?"

Myron sniffed. "It's temporary until I can find something more suitable."

Yeah. Maybe like prison. I wondered about the data stealing last summer. I could only figure he'd been let out on some kind of bond.

"Well, that's great. Nice to see you." Liar, liar pants on fire.

"Look, Mina – I didn't like working with you at EEJIT, and I'm somewhat appalled to be employed at the same location that would even consider you to be qualified as an elf."

"*Sidekick*," we all replied.

"Whatever. You stay on your side, and I'll stay on mine." Myron turned on his heel and marched back to his mall gig.

"Who do you supposed hired him to work Christmas?" Sheree asked.

"Scrooge?"

Barry shook his head. "You really worked with that guy?"

"Yep."

"You better travel incognito."

I stared down at my booties and vest full of Sparkle, and re-arranged my hat. "No problem."

I grabbed my coat and plodded back toward the mall entrance, along with a few hundred of my colleagues. The crowd lined up to exit was actually longer than the 'Mail-It-2' line. Then I realized I had bills to pay, and mail, if I wanted to keep my own lights on at home.

"What'll it be, Toots?" The Vito clone stood behind the counter, waiting on me.

I stared at him.

He shrugged. "Sorry about the little skirmish in your driveway. Family business, if you know what I mean."

I gulped a bit. "Sure. Completely understandable."

"So what'll it be? You got some goodies you want wrapped?"

"Just a book of stamps, thanks."

"One book of stamps, coming right up! You want the Virgin, or the Snowmen?"

"Either one, thanks."

He looked me up and down. "No offense, but you don't look like no Virgin. Snowmen it is."

"Huh?"

"I got a sense for these things."

"All right, here you go. Take your break. Here is your lunch, such as it is." Myron came up from behind me, plopped a paper bag in front of Buddy, then turned and stared directly at me.

"You again! I told you to keep your distance!"

"Hey, you keep your trap shut! This here's a paying customer!"

Myron squinted his eyes and sniffed.

"That'll be $9.20, Miss."

I handed him my credit card.

Buddy shook his head. "I'm sorry Miss, we only take cash. Good thing though, with the power down and all."

"Oh, right." I fumbled around in my pocketbook for an eon and eventually found a ten dollar bill – I was thankful Hilda gave us our tips in cash.

Buddy handed me the change. "Thank you, come again."

I stepped to the side to let the person behind me get served while I attempted to re-pack my handbag, spilling the contents of my wallet everywhere.

"Oh, please go on break! You can't seriously think to eat that putrid stuff here, in front of people, can you?" Myron hissed at Buddy, just after he processed the next shopper.

"To each his own." Buddy opened up the wrapper, removed the bun and bit into what looked like a raw meat patty. Ick!

He chewed, considering Myron. "You might want to be careful how you talk to me. You never know if I'll get out of control."

Myron frowned. "That's completely ridiculous."

"I'm just saying."

"And you might want to be careful about who you befriend in this town."

"How do you mean?"

"That woman – who bought the stamps."

"Nice kid. Vito's neighbor. Could come in handy."

Myron shook his head. "Trouble. All kinds of trouble."

"C'mon? Whaddaya mean?"

"She cost me my job."

"But now you got me, right? See, everything happens for a reason." Buddy gulped some more raw meat down.

Myron shuddered, then noticed the next person in line. Then he saw me. "Are you *still* here?"

"Just leaving!" I swung around and smacked right into James. And his lunch.

James was, as usual, tall, blonde, muscular and perfect. Nary a wrinkle on his clothes, or a mussed hair. He probably looks ready for a GQ photo shoot in his sleep. Hence, the soup splayed across his chest was more than a jot out of character.

James shook Miso soup off his hand. "Well, I shouldn't want to surprise you."

"Sorry!" I grabbed some tissues from my handbag and pawed at him. "Oh wow, I've spilled all your soup!"

James peered inside. "No, I've still got a good bit left. And I've a Sushi roll. No worries."

"I didn't burn you, did I?"

James shook his head. "Heavens, no. I got it outside the mall. By the time I got across the parking lot it was tepid."

"Well, that's too bad. It looks like a pretty nice lunch, though."

"Yes, well, I'm celebrating a bit. Actually, it's rather good that you ran into me."

"Ha, ha."

He looked at me. "Oh, yes. I get it."

"What's up?"

"Actually, it looks like you will be a very busy girl after the holidays. Particularly around Valentine's Day."

"Really?" I wondered idly what kind of busy he meant in connection with Valentine's Day, and felt my face flush a notch.

"We've got a tremendous amount of massage party bookings. I was planning on emailing them to you this weekend, so you could get started with your menus."

"That's great! Thank you!" And it was great. It wasn't as great as my fantasy, but my checkbook would be ecstatic.

James shook his head and smiled at me. "Fine. I'll be in touch later, then."

And he walked away toward his massage booth. Well.

I headed back toward the van, the smell of Miso soup hanging heavily in the air. Well, actually it was hanging heavily on me - I'd dumped more on me than on James. Which made me hungry. Well, you know what they say about Japanese food - you're always hungry right after you wear it.

I hopped inside, making sure to turn the radio on before I even attempted to start her up - wearing frozen soup would be very uncomfortable. I thunked my head on the wheel in time to "I Wanna Hippopotamus for Christmas" while I wondered about the dry cleaning bill for my Sidekick duds. I supposed I was going to have to visit Lickety-Split Laundry and Mrs. Phang after all. It would be interesting to do dry cleaning business with them, now that they were actually a dry cleaning business.

Last summer, Mrs. Phang and Vito enlisted the senior crowd at St. Bart's for some not-too-kosher prescription sales, using my basement for storage and the dry-cleaning business as a front. It actually did run as a dry-cleaners, it's just that the prescription drug sales made a bundle more profit. They bailed out of that jam, and jumped head-long into the legitimate business, just before they got busted. I guessed things were doing okay since the doors were still open.

I pulled up into my garage. I opened the door to a cacophonous rendition of "Roll Out the Barrel!" played by what sounded like a brigade of accordions.

"*Vito!*" I mean, who else could it be?

Nothing. Not even Vinnie.

"VITO!"

Footsteps thundered hastily up from the basement. "Sorry, sorry, sorry, Toots." Vito hurried to turn the volume down.

"What are you doing in the basement?"

Suddenly Miriam appeared, a bit disheveled and flushed.

"Never mind."

"Hey, don't go so fast."

I looked at Vito, then I looked at Miriam. She was hastily re-arranging a lime green and purple polka-dotted velour costume complete with matching lime green and purple jewelry. Lots of it.

"We was just counting inventory, for the bizarre."

"Bazaar."

"Yes!"

Vito consulted his shoelaces.

"But I think we're all caught up and in good shape now!" Miriam exited out the front door, minus her shoes.

"Look, it's not what you think," Vito began.

"LA-LA-LA I can't hear you."

"Seriously, there was no hanky panky going on in your basement."

"TMI."

"I'm 66 years old for Crissakes!"

I stared levelly at Vito.

"I know, I know. I'm Polish. And Jewish. We're passionate people. But I swear, on Marie's grave, there was no funny business going on in your house."

I put my hands on my hips.

"Miriam wore spikes to impress me. They did. But they hurt her feet. We was just counting supplies for the bazaar."

I held up a hand.

The door knocked. I figured it was Miriam looking for her lost spikes. I opened the door to find Bauser, Norman and Jim.

Bauser and Norman got fired from EEJIT the same day I did. Or rather, Bauser and me got fired, Norman quit. But, as we found out, Norman could quit because he has more inherited bank accounts than Pee-AY has pork and sauerkraut for New Year's. Go figure. About the pork and sauerkraut, I mean.

Jim is Bauser's three-legged pooch. He's good at sitting pretty but only just before he hits the floor. His heart is in the right place. His legs, not so much.

"Wazzup?" Bauser asked, while Norman held Jim up.

"Just the usual."

Norman peered in. "You mean something's on fire again?"

"No, nothing that ordinary."

The boys shuffled in carefully.

"Hey, fellas. How's tricks?" Vito lumbered at us, his dishtowel back in place over his shoulder.

Bauser held Jim up with his knee. "Great! We're going to have a business lunch! Wanna come?"

I sighed inwardly, a tad jealous. "Congrats. Where are you working?"

"Anywhere we want!"

"Come again?"

Norman cleared his throat. "Actually, we're working for us."

I stared at them blankly. Vito clapped and let out a whoop. "That's great! You're in business for yourselves! *Mazeltov*!"

"You're setting up your own company?"

Norman shook his head. "Actually, we'll probably start out as a partnership. Or an LLC. After we figure out a name. That is, after we figure out a business."

"You don't know what you'll be doing?"

"Not specifically. But it will be an online service of some kind. We're trying to narrow it down."

I shook my head. "So what's the lunch about?"

Bauser stepped forward. Jim slid down. "To figure out what kind of a business we want to launch."

Vito nodded. "That makes good sense."

I looked at him.

"Taxes. You can write off a business lunch-- legit."

I rubbed my face and wished I would wake up.

"So, you want to come to lunch?"

"At eleven?"

"We want to beat the rush."

Vito stepped forward. "Hey, that would be just great. I still gotta Swiffer for Mina, and that doesn't work out so good when she's around."

I stared at him.

"I mean, Vinnie goes all over the place, following you. When you're not here, he'll just nap. See?"

I sighed. "Well, I've got to go to Lickety Split anyway."

Bauser and Norman looked at Vito.

"No, no, no! We're legit now. Mrs. Phang only does laundry and dry cleaning now, honest."

Bauser shrugged. "Okay. Let's go."

"Wait a minute! I gotta change!"

"You look all right."

Norman sniffed. "Maybe we should go to Lucky Palace, instead of PizzaNow?"

"Why's that?" Bauser asked.

"I smell Chinese food. That always makes me hungry for Chinese food."

I explained about the soup as I raced up the stairs.

Vito got started with the Swiffering as soon as we were out the door. There was a large black pickup truck in the driveway. "You got new wheels, too?"

Bauser shook his head. "Nope, that's Norman's ride."

"Helps with the horses," he explained.

"Does it have heat?"

"Of course. Why?"

I explained about the van as we clambered inside. We followed Norman's nose and wound up at Lucky Palace.

"Come in! Come in! Party of uh, three? Wait..." The cheerful hostess' smile turned upside down at Jim.

"He's a service dog," Bauser explained.

She scowled at Bauser. "You not blind."

"Epileptic."

She shook her head. "I no understand. Used to be dogs for blind. Now epileptic? Yesterday lady bring poodle. Say she has diabetes. We gonna need new license. Follow me." Our hostess led the way, muttering something in an Asian dialect we assumed was not repeatable.

We sat down and looked at each other. Except for Jim, who studied the menu.

CHAPTER 4

Friday

After gobbling bowls of steaming Won-Ton soup and eggrolls and sharing entrees, we freed our jaws to talk.

"I was a lot hungrier than I thought," I admitted.

"So was Jim." Bauser stared at him: Jim had devoured every morsel of a family size bowl of rice.

Norman stifled a burp. "The point is, we do think we know where we're headed."

"Where's that?"

"Online retail."

"You want sell online merchandise?" I all but fell out of my chair.

Bauser shook his head in disgust. As did Jim. "No, silly, we want to help other people sell online."

"So what will you do?"

Norman tugged open the wrapper of his fortune cookie. "Don't know yet. There's tons of possibilities. We need to examine viable options that lead toward long-term sustainability."

"Huh?"

Bauser smashed his cookie open on the table with his fist. "We have to make sure we're not shut down before we get started."

"Got it." I didn't, but felt it was incumbent upon me to say so. I opened my fortune cookie quickly. I had to. Bauser and Norman were munching theirs and Jim was looking possessively at mine.

I stared at my fortune. "What the—"

"What does it say?" Norman asked.

"*Help – prisoner 1465 Conch Avenue, Mantoloking, NJ!*"

"It does not say that," Bauser said.

"It certainly does."

"Give me that." He grabbed my fortune.

Norman made motions for the check.

"Son-of-a-gun. She's right."

Norman took the fortune. "It is a little disconcerting that it's actually handwritten."

I nodded, crunching on what remained of my cookie, since had Jim relieved me of the first half of it.

"Probably some practical joker." Bauser swallowed the rest of his cookie, much to Jim's chagrin.

"Of course."

After we argued about paying the check, with Norman winning, (or losing?) as usual. We left the tip and shuffled out into the cold toward the truck.

"Lickety Split?"

I nodded.

Norman pulled up at the corner of Orange and Prince Streets. I hadn't been there in a while, not since they'd gone legit, anyway. So I was kind of looking forward to it, in a nervous kind of way.

"I'll be right back!" I hopped out with my soiled Sparkle and into the store.

No one was there. I tapped the bell on the counter.

"Just a minute!"

Mrs. Phang's sister-in-law poked her head out from behind a curtained back room.

"Can you have this cleaned by tomorrow?"

The woman looked just as stumped as if I'd asked her about her last trip to the moon. Eventually, the penny dropped and she pulled out a three-ring binder from behind the counter. She opened a section, and ran her finger down the page, frowning. Then she nodded and smiled. "Yes, I can!"

I was beginning to understand who the brains behind the actual dry cleaning business was and worried a bit about Mrs. Phang not being in charge of cleaning my Sparkle.

"Where's Mrs. Phang?"

The woman scrunched up her face with worry. "You know her?"

"Yes. She's friends with my aunt. And my mom."

"What's your name?"

"Mina Kitchen."

The woman jumped a bit. "Oh, *you're* Mina."

My reputation preceded me.

"I'm Fen. Tina's sister-in-law."

She extended a hand warily and we shook.

"That's what I figured." I gazed down at the notebook of instructions, then quickly back to Fen, lest I offend.

Fen shrugged. "I don't know where she is. The last thing she told me was that she was headed for the mall. She hasn't come back. I figured she's just giving me a rest."

"How come?"

She sighed. "We had a tiff. She's really all business sometimes. Anyway, she's not returning my phone calls."

"Well, maybe she'll come back with lunch, as a peace offering."

"I sure hope not."

"Why?"

"She's been gone since Sunday."

I counted on my fingers and toes and realized this was more than forty-eight hours. Very unlike our Mrs. Phang. She was one of those people who didn't consider OCD a personality disorder. She embraced it as a lifestyle.

"Don't you think you should report her missing? I mean, what if she had an accident and is hurt somewhere?"

Fen, who didn't seem like the sharpest chopstick in the drawer, opened her mouth and gaped at me. "You really think so?"

"Probably not. But it would be awful not to call, if it were true."

"I never thought of that!"

Fen was on the phone and dialing before I could utter another peep. I stared resolutely at the cover of the dry cleaning manual, realizing that if I were going to wait for this conversation to be over, I would no longer need my Santa Sparkle - it would be Easter.

I read the instructions while Fen yacked at the police, then wrote out a ticket for my clothes, and a receipt for myself. I made sure to circle the 'one day pickup' option.

I waved bye-bye while she stayed on hold, and headed back to Norman's truck. It was nowhere to be seen.

I was beginning to wonder if being stranded in front of the dry cleaners was going to be a habitual practice. I shivered next to the traffic post. A zillion cars and workers passed by, doing their lunchtime thing. No sign of Norman.

Across the street, there was a new culinary shop, *Gourmet Gadgets Galore*. The window display sported some new-fangled garlic presses, and what looked like some high-end mandolines. And it was sure to be warm inside. I could wait for the fellas on the other side of Prince Street just as well as here, right?

Just as I dashed across the street, a motorcycle came up behind me and slid sideways into the parking meter.

"Oh my gosh, are you okay?"

"What the hell's wrong with you?"

"What?"

"You're lucky I didn't run you over!" The irate driver got up, brushed himself off, and tugged his jacket into place over a sleeve tattoo on his right arm.

"Sorry?"

"Cross at the green, not in-between, you know?"

I glanced guiltily at the specialty lemon zester winking at me from the window. "I'm very sorry. I didn't realize. Are you hurt?"

The man glared at me. "Lucky for you, I'm all right."

A crowd had gathered. I felt the urge to become invisible by hiding in the shop. At this rate, I'd be walking home laden with an entire kitchen.

The guy bent over to right his bike, and I saw several smashed boxes on the ground. I tried to help him pick them up, when several boxes of tape tumbled out.

"Tape!" a voice rang out.

"Tape?"

The guy held up a hand, while hopping back on the bike. "Hey, this here's a delivery!"

"A delivery? Where?" a woman shouted.

"Special delivery for Country Side Mall."

"Which store?"

"Mail-It-2." He revved his engine, then glanced nastily back at me. "Thanks a lot, lady."

Before I could utter a word, he was off. Several people around me texted frantically. A car peeled away from the curb in pursuit.

Bauser and Norman pulled up.

"What was that all about?" Norman asked.

"I don't know. I think I caused an accident. But not on purpose."

Bauser took in the kitchen shop, and shook his head. "You really have a problem, you know?"

I nodded glumly.

They dropped me off at home, where I found Vito in a content post-Swiffering mode, whistling happily with his dish towel over his shoulder. But so was Miriam – she was humming. The sudden image of their having a senior moment – that has nothing to do with senior moments as we know them – sprang to mind. I willed myself not to picture the particulars – especially under my own roof. I blinked a bit, and counted to ten, willing my blood pressure toward something normal. They were well past the age of grownups, yes? Well, at least they weren't sharing a cigarette. Although I had serious reservations. So did the rest of my undigested lunch.

"I just came back for my heels! Ain't they beauts?" Miriam held up a pair of 4-inch, lime green stilettos. Good Lord – Miriam had lime green knock-me-downs.

"Gee." It was all I could manage without losing my lunch all over my newly Swiffered floors.

Vito held up a hand. "Miriam got here just after I finished."

"Oh." I was glad to be spared the details.

"Your floors are still wet. You might wanna hang out upstairs for a little bit, 'til they dry."

"Sure! You don't wanna go traipsing around now! You'll get the floors all schmutzed!"

Miriam had a point.

"Actually, you might also wanna check your answering machine," Vito blushed.

"How come?"

"I kinda overheard part of a message, while I was Swiffering."

"Was it James?"

"Not so good. Basically, it sounds like your cable's getting shut off."

Vito and Miriam made a hasty exit – shoes and all – while I shuffled upstairs, reluctant to listen to my first collection notice.

I found Vinnie sprawled across my bed, yawning. Well, at least he had enough sense not to get his paws wet from Swiffer juice. I played the message, took down the contact information, and gently pounded my head against the desk. Vinnie patted me on the shoulder.

"Thanks."

I called the number and after several hundred dial-up menus, I finally reached a person: Edna.

"So, once I pay the remainder due, can I cancel the service for a while?"

"You could, but it would only cost you more to get reconnected later. You'd have to pay a $200 installation fee."

"What would they install? I've got all the equipment. Don't you guys just hit a button somewhere?"

"Not exactly. All I know is that if you disconnect your service now, you'll pay a whole new installation fee later."

"Crud."

"I'll tell you what you can do, though. You can put your service on 'vacation' – that's just $5 a month. People with vacation homes do that all the time."

"Let me get this straight: I'm collecting unemployment, and working enough part time jobs to qualify for a personality disorder, but I can't get a break because of financial hardship?"

"Nope."

"But someone who's rich enough to have two homes can put their second home satellite receiver on vacation for five bucks a month?"

"Oh, you don't have to be rich. Anyone can do this."

"The benefits of this being?"

"You don't have to pay a new installation fee."

Edna had me there. I gave her my financial particulars to take care of the truant amount, and told her I'd get back to her about vacation status. As much as I hated the idea, it probably would be sensible to put the satellite on hold until I was employed full-time again.

I stared at the pile of bills whimpering in the corner from neglect. I wondered which system of payment to try out this month: toss them on the floor, and the first five get paid? Pay just the little ones? Or pay the ones in the pink and blue envelopes screaming at me? Well, at least I had my stamps at the ready.

Luckily, Vinnie volunteered to be this month's financial advisor, so a few calculator clicks and tail thwackings later and I soon had all the past dues paid.

Mostly, anyhow. The current ones would have to wait in line until the next paycheck. Maybe if I got called by another collection office, I could say it was a fermentation process? Like wine? I had a funny feeling they would prefer payments that were a lot less vintage.

The phone rang, and I cringed, fearing another bill collector. I let it go to the answering machine.

"Hey, it's me! Trixie! You there? Pick up!"

I pounced on the phone. "Sorry!"

"What are you doing, screening your calls?"

"Yes."

"Why? You getting obscene callers?"

"Nope."

"That's too bad. Who're you screening?"

"Bill collectors."

"Yikes!"

"Wazzup?"

"Mike's taking me to dinner at that cute new place by the movies. He was thinking of inviting his co-worker. Do you want to come along?"

"You're setting me up on a date?"

"That was the general idea."

"Sorry. More work plans."

"Oh for crissakes, you're not being Santa's Sidekick at night, are you? Those little monsters will bust your kneecaps."

"Agreed. Happy to report it's not that. I picked up an extra shift for a dinner party."

"Oh. Well at least it's the kind of part-time job you like. Even if it is at night."

"Thanks. Sorry."

"No biggie. Actually, I was kind of hoping to not double-date tonight. Mike's schedule has been at polar opposites with mine for weeks."

"You have a schedule?"

"Ha, ha."

I heard Trixie exhale. "Hey, you're not smoking again, are you?"

A cacophony of coughing responded across the wire. "Whoops! Sorry, gotta go. Catch you later."

Trixie had quit smoking. Several times. I had a suspicion Mike was behind it, which bore the hallmarks of a serious relationship. Trixie and Mike. Vito and Miriam. Gosh.

Well, at least I have Vinnie and Marie.

I checked the time and realized I'd better get moving and changed into service wear. Which meant I didn't have to worry about Vinnie attacking my costume – he was cool with the orange crocs.

I dressed and hustled downstairs, and held up two cans of Finicky Fare to him. He stared at me, and pointedly meowed at the kitchen clock: it was only a quarter past four.

"I know, I know. But I have to leave in fifteen minutes. Do you want to eat now, or at ten o'clock?"

Vinnie muttered something about being ill considered, comparing himself with some fluffy faced cat he'd seen in a television commercial, who at least had staff, and wasn't he clearly the more intelligent, given his recently demonstrated financial prowess?

"Of course you're smarter than that brat cat. But I gotta go. What'll ya have?"

He turned his back to me and knocked one can from the counter onto the floor with his tail.

"Beefy Bottoms it is."

He settled down to eat, while I pulled on my jacket. "Now be good, and no shenanigans, okay?"

He looked at me, winked, and returned to his feast.

I slalomed across town toward my last job for the day. I headed up 741 toward Route 30, realizing I'd better mail my bills – pronto – before tomorrow. Luckily, 741 crosses Harrisburg Pike, where the main post office has late hours. I pulled in, tossed the bills in the mailbox, and wished for nano-second delivery to avoid any further late notice nasties.

By the time I reached Squirrel Run Acres, Chef was almost finished loading the van. Crap.

"Do you need any help?" I asked.

"There are two hotel pans on the counter; can you get them?"

I nodded and hurried away, while Chef re-arranged the cambros.

I spotted Hector in the kitchen on my way out with the pans.

"Still here? You late! Hurry!"

"Okay! Sorry!"

Hector waved me off and walked away shaking his head, muttering something about vans and lost advertising opportunities. I ignored the leap in logic and hustled out the door.

"Here you go!"

Chef responded by whacking his head on the van's roof.

"Oh-my-gosh! Are you all-right?" I put the hotel pans down on the floor of the van and rubbed his forehead without thinking.

Chef looked at me funny. Well, who wouldn't when someone starts feeling up your forehead?

I quickly shoved my hands in my pockets. "Right! Sorry! Hey, isn't there ice in one of the cambros?"

"It's okay. It just sounded bad."

"Are you sure?"

"Yeah." He took the hotel pans, and stacked them along with the others. "You ready?"

"Sure. Just give me a minute to start the van. Do you have the address, in case I lose you?"

He shook his head. "You get to ride gun. The dinner's in Ephrata."

"Oh, okay thanks. You sure?"

Chef nodded toward the Doo-doo. "I want to make sure you get there, in case your radio loses its signal."

Ha, ha.

I went to hop in, and noticed some snow still on the van's roof. I grabbed some and bunched it into a ball. "Here."

He looked at me funny.

"For your forehead – you don't want to have a lump, do you?"

"I don't need a stupid snowball."

"It's not a snowball. It's an ice pack. Here."

"I don't need it." He rubbed his head.

"Oh for Pete's sakes!" I held the snow lump to his forehead, while it melted down my arm. "Could you please hold this on your own forehead?" I shook my arm free of water.

He held the snow lump, and looked at me. "Thanks. It actually does feel better."

"See?"

"I'm beginning to." He gave me a sidelong smile, and started the van, and off we went.

The trip from Squirrel Run Acres to Ephrata was about half an hour. Which was good – it gave us time for Chef to fill me in on the party set-up, menu and details.

We pulled into a reserved parking space on Main Street, in front of a humungous Victorian that had long ago been converted into offices. Now it appeared to house a financial consultant, a tax attorney and a coffee shop.

"Wow, this must have been something back in the day," I mused.

"You like old buildings?"

"Almost bought one downtown."

"Really? Ever been to Cape May?"

"It's my favorite place!"

We finished our chatter just as we reached the front door. Chef rang the bell. "I need to find out where they want us to unload, and see if they have a kitchen entrance."

I nodded. Funny - I had Chef pegged for a chrome and steel guy. Victorian Cape May – who knew?

A matronly middle-aged faux blonde, wearing lots of velvety sparkle and earring bling answered the door. We were quickly given directions to a side entrance.

I picked up a couple of half hotel pans. Chef carried in four whole ones.

He set them down with a thump on the counter. "Look, you set these up. I'll get the rest."

"I can help you carry the rest." I turned around and he was gone.

Well. I commenced with my non-marching orders.

We quickly had things heating and warming, and soon set out a buffet in a room that served as a conference room, but must have once been a showcase dining room.

The guests arrived and everyone was fed hors d'oeuvres and cocktails. Before long, we met Tipsy Town Gal.

"Tell you what I'm gonna do," she slurred at a poor newbie accountant type. "I'm gonna fix you up with my sister."

The object of her affliction gave rapid glances toward another man leaning in the doorway, smiling and shaking his head.

"My kid sister's great! You're gonna love her!"

The man glanced back at doorway man, who was determined to hide his laughter behind some fake coughing. A woman's face appeared next to him.

"Julie! There you are! Hey, can you help me find some coffee?"

"Coffee? This is a party."

The woman smiled and escorted Julie back toward the party. "Precisely."

The accountant fled to the man in the doorway.

"Really! You could have said something!"

"Oh no, not me. Come on, let's find you a beverage."

"Please!"

I was just finished replenishing platters when the coffee gal came back in, picking up a buffet plate. A chorus of laughter came from the other room.

"Great party," I said.

She looked at me. "Hey, I know you!"

I looked blank.

She snapped her fingers. "The elevator - the old Armstrong building on Chestnut?"

The light went on. "Of course! I guess you got a new job?"

She nodded. "Almost a year now."

"That's great."

She shrugged. "It's great until the Holiday party."

"It seems like a nice party."

"It is - until they get to the Kringle game."

"Oh, you mean where everyone trades presents and you all open them at the end?"

"Kind of. But with this company, we open the presents first - then we trade them."

"You mean, if you bought something you thought was nice, it gets traded?"

She nodded. "Traded up."

"Are they all white elephant gifts? Like gag gifts?"

She shook her head. "No, that's what makes it awful. And we all have to spend at least fifty bucks, too."

Yikes. Talk about insult to financial injury.

Julie came back in, looking for my elevator buddy. "C'mon - you're going to miss it! Hal got your espresso maker - he's going to Kringle it!"

"Can't wait." She followed in Julie's wake, rolling her eyes back at me.

Of course, I sympathized. And once again, was glad my EEJIT days were in the rearview mirror.

Chef stared at me from the doorway. I quickly busied myself by cleaning and replenishing the repast.

Later, we deconstructed the party and cleaned up.

"You were a lot of help tonight, Mina. How'd you like off premise work?"

"It was fun. And it was a lot of work. It's funny being in someone else's kitchen, and not knowing where things are."

Chef nodded. "That's why we always carry some back up."

"You mean more food?" Maybe my catering crazies were a requirement, after all.

He smiled. "No, I mean you always take some extra linens, serving utensils, sterno - things to serve with."

"Gotcha."

"Who was that gal you were talking to in the dining room? An old office buddy?"

"Elevator buddy."

"Maybe she has a job lead for you?"

I sighed. "I hadn't thought about that. But probably because I'm thinking I don't want to go back to office work again."

"Really?"

Soon we were headed back down Main Street, toward Route 30. We waited for a traffic light.

"Hey, before I forget, here you go." Chef handed me eighty dollars - cash.

"What for?"

"Your share of the tip from tonight."

"Oh wow - thanks! Maybe I can watch TV next month, after all!"

Chef looked at me. I turned red. The light turned green. The beeping car behind us confirmed that fact.

Chef turned on the radio. Some vintage jazz played softly.

"You like jazz?"

"I like anything that doesn't sound like a hymn."

He laughed. "The Doo-doo's selections are getting pretty old, huh? Well, at least Christmas carols aren't so bad."

"Bah, humbug."

Back in the parking lot of Squirrel Run Acres, we hurried to get the van unloaded in the cold. What trays and platters we couldn't wash right away, we set to soak.

"You need help washing these tomorrow morning?" I asked.

"Would you mind?"

I shook my head. "I don't have anything else planned."

"No Side Kick action?"

I explained about the power outage.

"That's tough."

"Yes and no. My shins could use a break. And, I had to have my Sparkle dry cleaned."

"Sparkle?"

"It's complicated." I stifled a yawn as I put the last pan in the sink to soak. I turned around and found Chef beside me, his arm resting casually on the shelf above my shoulder. He stood close enough to embrace me. Heck, he was close enough to smell his breath mints. He held my gaze for a moment. My feet tingled. I stomped them.

He looked back at the clock. "Okay. Fill me in tomorrow morning. Nine okay?"

"Yip."

Later, I pulled out of the parking lot accompanied by Judy Garland and "Merry Little Christmas". I looked to see Chef in the kitchen doorway, waving good-bye.

I beeped back.

At home, Vinnie sat waiting by the door for me, insisting that he have a second dinner. "Not at ten o'clock you don't, buddy."

"Mwow! Mwow!"

"Okay, we'll compromise." I entered the kitchen and tossed a few Kitty Cookies in his bowl. Vinnie came running in with a clatter, his name tag jingling all the way.

That's when I saw Vito's note. And his latest experiment: Choucroute Garnie. Poor Julia.

A large size Fiestaware dinner plate lay ominously on the counter, covered in foil. A note taped to the top read, "Microwave me - 2 minutes."

I considered it, mostly because I had never destroyed a microwave before and always wondered what the fireworks would look like. Since I was not in a position to contribute to the small appliance industry's profit margin, I nixed it. I wasn't quite adventurous enough yet, to peek beneath the lid. A large slice of kielbasa stared back at me swimming in an ocean of sauerkraut, along with something green. I put it in the fridge, and poured myself a Mug o'Merlot to ease the transition - and my inhibitions - and opted to keep the sofa company for awhile.

CHAPTER 5

Saturday morning

The phone rang off the hook. I woke up underneath dead weight, surfacing from a dream a lot like *Sharknado* but with chorizo. Vinnie yawned and the "no signal" sound blared forth from the TV. Ah, yes. Chateau Kitchen.

"Hello?"

"Are you up?" It was Trixie.

I blinked at the time on the television. It was six-ten. "I am now."

"He dumped me." She stifled a sob.

"Who?"

"Mike!"

"*Mike?*"

"Yes!"

Well, this was significant. Trixie never gets dumped. Except for the one time when she was the other gal. Which we agreed technically didn't count.

Generally speaking, Trixie is always the dumper, never the dumpee.

"What happened?"

I heard Trixie exhale strongly. "He said I had to quit smoking."

"And?"

"I did. Four times."

"That's pretty rough."

"Tell me about it. I know it's not good for me. I'm a nurse, for crissakes."

"Of course."

She exhaled again. "And I'm gonna get fired."

"Huh?"

"New rules, new supervisor. Complete no-smoking facility, including the staff."

"Look - I'm not going to stand up for smoking. But so long as you don't smoke at work, none of their beeswax, right?"

Trixie exhaled again. I could only assume she was blowing huge smoke rings at this point and poking at them vehemently with her middle finger. "Same kinda deal as off-duty recreational drugs and alcohol. It's a whole new ballgame. Matter of fact, before my last promotion, they ran my credit rating."

WTF?

"Turns out, thanks to the last loser, since I'm still bailing myself out of his running up my VISA, I didn't qualify for a pay raise."

"But you work like, sixty hours a week!"

Another exhale. "Actually, sixty-eight."

"That's not fair!"

"Yep. Can you spell me a breakfast? I can't wander around this apartment by myself anymore. I don't have pets, like you do. And my houseplant died." She blew her nose loudly.

"But K. told you you're not allowed to have another houseplant until..."

"I know, I know - spare me the lecture. Mike gave it to me. Now I think it's symbolism. Are you scrambling me some eggs or what?"

"C'mon over."

"Can I come in my jammies?"

"Sure. You can hang as long as you like. But I'll have to duck out on you for a bit."

Trixie heaved another sigh which I imagined was full of nicotine. "James?"

"Squirrel Run. Helping with dishes from last night."

"Sounds major."

"Do you want breakfast or not?"

Trixie arrived on my doorstep looking bereft, clinging to the remains of a rubber plant. "Are you sure we can't save it?"

I peered at it, then at Trixie. "Would you like me to keep it in my garage?"

She brightened. "Why, sure! Maybe it's just gone dormant for the winter!"

I placed the dead plant on the steps, wondering if there weren't also dormant waterfalls in the Sahara.

Trixie tossed her coat on the newel post, while I tossed some eggs into a pan, alongside some sausage I'd started after we hung up.

"So, the thing is, he's a total hypocrite."

"Right."

"I mean, I have one lousy habit."

"Right." I stirred the eggs.

"And he's got like a thousand of them!"

I nodded. I knew the drill. I figured ranting was a time-honored code for beer and sympathy and not much else.

"Is there one G-D good reason he can't put his underwear inside the laundry hamper? It lands, without fail, just four inches next to the G-D basket!"

I looked at her.

"I measured!"

I stirred the eggs and put some bread in the toaster.

"And the nail clipping!"

"It's necessary sometimes, I guess."

"Of course it is! But you trim you nails over the sink, right?"

"Yeah?"

"He doesn't."

"You mean…"

"In the living room. In the kitchen. In the car, for godssakes."

"But not over a sink?"

She shook her head vehemently.

I felt a little squeamish.

"And you know what else? He poots!"

"Poots?"

"*Poots!*"

"Oh." The rant was threatening to lurch well beyond TMI. "Maybe it's the fast food he has to eat, while on stakeout and all."

Trixie snorted. "Probably all the *coffee*. I've never seen anything like it. He drinks it by the gallon. He can't be at home without a mug in his hand. I'm amazed he's able to sleep at all."

"Hazards of the profession?"

Trixie shook her head. "I know nurses with less caffeine addiction."

I buttered the toast, and scooped the eggs and sausages out onto our plates. "Voila!"

Trixie cried.

I hugged her. "There, there. Sounds like he was just a stinky, messy bastard anyway."

She nodded and sniffled a bit more.

"C'mon. You came for breakfast, and breakfast you shall have. Come and eat your strangled eggs."

"Strangled eggs?"

"Yeah. The kind of eggs you make when you want to strangle someone."

She blew her nose and picked up her fork.

"Coffee?"

"I'm off my last shift and have the rest of today and tomorrow off. I wish you had real beer. And Bauser's leftover Krumpthfs doesn't count, sorry."

"Hey!" I dashed to the fridge and pulled out the sole bottle of the artisanal ale – thank you K.

"Wow. Fancy!"

I explained as I uncapped it. "Look, I've got to get washed and dressed for work. Sorry to run out on you."

She waved me off. "I barged in on you."

"You didn't barge," I fibbed, dashing upstairs and over Vinnie.

Crap. I'd forgotten about Vinnie's breakfast. Again.

"BEE-YOU!!!!"

And I'd also apparently forgotten poor Marie, too. Double crap.

"You need help feeding your pets? So you can get going? I can help!"

I considered it. How bad could she do? Baby steps, right?

"Vinnie gets three scoops of Kitty Cookies in his bowl. Marie gets her seed cup refilled with Cockatiel Clusters."

"Got it! Now you hit the shower and I'm on it!"

I showered and dressed into clean service gear and flew back down the stairs before her eggs got cold.

"Wow, you look crisp!"

I stared down at my usual uniform. "Well, I'm not covered in Vinnie or Marie fluff, anyway. Or food. Yet."

Trixie began a smile, then her lip quivered. "Okay, so you get a little fluffed. But at least you have someone who loves you, waiting for you to come home, right?" She dissolved into a puddle of tears.

"There, there. You have people who love you."

"But they don't live with me."

"You don't really want to live with your mother again, do you?"

She shot me a baleful look.

"See? Things could be worse."

"I know. I'm just feeling sorry for myself. I almost never have a day off, and now I have practically two whole days staring me in the face. I don't know what I'm going to do with myself."

"Laundry?"

"Ha, ha."

"Look, I promise I'll call you the moment I get home. And if the rest of the decks are cleared for the day, we'll do something."

"Actually, I probably should focus on laundry."

"I was just kidding!"

"No, it makes good sense. I've got mountains of it. And I never have time to do it. I'm forever buying new clothes because my uniforms are in the hamper."

I looked at her. "That can't really help your credit card, can it?"

She sighed. "Tell me about it. Work a gazillion hours, no time for the wash so you buy new. Don't work a gazillion hours and have time to do the laundry, but not enough cash to make a decent dent in the charge card balance. It's a vicious cycle."

I patted her on the shoulder. "Why don't you bring your laundry here?"

"Really? That would be fabulous! Thank you! I hate the laundromat."

"Who doesn't?"

After promising Trixie – again – that I'd call her soon as I got home, I shooed her away under the valid pretense that I couldn't back down the driveway while her Jeep was parked in the middle of it.

As soon as she was out the door, I tossed the bird seed out of the cat bowl and the Kitty Cookies from

Marie's seed dish. They both looked at me oddly until I replaced their feed with the proper stuff. "Don't worry. Aunt Trixie won't be babysitting again anytime soon."

Vinnie muttered a snarky feline critique, just after I left Marie munching in time to, "Top Hat." It's her favorite musical and I thought it only fair to give her a morning matinee to compensate for the cuisine confusion.

I hot-footed out the door and into the van. Soon I barreled toward Squirrel Run Acres and through the kitchen door. The lights were on but it looked like no one was home. "Hello?"

Hilda trundled forth into the kitchen from her office. "What are you doing here?"

I explained about the dishwashing.

Hilda eyed the dozen or so hotel pans, pots and the like on drying racks next to the sink. Everything was spotless.

Chef ran in, sliding on the floor and looking from Hilda to me. I glanced over my shoulder at the spotless pans on the counter.

"Wow, Hilda, did you do all these? I thought you had off today?" Chef asked. He seemed surprised and flushed. Very flushed. Or was he blushing?

Hilda rested her hands on her hips to consider the lunatics before her. "Arnold washed them. Like he always does after off-premise parties. What are you doing here? You're supposed to be off."

After some clarifications where Chef explained he thought he was leaving a mess and Hilda reminded him he had a full-time dishwasher who wasn't me; we buttoned our coats back up and headed out the door.

"By the way," Hilda added, "today *is* my day off."

Chef stopped dead in his tracks. "What are you prepping? Can I help you?"

She shook her head. "I just came in to finish some bills. But I would like to get them into the mail. Would you mind taking these to the post office, and getting stamps for them? I'll give you petty cash."

Chef shrugged. "Sure."

I spun around. "No, wait! You don't need to make a special trip. I've got stamps!"

Hilda took the stamps, and handed me some change. "Thanks. You're a real life saver."

"No problem." I couldn't help but ask, "But how come you don't pay your bills online?"

"Hector. He's two years older than me, but acts older than my grandpa. Doesn't trust internet technology with finances."

Wow. So I'm not the world's most looney Luddite – I have competition.

"So now that these have stamps, would either of you mind throwing them into the mail box? They need to get picked up today and the mailman usually comes about this time."

"Got it," Chef said. "Team effort." He smiled warmly at me. My feet tingled. I felt myself begin to blush and got embarrassed.

Which was probably why I bumped into a steel cart and launched a hundred muffin tins clattering to the ground. Chef rescued the tins then cleared the obstacle course I'd invented for myself. He held the back door open for me. I wasn't sure if he was being polite or giving me a nice shove out of harm's way. We stood awkwardly in the parking lot, looking down at our shoes.

"Sorry I made you come all the way out here for nothing. I didn't think Arnie was scheduled to clean today."

"He works part time at Save-A-Lots, nights mostly. So it makes good sense. He probably stopped by on his way home this morning."

Chef nodded. "Well, the rest of my day is actually free. How about you?"

"I've got to pick up my Santa Sparkle from Lickety Split. If the power comes back on, I might get my Santa's Sidekick shift back. And I'm kinda hoping I hear from James."

"Oh."

"He hasn't given me a lot of work lately. But he's been very busy with his Stressed Shoppers station at the mall. So I'm hoping he's picked up some new clients."

"Oh, *that* James."

I looked at him. "What other James would I mean?"

"Sorry. Must have confused him with someone else." Chef smiled back brightly.

I rubbed my arms to keep from shivering. "Well, I'd better get going. It's a little brisk out here."

"Brisk? Oh, yes."

"See you."

"Mina?"

109

"Yes?"

"If there's anything I can help you with, just let me know, okay? I've got most of the day open."

"You've got *nothing* to do?" I was incredulous. I always have something to do. It doesn't mean that I actually do anything. It's just that I've got miles of things on lists to which I pay little attention. They keep the paint swatches company.

"Well, yes and no. I might go through a box of recipe books I should have unpacked long ago. But that's about it until the dinner party later."

I considered it. Chef's recipe books had to be real recipe books. Professional. It was very tempting. Then I remembered Trixie and her love-lorn laundry. A promise is a promise.

"I told Trixie she could do laundry at my house. From the sound of it, it could last all day." Or all month, I thought.

"All day?"

"It seems she hasn't done any since July."

He shook his head. "You're a real trooper. I hope Santa brings you everything you want for Christmas. Any wishes?"

"Do you think he does vans?"

"Doubtful."

We smiled hesitantly at each other. "Thanks anyway. Although I'd rather look at recipe books than dirty duds any day."

"Call me if you need an excuse."

"Thanks. But this is sympathy laundry."

"Who died?"

"Her boyfriend."

"What?"

"For the moment, anyway. It's complicated."

"That's a shame. You know, not all relationships have to be complicated." He looked down at me, his blue eyes sparkling in the bright winter light. My feet tingled and I stomped them.

"Geez, you are cold! You better get going." He held open the door for me, and I hopped in. Well, that was that.

I drove away, wondering if I was reading too much into a nice guy's polite conversation. I pushed away the double entendre thoughts beginning to form – it probably wouldn't be a good idea to fantasize about a part-time boss. It would get in the way of my fantasizing about my other part-time boss.

My thoughts and the steering wheel turned in the direction of ransoming my vest from the cleaners.

My luck abruptly changed for the better, when I slid – literally – into a parking space right in front of Lickety Split. I hopped out, only to find the door locked. A sign read, "7:00 a.m. - 5:00 p.m." I certainly was in the ballpark. I banged on the door. I waited. Then I banged some more. How the heck was I going to get my vest?

Some scuttling sounds came from inside, and the door opened a crack.

"Mina?"

"Fen?"

"Quick – come in!" She opened the door to let me in. She glanced furtively around outside, then shut and locked the door.

111

"Why did you lock the door? Are you open for business or not?"

"I have no idea."

"But your sign says 'Open'?"

"Sign?"

I pointed. Fen looked to the door, then, spun the sign around with Ninja-like precision. She leaned against the counter, shaking her head. "I got so overwhelmed. I didn't know what to do. And I still haven't heard from Tina."

"What did the police say?"

"They're looking into it. They want to access her place, to look around."

"Well, that makes sense."

She nodded. "I know. They'll probably want to question all of Tina's friends, so they might contact you, too."

Thoughts of being another front for Vito's new stash in my basement paraded through my mind. This could become a little more interesting than anyone wanted.

"I'm sure she'll turn up soon."

"I hope so. I'm not good at this business on my own."

Truer words were never spoken. "Maybe she's visiting a friend?"

"Probably. But she would never leave the business without instructions for me. She's so organized - even her lists have lists. She could have at least called."

"I probably just over-reacted yesterday. Hey, maybe she ran off with a boyfriend. Ha, ha."

Fen nodded. "The police said they'd be questioning all of them."

"What?"

She giggled, then whispered, "She's a cougar."

I blinked. After Mrs. Phang's initial rabid treatment of me, as well as most everyone else on the planet, it was absurd to think of her interacting with anyone sans snarling and bearing of teeth. Even though she'd started paling around with Auntie, she didn't really strike me as the flirty type, much less a cougar. Yikes. "I hope you don't mind my asking, while all this is going on...but, errm... you wouldn't happen to have my vest ready, would you?"

"You have ticket?"

I produced the crumpled ticket from my wallet, and waited several lifetimes while Fen fumbled among the hanging conveyor racks behind the counter.

She finally emerged. "Here it is!"

Well, it looked like a vest. And she hadn't shrunk it. Unfortunately, instead of being a solid red, it now sported a bright orange patch on the right pocket.

"What happened?"

Fen sighed. "Look, it's clean, right? You have any idea how hard it is to get food and gunk out of felt?"

She had a point. Of sorts. I re-examined the vest and suddenly fell into abject panic. "What did you do with all of my Sparkle?!"

"Sparkle?"

"The buttons! The store discount buttons! They won't let me work my shift without them!"

She tsked. "I took them off, of course. Couldn't clean your vest with all that bling on it, right? Here." Fen handed me a Ziplok bag containing several hundred campaign-like buttons.

"Oh, sorry. Thanks."

"That'll be $10.50."

I grimaced and dug for my wallet. "You know, I'm glad you were able to get this done before... you weren't able to get this done. But there is a very large orange spot on the front pocket now, where there wasn't one before."

Fen threw her hands up in the air. "What is this, some kind of uniform?"

I must truly need a wardrobe consultant. Did she really think I dressed this way? "Well, actually, yes." I filled her in about being Santa's Sidekick.

Fen shook her head. "I had no idea. I guess they'll make you return it, after the holidays? Do you think they'll fine you for the spot?"

"Actually, they made me buy the vest outright, before I began the job."

"What? That's terrible."

"I'll say."

"Yeah. That's one ugly vest."

I nodded.

"Here take it. No charge."

"Are you sure?"

She shrugged. "I really wasn't sure what to charge you, anyway. I can't make sense out of Tina's payment matrix. Polyester shirt or silk shirt. Wool trousers or chinos. Sweater coat or pullover – not a goddam thing about felt."

114

"That's a problem."

"No kidding!"

Another confused customer banged at the door. Fen winced.

"Don't you think you should, umm... let him in?"

She sighed. "I suppose so. But I'm going to get burnt. I didn't finish all of it. It's not all done."

"Maybe you could offer him some kind of discount?"

She brightened. "A delay discount! I never thought of that! I love discounts!"

I hoped Tina returned soon, before Fen gave the shop away.

I skidded home and into the garage in record time, thanks to Straight No Chaser's, "Christmas Medley." I grabbed the dry cleaning bag with my vest, then thought better of it. It would be safer to don my gay apparel at the mall - far, far away from Vinnie. Hopefully, that would be in the very near future, after the juice was back on.

As I entered, the smoke alarm blared. Vito and Miriam's voices bellowed over the din.

"You never listen!"

"I know what I'm doing!"

"So does the fire department!"

Vito shouted a Polish retort and raced into the front hallway, waving one of my chip baskets and a dish towel at the screaming smoke alarm.

"Hiya, Mina!"

"Hey, Vito." I squeezed past him into the kitchen, turned on the exhaust fan and opened the back door. There on the stove top, I saw what

remained of my very best cast iron skillet and the remnants of some mummified sausages.

"He has good intentions, you know?" Miriam waved her hands at the smoke.

I nodded resignedly, remembering something about the path to Hell being paved with them, and reached for a silicon oven mitt. I grabbed the handle of the blistering pan and set it outside on the deck. It sizzled and tattooed a circular burn mark. I swore silently and tossed the pan out into a snow bank. It cracked in half. I swore not-so-silently and returned inside.

The smoke alarm stopped.

"So?" I looked squarely at Vito and Miriam.

Vito threw the dish towel over his shoulder. "Sorry, sorry, sorry, Toots."

"He was just trying to make you some brunch. On account of new car shopping, and all," Miriam chirped from behind.

"New car shopping?"

Vito shrugged. "I need new wheels. They totaled the Towncar."

"He thought we could have a nice brunch together, before we all head out."

"We?"

"Well, sure. I mean, if you don't mind?" Vito blushed.

"Of course she doesn't mind! Everyone likes to go car shopping! Besides, we need to borrow Mina's van, anyway. We got a grill to pick up."

"Grill?"

Vito blushed some more. "Miriam got me a Christmas present."

"A four burner grill! With extra side burners! They put it together free! With a fancy cover!"

The phone rang, it was K. "I'm bored."

"Trade you."

"What now?"

"It looks like I'm going car shopping. Then I pick up a grill."

"Car shopping! What fun! Can I come?"

Miriam piped up from behind. "See? Everyone likes to car shop!"

I sighed. "Sure."

"When are you leaving?"

I turned to Miriam, our newly appointed Director of Activities.

"How's about now? We can grab a bite out! My treat!"

Vito shrugged. K. agreed and we hung up.

Once K. arrived, we all squeezed into my van. I turned on the radio but my usual hymn factory was on a news break. I turned they key. The ignition coughed and I pumped my fist against the dashboard a few hundred times.

K. grimaced. "Great, at this rate we won't get anywhere until the Spring thaw!"

"Why?" Miriam asked.

Vito explained.

Miriam perked up immediately. "This is a synch! Vito, you and K. start singing 'Deck the Halls' and Mina and me will jump in later – like a circle!"

I think she meant a round, but who was I to quibble with a dysfunctional ignition? While it was a circuitous route to starting up the van, it beat the heck out of waiting until news got past the top of the hour.

After some group embarrassment, our ride complied and off we went, toward Manheim Pike and Lancaster's car dealership mainline. Soon, we turned left from Dillersville Road and were on our way.

"So, Vito, what kind of car are you looking for?" K. asked.

"Towncar."

"Hyundai!" Miriam chimed in.

"I see. Maybe you could use a bit of a change?"

"Nope."

"Agreed!" Miriam's voice sung on top of Vito's once more.

"Mina, be an angel, and pull in here?"

"Here? This is for Mini Coopers."

"Precisely."

After satisfying K.'s newly-found lust for Mini's, we went onto the Hyundai dealership at Miriam's insistence. We finally landed at a dealership that sold Lincolns for Vito, the actual buyer of the vehicle.

Vito and Miriam eventually emerged from a behind-the-door discussion with someone who appeared to be the King of the dealership. Vito bore a packet of papers under his arm, bearing witness to his having bought a brand new Towncar. "Nothing fancy."

"When do you pick it up?" K. asked.

"Monday. They're gonna call me."

118

Miriam scooted up beside him. "The inside is beautiful! We really lucked out!!"

We collectively held our breaths, then looked at Vito.

He sighed.

"He wouldn't get talked out of nothing but black, for the outside color." Miriam wagged her finger a lot.

Vito sighed some more.

"But we got a real good deal about the interior package! It's a custom job! But it got returned!"

"Really?" Clearly K. already had return deal swinging plans for his Mini Cooper future.

"If you know the right people! If you catch our drift! Right honey pot?" Miriam elbowed Vito chummily in his side with her elbow.

Vito rubbed his forehead.

"So what kind of interior did you get?" I asked. I had to. I was curious, and besides Miriam was bursting at the seams.

"The seats are a dark purple velour! And the dash is this new thing, *experimental* - not like fake wood. It's a 3-D print of a golden metallic basket weave!"

My.

"So – who's up for a nosh? My treat! Vito and I want to celebrate!"

Vito weighed the tome of contracts in his hands.

K. took the lead. "I'm famished. How about the Lancaster Diner? It's on our way back."

Everyone agreed. Off we went like a herd of turtles.

Vito helped Miriam into the van, while the rest of us scooted inside. Suddenly, an expensively appointed Towncar pulled up alongside Vito. Vito shut the van's door with a thud.

"Hey Vlad! How's tricks? What are you doing with the van? Slumming it? Ha ha!" Buddy stared out the tinted window at Vito from behind Elton John size sunglasses. I noticed his Towncar was a very dark navy blue – nearly black. It had a conservative dark grey leather interior. There wasn't an inch of velvet or metallic gold to be seen.

"I'm doing all right."

"Sure you are."

"Sales are good, huh?"

"Can't complain. You see?" he indicated the new Towncar.

"Me neither. Catch you later."

"I'll look forward to it."

Vito hopped in, as Buddy's car vanished from sight. We meandered along and made our way to the diner without further incident – other than a rousing chorus of "Santa Claus is Coming to Town!" to propel us there.

We'd just ordered, when K.'s cell phone chimed. "Hello? Sure. You want quarters for what again?"

The waitress refilled our coffee mugs. We stared at K.

K. shook his head a few times. "Just a minute." He cupped his hand over the mouth piece. "Mina, did you promise Trixie she could do laundry at your place?"

OMG.

K. grimaced at me, and returned to the phone. "Well, of course she hasn't forgotten you. She's been out doing a Good Samaritan mission for Vito. And Miriam," he added quickly.

Miriam bobbed good-naturedly. Vito grimaced. I slid down in my seat a notch, having completely forgotten about Trixie.

"Look sweetie, they're just bringing our food now." Everyone turned around, looking behind them and under the table for the invisible food K. mentioned. He clinked silverware about the phone. "We'll be finished up in no time. I'll make sure she calls you as soon as we're headed back." He shut the phone and stashed it in his pocket. "Laundry? Trixie?"

"I promised. I forgot."

K. shook his head. "What possessed you? Trixie hasn't done laundry since aught twelve."

I gave everyone the thumbnail sketch about Trixie and Mike and Christmas Past.

"Geez, that's too bad," Vito commented.

"Just awful!" Miriam agreed.

"You know, I'd be happy to let Trixie in and out of your place so's she could do her laundry, if you've got other plans. I mean, so long as it's okay by you?"

"I don't have any plans, really. But I'll let you know if something comes up. You still have the spare key, anyway."

Miriam choked on her coffee.

A waitress and her burly sidekicks began to heft our breakfast platters onto the table. They were stacked high with enough food to feed a goodly portion of Harrisburg.

We ate and ran, leaving piles of leftovers in our wake. It was a real waste. I made a mental note to ask Chef about profit amidst leftover loss.

"We're on our way!" K. proclaimed and snapped his cell phone shut. "Trixie's on her way, too. And you were right. This is definitely sympathy suds. We can't afford to have the Doo-doo stall out." He searched the radio frantically. "The Christmas Song" and all its chestnuts thankfully sang forth.

Vito burped quietly from the back seat. "Sorry, sorry, sorry. Just couldn't imagine any more food – even chestnuts – after that spread."

We all agreed. Miriam shared her Tums.

As we turned onto Columbia Avenue, Miriam face-palmed herself. "Geez! We forgot all about the mall!"

"Mall?" K. practically slathered at the notion.

Vito shook his head. "Honey, another time, okay?"

Miriam pouted. "But the grill!"

"What's at the mall?" K. asked, then patted my arm. "I mean, besides you."

"Ha, ha."

"I got Vito this top notch grill. It just didn't figure to me I couldn't have it delivered."

Vito turned to her. "They do deliver."

"For seventy-five bucks! I could buy a half another grill for that!"

Wow. Were they romantic or what?

We reached my driveway and found Trixie parked at the top.

"This is worse than I thought," K. whispered.

I nodded.

We hopped out and stood by Trixie's Jeep. The back seat was loaded stem to stern with laundry baskets heaped on top of each other. The front seat was loaded with Trixie, puffing vehemently on a cigarette.

I tapped on the window. Trixie rolled it down, and billows of smoke wafted out, along with the sound of a man's sonorous voice.

"Whatcha listening to?" I asked, waving the smoke away.

"Cease Smoking Forever."

K. waved his hand in front of his face. "When do you get to the 'cease' part?"

Trixie shot him a look. "He says to get it all out of your system before you start. I have almost a whole pack left."

Vito nodded. "Stands to reason."

"I'll say. Cigarettes are so expensive nowadays. I don't know how anyone with any sense affords it," Miriam chorused.

Trixie shook her head.

"Oh! I mean – unless you get a deal! You probably get a discount, working for the hospital and all!"

K. looked at her. "Of course, that makes perfect sense. Wholesale carcinogens. Keeps the hospital's volume up."

123

Vito took hold of Miriam's elbow and quickly led her into his house.

K. and I helped unload Trixie's laundry while she unloaded on us.

We loaded up the first batch while Trixie sat on the sofa next to Vinnie, and spun her tale of woe. Vinnie snored.

"Sweetie, I'm sorry. They say these things happen for a reason, you know," K.patted Trixie's shoulder.

"I know. It's just that it's right before Christmas." Trixie blew her nose again.

"Maybe you'll make up?" I suggested. "You never know."

K. and Trixie stared at me. My statement hovered in the air like toxic fumes.

The phone rang, and I found myself wishing it was Chef. An afternoon pouring over recipe books with tall, dark and handsome would sure beat pouring unappreciated tea and sympathy.

"We're on! How soon can you get here? I'm flying solo!" Barry rattled into the phone. Screams and crying and things being broken sounded in the background.

"Barry?"

"Who else? *No, you cannot do that little girl!* Santa won't be happy…" A man's shouting bellowed in the background as a child wailed. Clearly, the little girl had discovered that Santa wasn't happy with her.

"Is the power back on?"

"No. Just some temporary generators. But we're all hooked up. Ow!"

I sighed. I wondered when they would finally come up with Santa sanctioned shin guards. "When do you need me?"

"Yesterday!"

I made another promise I was sure I'd regret, and hung up.

Vito poked his head inside the front door.

"Sorry, Toots. But Miriam's pretty set on picking up the grill today. Mind if I borrow your van?"

"I wish I could. But I just picked up another shift."

"For the chef?"

"Santa."

"Hey, that works out great! We could drop you off at the mall, and pick you up after we get the grill."

"The mall! We're going to the mall! Woot!" K. loves Christmas. And the mall. Nirvana. Mecca. Whatever.

Trixie pouted. "I guess you can just leave me a key, to lock up."

We glanced at one another guiltily.

"Oh, no you don't, missy! You're going to have a load in the dryer, and another in the washer. Vito, how long will it take to pick up your grill?"

"Only about an hour!" Miriam piped up, pouncing on the tail end of the conversation.

"You and I will shop while Vito and Miriam pick up their grill. We'll drop Mina off to play with Santa. Mina, what time will your shift end?"

I shrugged. "Maybe six? Dunno."

"Right! I'll check in with Mina. When she's ready to call it quits, I'll call Trixie's cell phone and she'll let Vito and Miriam know. Then we'll all meet back at Chi-Chi's.

"This is terrific! I love shopping!" Miriam pounced at the chance.

Vito sighed. "Okay."

"After we come back with the gang, you'll finish your final round of duds!"

Trixie blew her nose a bit. "It sure sounds better than sitting here waiting for the spin cycle."

"Precisely."

"Sure! Nothing cheers me up better than a little shopping! Especially if you find a good sale!" Miriam enthused.

"It's too bad I don't have Mike's presents with me. I could return them. I wouldn't have to waste a trip," Trixie blew again.

We rolled our collective eyes. K. patted her some more. Miriam offered her a Tums. Vito examined the ceiling.

"Well, I hate to break up a good time, but Barry sounded kind of desperate."

We launched into our winter gear and out the door. I glanced back to see Vinnie, still snoring on the sofa. Clearly, he wasn't worried about any laundry, or his love life.

CHAPTER 6

Saturday afternoon

Vito and Miriam dropped us off in front of the Mall Entrance North. I stared guiltily at my employee counterparts as we drove past, plodding their way across the vast parking lot the way I normally did. Had no one thought of employee shuttles?

K. led Trixie gently by the arm. "You see, it's Christmas. And you're a grown-up. That means, even if you're happy, you're blue. It's nostalgic."

"So, even if I were still with Mike, I'd be miserable?"

"Precisely."

Trixie took K.'s arm, and they trotted together down the lane toward tandem holiday budget destruction.

That is, after we squeezed past a line that stretched into the parking lot. Apparently, 'Mail-It-2' was doing a brisk business. As I reached the kiosk, I saw Buddy's forehead slick with sweat, as he hefted package after package across the counter. I wondered if he wasn't a little too long in the tooth for that. I looked around for Myron but didn't see him. I figured he was probably doing all the easy work like rolling coins and counting bills in the back. It looked like Buddy was definitely ready for a break. Either that or a stroke.

I turned around and a guy with a handcart barreled into me – boxes flew everywhere.

"Hey, watch it lady!"

"Ouch!"

"What the hell you do think you're doing?"

"Walking?"

"Yeah? Walk someplace else, would ya?" The rude guy leaned over me to grab his boxes.

I scrambled out of the way, then recognized the tattoo. Its owner recognized me, too.

"You! Again!"

"Small world?"

"You have any idea how much damage you did to my bike?"

"Well, at least your hand truck's no worse for wear."

He muttered under his breath, shoving the last packages back onto the cart, "Stay outta my way." He dodged out the door, ferrying his burden toward a waiting white cargo van.

I counted to ten, and tried to get my blood pressure under control before I went on shift. I was going to face a lot of angry, insulting parents and their kids for the next few hours. I might as well consider this a warm up.

As I worked my way through the crowds toward Santa's station, I consoled myself with the idea that the tattoo guy might actually have a worse job than mine. He must have been late for his deliveries. At this time of year, there would be heck to pay.

I reached the stand and pulled on my Sidekick wear behind a clump of aqua tinseled Christmas trees. Barry was waving at me wildly from behind the computer monitor.

"Did Sheree break it again?"

"Worse!"

"What?"

"She quit." Barry mopped his brow, then zipped past me to pop the next little tike onto Santa's knee. He ran back to snap the pix, then ring them out. He scuttled back to me just as I was pinning on a Sparkle button.

"Where's all your Sparkle? Are you nuts?"

"I'm putting it on. See?" I held up my buttoned lapel.

"You better add more than that pronto! I can't afford to have you sent home again! I cannot do this all by myself!"

"I'm pinning! I'm pinning! Who would send me home, anyway? I've got it all here." I waved the baggie at him.

"Jane."

"She's never here. She wouldn't know anyway." Jane is the HR manager in charge of ensuring the proper behavior of Sidekicks – including the wearing of Sparkle. She's also the fascist who sent me home for forgetting my hat the one time she did visit. I hoped Santa would bring her a large lump of something.

Barry's eyes popped at me. "Jane…"

"I know, I know. 'Wear the Sparkle!' 'Shine like Sparkle!' 'Sparkle is as Sparkle does!' Where does she come up with this crap?"

Barry clapped his hand over his eyes.

"Actually, the marketing department comes up with this crap."

"Jane!"

"Kitchen."

"Wow! You finally found time to visit us here with Santa! Great!" I should have tossed my baggie and ran out the door. As it was, I just felt like tossing my cookies.

"I see you're still willfully disobeying our Sparkle statute?"

"No! No! See? Got it all here!" I held up the plastic bag. It looked a little soggy now from my nervous sweaty hands.

"It's supposed to be on your vest, Kitchen. Your entire vest has to have all the participating store buttons. See... *Kitchen, what happened to your vest?*" she pointed directly at the large orange splotch on the pocket. It glowed back at us like a psychedelic version of the Japanese flag.

"I had it dry cleaned."

"This does not conform. You are out of uniform!"

Barry groaned softly in the background.

"No! I'm not! Honest! See?" I hurriedly plastered some more buttons over the orange circle.

Jane shook her head. "You are not up to code, Kitchen. It will have to be replaced before you go on shift."

"You mean I have to buy another one?"

"Of course."

"But they're thirty bucks!"

Jane smiled sweetly at me. "Not to worry. I certainly wouldn't expect you to have the cash on you. We'll just deduct it from your next paycheck. Luckily for you, I have an extra vest with me. Otherwise, I'd have to send you home."

Barry groaned again.

"Good thing I came to see how you were doing, Barry. I was worried when I got Sheree's notice. We weren't sure you'd reached anyone to help you."

"Thanks."

"And Kitchen, make sure you have *all* your Sparkle on your new vest right away."

She tossed the vest in its wrapper to me, and clicked away on high heels.

"I can't believe I have to buy another one of these freakin' vests!"

"I can't believe she almost wouldn't let you work today! I would have bought you the vest!"

"Wanna buy me a Christmas present?"

"No."

A few bruised limbs and egos later, Barry and I came up for air and took a short break. He offered me a root beer. I removed and folded my vest and sat on it, then carefully sipped the soda.

"Excuse me, I'm sorry to bother you, but do you work here?"

I considered the rest of my outfit– Santa hat and fake booties – and wondered how the rest of Lancaster must dress for me to be mistaken for a civilian.

"Yes, we do, ma'am," Barry replied, gesturing to the "Santa's Cookie Break" sign standing next to us. "We'll go back to doing pictures in just a few minutes."

"Oh, that's wonderful! I was afraid you'd stopped for the day."

"From your lips to God's ears."

"Pardon?"

"Wishing you a *lovely* New Year's," Barry fudged, then directed the young mommy and her little boy toward the end of the line.

We guzzled the rest of our sodas. Then Barry flipped the cookie break sign around, and we arose to accept our fate. We no sooner had the four-year old (Charles) settled onto Santa's lap, when his mommy (Latisha) screamed and pointed at an enormous bull mastiff careening toward us.

Charles pointed and giggled. "Look, Mommy! Kwe-o!"

"Kwe-o?" I asked, looking around for the interpreter.

"Cleo! Cleo!" the mommy snapped, speed dialing her phone in a frenzy.

"Who's Cleo?" Santa asked.

"Him's my biggest puppy dawggie!" Charles answered happily.

"You might think you have him, but you do not!" Latisha spat into her phone. "No, he is not getting his nails clipped! He's just sped past me and looks like he's racing into Chi-Chi's. You know what's right next to Chi-Chi's, right? Damn straight, it's Cluck 'n Claw. Uh-huh, you heard me. He eats that stuff, we're done for."

"What's wrong with Cluck 'n Claw?" Barry asked. He had to-- he ate there three or more times a day. It was his disaster food place of choice.

"Nothing for you or me. But we got a dog with dietary issues. *Expensive* dietary issues. You understand what I'm saying?"

"Kwe-o go poo-poo on the caw-pet." Charles giggled the explanation. Barry and I stood aghast.

Latisha bobbed her head up and down. "We can't even give him dinner scraps. He's got a digestive disorder. His food costs almost more than ours."

Barry attempted to calm the waters. "Well, sometimes our furry kids have accidents. I'm sure it will be all right."

She stared at him. "You have any idea how much diarrhea a mastiff makes? We already replaced our wall-to-wall – twice."

I briefly considered the wisdom of suggesting linoleum, when a flock of parakeets flew past. Which made sense, since they were being chased by a half dozen puppies.

Barry threw up his arms. "What is this? Jumanji?"

"Look, Mommy! Puppies!"

Latisha returned to speed dialing. "Why aren't you chasing him? I don't see you yet. Where are you?"

"I wanna get down!"

Latisha snapped her phone shut and shushed Charles. Santa bobbed his knee a lot.

"I want puppies!"

Latisha swung around and grabbed me by my vest. "I need your help."

"Hey, careful! This isn't paid for yet!"

"I can't leave him here alone!"

"You want me to watch your kid? Umm..." I nodded toward the line of parents and children snaked behind her, backed up toward the parking lot.

"No! No! I need you to get my dog!"

"What?"

"He's real friendly! He's just big!"

"How am I supposed to find him?"

"He'll be the only mastiff in the store."

"Mina..." Barry pointed to his watch then Charles, fast on the brink of a meltdown.

Latisha thought fast. "I'll give you fifty bucks."

That was one vest plus some non-taxable gas income. I could bribe Barry later.

I looked at him He sighed. "Fine, go. I'm used to working solo. Get back quick."

I dashed toward Chi-Chi's.

I found Cleo right outside of the Cluck 'n Claw, like her human mommy figured. Some kids were petting the hound, a couple shared their milkshakes. They may have been stalling. Surely there were others looking for a saddle.

"Hey, great job guys! Thanks for holding onto the dog!" I panted.

"Is this your dog?"

I shook my head. "No, she's... a friend's."

"What her name?"

"Cleo."

"That's a weird name for a dude."

Cleo sat pretty and demonstrated that he was, quite definitely, a dude.

"It's spelled with a K." I fibbed. Can I think quick, or what?

"Where's your leash?"

"Good point. I umm...forgot it. Hey, can I borrow a belt?"

The boy looked at me oddly. Once I saw his pants were around his knees, I realized he didn't know what a belt was. He certainly was in more need of one than Cleo. Kleo. Whoever.

"You can have my scarf," the girl standing next to him offered.

"Thanks. Lots. I'll get it back to you." Although I had a fleeting urge to suggest she give it to her boyfriend for Christmas.

"It's okay. It's from my ex. It makes Jacob jealous, anyway."

"Does not!"

"Does too!"

I felt like I was back home with Vito and Miriam.

I led the dog away from his non-canine cuisine at the end of a glittery purple scarf, and hoped he wouldn't pull my arm out of its socket. As luck would have it, he was a very complacent, obedient dog. I wondered how he got loose. He didn't seem like a bolt and run kind of pooch.

Just as we ambled past Barney's Books, someone yelled my name.

I swung the Titanic dog around and saw Ida Rose waving wildly at me from just outside the bookstore.

"You're just the person we need!"

"We?"

"Walter's book signing! Did you forget?"

In fact, I had. "Sorry. How's it going?"

She made a face. "It was a complete and utter bore until a few moments ago!"

"What happened?"

"A big bird flew in and sat on Walter's shoulder!"

"That must have drawn a crowd!"

Ida nodded "It did. But it's making Walter a nervous wreck. He's trying to be good about it, but he's terrified of birds."

"Really?"

"Really."

Wow. I've known Walter for a long time, and never knew he had an avian aversion. I met him through Ida Rose, and he somewhat ran with our crowd when he could tear himself away from his virtual crowd. So I had no idea about this phobia.

He'd finally released a novel under his own name, and I should have remembered the signing. He was very excited about it and described it as a take-off on a Wolfgang Puck-type cookbook for vampires. He explained that vampires are very 'in.'

136

Walter works free-lance as a ghost writer for a whole bunch of publications. He also reviews cookbooks, which explained the gist of his fiction, as well as some of his tonnage. Walter is exceedingly heavy, well past the point of concern and smack dab in the middle of OMG.

"But he knows about my Marie, my cockatiel?"

"That's why he doesn't visit."

"Oh. I thought it was because he might not fit."

"With what?"

"The door."

Ida waved me off. "That's why we need your help. Can you take this bird with you?"

"I can try, but I'm not making any promises."

Inside the shop, Walter sat stoically at a table, with an African Grey sleeping on his shoulder, nuzzled next to his ear. A crowd of on-lookers cooed, took pictures and tweeted. Walter smiled tightly, but brightened when he saw me. "Mina. Help."

I nodded and indicated the dog with a shrug.

"Trade you?"

"Sorry. Not mine. Returning him to his owner."

"Please!"

The cash register rang, and I looked up to see Buddy coming toward us. "Hi, Mina. Hey, Walter, thanks again for the autograph!"

"No problem. Thanks for picking up a copy," Walter said through gritted teeth, careful not to awaken the conked creature.

Buddy left, and Walter regarded me. "You know that guy?"

"Sort of. In passing. He runs the Mail-It-2 stand."

"That guy is weird."

I considered it. "He is a bit eccentric."

"Eccentric! The store manager threatened to throw him out if he continued to drink his beverage in the store," Ida said.

"Well, that's understandable."

Walter shook his head, carefully. "No, they serve lattes here, chai – you name it. He was just gross."

"Was he slurping?"

"No. It was *what* he was drinking."

I thought about it. "Beer?"

Walter leaned in with a whisper. "Blood."

The parrot woke up, and lazily stretched its wing. S/he took one look at Rover and hopped onto his back. Luckily, the dog didn't share Walter's phobia.

I waved bye-bye at my pals and left quickly. I wasn't sure how much longer I could play Dr. Doolittle. Or how to even begin playing Nancy Drew and the Case of the Disgusting Drink.

I made bye-bye waves and headed back, Hound of the Baskervilles and pirate bird in tow. A second later the hound raced toward a fountain in the center court. The bird hopped onto my shoulder just as the scarf ripped from my hand. That was, until it saw the dog lapping from the fountain, and figured this was a great time to take a bath, too.

Aside from the obvious, I wasn't so sure how great drinking or bathing in extreme chlorinated water would be for anyone, especially pets. That, and the water was dyed bright green for Christmas.

After dragging the dog away from the fountain, the bird climbed back up my arm and decided to doze on my shoulder on our trek back. I'm sure this is an "aww" moment for someone. But as the owner of a cockatiel, namely Marie, I knew this would eventually morph into an ewww moment.

I no sooner thought it than I felt the parrot let loose down my back, all over the new non-paid-for vest.

"Crap."

"Rawwk!" the bird concurred.

I led our pilgrimage on a slight detour down a cinder block hallway and toward the restrooms.

Inside the ladies room, I tethered Rover next to the sink, wiped it as best I could (who knows?) and turned on the faucet for him. Since the pooch was well over counter height, he lapped water from his impromptu water bowl sink easily - no worries.

After slipping the cockatiel to perch on the side of the stall, I removed my vest. Completely schmutzed. Yeeshkabiddle. I dabbed off the gunk and made a mental note not to get too mental. S/he was only a bird, who was lost, with or without owner. If it had been me, I'd have crapped, too. As it was, I still wasn't sure who my owner was and life was apparently doing its due diligence in the crappy department. Oh well. Boo flippin' hoo.

I hitched up my virtual big girl panties and headed out the lavatory door with the parrot back on my shoulder, and Kweo in tow. (I tried to encourage the bird to sit back on the dog, but it wasn't having it.)

Just as we came to a bank of lockers near the Men's Room, I heard Myron Stumpf's unmistakably snotty voice.

"You're absolutely sure you have everything settled now?"

"No problem. Bernie won't know what hit him. Thinks he's going on vacation."

"Yes, quite."

"A permanent one!" The other guy sniggered.

"Precisely. This little charade has become quite tedious."

"Huh?"

"Never mind. You've memorized the directions, haven't you? You know exactly where to go?"

"Got it."

"And you know where to find the boat?"

"Absolutely. You're a real genius, you know? Who'd have thought of hiding a boat in..."

"Shhh, you fool!"

That was when Kweo decided to galumph for all he was worth straight into the Men's room.

The parrot thought this was a blast, too. "RAWWK!!"

"What the fuck?"

I scurried up from behind. "Sorry, they really do have minds of their own."

"Mina!"

"Hiya Myron!" I tugged at the dog. He responded by slobbering all over Myron's waist, and pawing at the knees of his trousers. I looked down

140

and saw wet, brown stains on Myron's knees. What the hell had been kneeling in, anyway? Manure?

"How long have you been eavesdropping, Kitchen?"

"Huh?" I pulled at the pooch. He pulled back.

"*What did you hear, bitch?*" It was the guy who ran into me with the hand cart. And the motorcycle. With the weird tattoo. Small world, no?

"Now, now, manners Dexter."

"*Dexter?*" I nearly shrieked. He definitely did not look like a Dexter. Tatt Dude, maybe. Dexter, not so much.

"You gotta problem with that?" Dexter shouted, about a hair away from my face. He could have used a breath mint. Or a tongue scraper.

"Oh, no, no! It's a lovely name! I just wasn't sure I'd heard Myron right. Hey, how's sales?"

"Very well, thank you."

"Great! Hey, look – would love to kibbitz with you and all, but I got a dog and a parrot to return, you know? Hey, fabulous seeing you! Bye!" I desperately tugged the maverick canine toward the exit.

"*Absolutely. Bernie won't know what hit him. Rawwk!*"

I stopped in my tracks, and stared at the bird.

"*Pick up the boat!*"

I didn't want to turn around. But I had to. Myron and Dexter's death ray stares were boring into my back and pulling me toward them. They glared malevolently at me. Actually, they glared malevolently at the African Grey.

The bird responded. "*What the fuck?*"

Myron and Dexter marched toward us.

I shook my finger at the bird. "Now, you know what your mommy said about blue language! Ha, ha! Parrots these days!" I grabbed Rover by the collar and headed Exit, Stage Left like nobody's business.

"I told you she was going to be a problem! She's going to give us away!" Dexter said.

Myron put a hand on his arm, stopping the chase. "No worries. Just eliminate this problem along with our original one."

"You wanna do her, too?"

Myron sniffed. "That's a very colorful way of putting it."

"C'mon, you know what I mean."

"It should be fairly easy to accomplish."

"It'll cost you."

"No worries."

I panted a bit after I reached Santa's Station. I was relieved Myron and Dexter hadn't followed me. But dressed up like an elf, with a parrot and a Bull Mastiff, I sure wasn't hard to spot in a crowd.

Cleo's mom found me, and we swapped her fifty bucks for the canine in question.

"Thank you so much! You are a real life saver!"

"No problem."

"Kwe-oo!" Charles cried with delight, hugging the hound by the neck and hanging a foot in the air.

"He really is one of the family. Would have broke our hearts to lose him."

"Actually, I thought Cleo was a her."

"It's short for Cleophus. It's Greek. It means 'seeing fame'."

"Huh?"

She sighed. "My husband's a jazz pianist. We're hoping."

"Wow. That's a complicated name."

She sighed. "He's a complicated dog."

"Pet people, huh?"

"Definitely."

"Want a parrot?"

"What did you hear, bitch? Rawk!"

Latisha raised her eyebrows. "No thanks."

I went to find Barry, to let him know I wasn't quite finished with my pet finders' improv. I found him with about a half dozen happy families, each holding a wriggling puppy.

"There you are! Back just in time! Business shot up!"

"What else is new?"

"No, really! The animals that got out were all up for adoption!"

"So?"

"So they all got adopted! And now everyone wants Santa pictures of their kids with their furry kids! We have to work fast!"

"Why?" I looked around. The crowd was definitely not going anywhere.

Barry leaned toward me and whispered. "We don't have a pooper scooper."

I could relate.

"Now, put that parrot down and start rounding up… what are you doing with a parrot?"

"Practicing to be a pirate?"

"Very funny. You can't wear a parrot! It's not Christmassy."

"Maybe he'll get adopted?" Then the bird relieved itself – again – down my vest. I sighed.

Barry grimaced. "Maybe not."

"Wow! You got him! Thanks! Oh, this is awesome!" A kid wearing an "Adopt! Don't Shop!" t-shirt dashed up to me, and held out his arm to the parrot. The bird hopped on.

"Is he yours?" I asked.

The kid shook his head. "He's up for adoption. I take care of him. I'm a volunteer."

The parrot leaned over to me, and nibbled at my Sparkle buttons.

"Hey! He really likes you! Want to adopt him?"

I turned around and showed the kid my back.

He shrugged. "Goes with the territory. But they're really smart birds. They can even talk sometimes, too."

"Rawk!"

I considered the parrot's new vocabulary and quickly decided to put a good distance between us.

"Hey, c'mon! We gotta get the rest of these guys back in their crates!" A petite girl with a shaved head and nose ring came up to us, holding an impossibly plump Persian.

"Hamlet! You found Hamlet!" the boy screeched.

The girl snorted. "Wasn't hard. I just went to the food court."

The cat shot the girl an exceedingly harsh look.

"Is he up for adoption, too?" I asked.

The girl smiled. "Yeah, but I have two families interested in him, since he got let out. It was pretty sad, the owner died and no one in the family would take him."

"It's great that someone's interested, though."

"It is. Actually, it was lucky that they got let loose. Hardly anyone was visiting the adopt-a-thon at the pet store. And after all those families stood in line for Santa with the puppies, that was the best!"

"Madison, we should do that next year!"

"Let them loose?"

The boy rolled his eyes. "No! See if we can set up the adopt-a-thon right next to Santa!"

"Leo, that's so cool! We should definitely check that out.

He turned to me. "Thanks for rescuing Sammy."

I patted Sammy's feathered head bye-bye. "Sure."

"Leo, those families are meeting me soon. I gotta get back with Hamlet."

"Gotcha. Let's go."

Barry exhaled a sigh of relief, then spun me around and pawed at my back. "Now hold still – don't move."

"Is it gone?"

"Yick. Mostly."

"What'll I do if Jane comes back?"

"Tell her it's baby puke."

"Does it look like that?"

"No."

A few thousand years later, after posing the kiddies and their canines and several hundred other children sans pets, Barry and Santa and I closed out our shift.

Barry rubbed his head. "Oh, my nerves! My head is throbbing."

I rubbed my knees. "Ditto. But at least you're not crippled."

"What are you two grousing about? Anybody tinkle on you today?" Santa put in.

"I got pooped on."

"Not bad enough little kids are going on me, now I get puppy pee-pee?"

"I think I'm still wearing it."

Santa snorted. "Yeah, you've got some bird poop. Big whoop. I got a bath! It's soaked right through to my skin."

"Yuck!"

"You're telling me."

Barry popped some aspirin with the remains of his soda. "I'm going home and having a hot bath."

"That sounds like a good idea," I said.

Santa grunted. "I'm going home and having a cold brewski."

"That sounds like a good idea, too."

"What are you going to do?" Barry asked.

"I'm thinking of sautéing a few pounds of onions."

Barry and Santa exchanged looks.

"There you are!" K. bounced up to me, beaming.

I looked at him. "Why are you happy? You're empty-handed."

He waved a finger at me. "No, no, no! All purchased and packed. We'll be lucky if there's room for us in your van!"

"Where's Trixie?"

"She's helping Miriam pick up the grill."

"With Vito?"

He shook his head. "No. The heat's on. He's trying to buy Miriam's present, now that she's distracted. Really, I've never seen anything like it – she's like glue!"

I quickly introduced K. to Barry and Carmine, aka Santa, before we all departed.

I took off my vest, folded it and put it inside a shopping bag. I'd have to deal with the mess myself later. K. held my coat open for me.

"Thanks."

"Sure." K. sniffed and made a face. "Oh, we need to get you home. You're ripe."

We traipsed across the mall and headed toward the loading area. Trixie and Miriam were standing just inside the entrance, waiting for us.

"Where's Vito?" Miriam asked. "I thought he was with you?"

"He'll be along shortly. He had a little personal errand," K. explained.

"Oh, for heaven's sakes, why didn't you just say he went to the Men's Room?" Miriam pulled her gloves off and thrust them in her pockets. We stared at her blankly.

A few moments later, Vito made his way toward us – sans shopping bag.

"Weren't you successful?" K. whispered.

Vito patted the inside of his coat. "Very."

K. and I exchanged glances. You never know with Vito.

We climbed into the van, and K. immediately began a rousing chorus of "Deck the Halls." "I'm not waiting around to see if the Doo Doo can be assuaged by Top 40 Christmas carols. I'm freezing!"

"Ditto that!" Trixie agreed.

We trekked back across town with our bargains packed solidly around Vito's grill.

Halfway home, Miriam waved her hand in front of her face. "Oh, pew! What is that?"

"I don't know. But it don't smell good." Vito rolled down the window.

Trixie held her nose. "Amish fertilizer?"

K. swirled around. "No, it's not Amish fertilizer. It's Mina. And opening windows isn't going to help. Besides, it's freezing!"

Vito reluctantly rolled the window back up. "This smells too bad to be just one person. Sorry, Toots."

I hung my head, suffused in the scent of eau de malodorant.

Eventually we slid up my driveway and bailed out quickly. We were all gasping after holding our collective breath for several miles. "Hey, Mina, I thought you told me you got the van cleaned, after that last time with all the dog poop?"

I sniffed inside the van and made a face. "I did. But it sure seems like it came back."

K. and Vito unloaded the grill and set it down. Vito looked around the van. "Well, at least this time there's no flies."

Am I lucky, or what?

"I'm a little disappointed with my buddy's work, if this is the case. I'll take a look at it tomorrow, if you want. Okay Toots?"

"Sure. I'll leave her parked here for you." I waved my hand vigorously in front of my face and shut the door quickly.

K. helped Vito ferry the grill to his front porch.

"Thank you so very much!" Miriam squealed with delight.

Trixie and I hauled the rest inside my house.

Vinnie sat purposefully inside the front hallway, waiting for his dinner. That is, he sat quite still until he saw my elf shoe covers that I forgot to remove. He dove at my right foot and gnawed away.

"Hey, cut it out! I mean it!" I shook my leg but he hung on with renewed fervor.

"Geez, good thing you're not wearing sandals," Trixie said.

"Ha, ha. Gimme a hand here, will you?"

"Not on your life. I don't put my fingers near fangs."

Vinnie growled.

I flapped my arms. "Just go into the kitchen, and open up a can of cat food. That should get his attention."

No sooner did Trixie crack open the can than Vinnie bolted down the hallway for all he was worth. I examined my bootie: it unfortunately complimented my vest. It was covered in slobber and tooth marks. I quickly removed the shoe covers and tossed them on a shelf in the coat closet, far, far away from feline fangs.

"Hey! Get down! Leave me alone!"

I went in the kitchen to find Vinnie standing on his hind legs, swatting his paws at the can of food that Trixie held over her head.

"I mean it! Shoo!"

I took the can away from Trixie, and plopped the contents into Vinnie's bowl.

"He's a big cat! He could bite your finger off!"

I shrugged. "I doubt it. Not unless you're keeping his Finicky Fare from him."

"Hey, maybe you could hire him out as a spokesperson?"

K. popped in the front door and stomped his feet. "So, what should we order for dinner? How's the laundry? Are we on the last cycle?"

"That's a good question. I better go check or I'll be paying Mina rent." Trixie hurried down to the basement.

"Where are Vito and Miriam?"

"At Vito's, arguing over what to make for dinner. It's their date night."

"Oh, jeez."

"However, it looks like the Grill Gods have spared us."

"Why?"

"They were completely intent on grilling a 'special appetizer' for us. Until they discovered that gas grills do not come equipped with fuel. They have to purchase the tank separately."

I shook my head. "That won't stop them. They've got an unguarded kitchen."

K. looked aghast. "In that case, we'd better order quickly!"

CHAPTER 7

Saturday evening into Sunday

Bento boxes devoured, we plotzed and half-listened to a made-for-TV Christmas movie.

K. helped Trixie fold her laundry. "Oh, this is nice! Where'd you get this?"

Trixie lowered a pillow case and sniffed.

"Whoops! We almost used the M-word again! Now, now!" he tossed the Liz Claiborne shirt aside.

Trixie's cell phone rang. "Hello. Oh. Yes, sort of…" she trailed away into the front hall.

"Do you think that's Mike?" I whispered.

K. peered around the corner, and nodded his head.

"I wonder if they'll get back together?"

K. waved one of Trixie's socks at me. "Of course they will! It's Christmas!"

K.'s phone went off and he answered. He took the call and wandered into the dining room.

I stared at Trixie's mountain of laundry, and looked for the remote. Then, my phone rang. I went into the kitchen to answer it, and found myself looking at Trixie and K. talking on their phones. We looked like a telethon.

"Who?" I asked again, trying to focus on the conversation at hand, which had a very bad connection.

"Jack!"

"Chef?"

"Yes!"

"Where are you calling from?"

"Sorry – hold on…there, is this better?"

"Lots."

"Sorry, I just walked out of the freezer. Hey, we might be in a jam tomorrow. Are you available?"

"Sure!"

"That's what I was hoping."

"What time?"

"Huh?"

"What time do you need me?"

There was a moment of silence on his end. "Dunno. I think Hilda picked up some new orders, and I have to go over them with her. I'll call you later, okay?"

"Great. Thanks for the extra work."

"I'm sorry it's last minute. But I'm looking forward to seeing you."

I looked at the phone. Did I just hear that? "Oh, well…"

Clattering and yelling erupted in the background. "Catch ya later. Gotta roll." And he hung up.

Well.

Trixie and K. had just hung up, too. We stood staring at each other in the middle of the kitchen.

K. pointed to Trixie. "You first!"

"Mike said he was sorry. He really cares about me, and he didn't mean to be so harsh and unsympathetic."

"And?"

"And I told him he was a big dumb jerk."

K. rolled his eyes.

I knew better. "So when are you exchanging Christmas presents?"

"Christmas Eve. Then we're driving to his folks for dinner."

K. pantomimed clapping motions and did his happy dance.

"Now you," he nodded to me.

"I got another shift. I'm working tomorrow."

"What else is new?" they chorused.

K. shook his head. "You are the most working, non-working person I know."

"It's true," Trixie agreed.

I shrugged. "So what's your news?"

"I'm going to Lincoln Center! To see the Nutcracker!"

"Wow! Who's taking you?"

"A client, but it should be fun. Someone in her party fell ill, so she has an extra ticket."

"Sweet!"

"Thank you."

My phone rang again. "So when do you want me?" I asked, figuring it was Chef calling back.

"Really, Kitchen, you are a bit odd at times. I shall now spend the rest of my evening contemplating that very question."

It was not Chef. I blushed down to my toes.

"Who is it?" K. mouthed.

"James!"

K. hopped lightly up and down on his toes, and grabbed Trixie, who had just pulled up a stool to watch. "C'mon missy, a-folding we will go…"

"Rats. Just when her love life's getting a love life."

I shushed her away, and tried to put the conversation with James back on an even keel.

"Sorry. Thought you were someone else."

"My. Now I'm hurt."

"A client."

"In that case, I'm jealous. I thought I was your only client?"

"Catering client. The other clients I work for."

"I see. Actually I don't, but it doesn't matter. What are you doing Tuesday evening?"

"This Tuesday? Wow, that's pretty short notice for a party menu…"

"No, no, don't fret. It's to discuss future massage parties."

"A business meeting?"

"If you like. Can you meet me at the Barn Door, say five o'clock?"

We made our arrangements, and hung up.

"Is it a date? Where's he taking you?" K. asked.

Trixie shook her head. "It's more work, isn't it?"

I shrugged. "Sounded like it. But then it didn't sound like it."

K. rolled his eyes. "Are you going out?"

"Yes. I'm meeting him Tuesday night. The Barn Door."

"Ew! Yech! The Darn Boor! Oh, that's too bad."

I looked at him. "I guess you've been there?"

"Once! And that was enough!"

"What's wrong with it?"

"Take it from me," Trixie said, "when you order a beverage, make sure it comes in its own bottle. Don't order anything that comes in a glass."

K. nodded. "It wouldn't hurt to bring your own utensils, either."

Swell.

A little while later, we loaded up K. and Trixie's cars. I waved, holding a covered plate of non-pecan pie thrust upon me by Miriam, after she saw us on the front porch. "We didn't have any pecans. So we used crushed candy canes instead. Clever, right?"

I went inside and took a peak at the pie. It sparkled back at me, winking with a gleam only a dentist could love. I tossed it in the garbage and covered the evidence with some newspaper, in case Vito stopped by to Swiffer again.

I poured some wine, flipped the remote, and settled for the last of the news.

"Keep those tracking numbers, folks," the news anchor warned. "The United States Postal Service is investigating a flurry of missing packages."

"At this time of year, that's a real worry." His co-anchor smiled broadly.

He nodded. "It could be a Grinchy Christmas for many of you out there. So if you're mailing presents, keep track of those tracking numbers."

"It wouldn't hurt to let the recipient know to expect a package, either."

"Good point. You don't have to give away its contents; but you sure would want to know if it doesn't arrive."

I clicked off the remote, dimly thankful my presents went direct via Mom-mobile to my sister. I wondered when I would catch up with them. Then I thought about the Barn Door non-date. It made me a little uneasy. So I decided to whip up a lasagna, to take the edge off.

Later, I padded upstairs to hop in my jammies, and put on the night light for Marie, as Vinnie cat-chirped behind me about early to bed, early to rise, and please don't forget to make his breakfast a top priority in the morning.

Outside the wind swooshed; hail battered against the window pane. I heard it all as I woke up to the phone ringing, trying not to roll on top of Vinnie to answer it.

"Good morning."

"Hello?"

"Mwa-gwuph!" said Vinnie.

"Huh?"

"Who is this?"

"It's Jack. Did I wake you?"

"Uh-huh." I looked at the time. Of course he woke me. It wasn't even dawn.

"We need you here at seven. Can you make it?"

I yawned. "Sure."

"Great. Hey, I'm glad I woke you." He sounded exceedingly pleased with himself.

"Huh?"

There was an odd little silence. Maybe his cell phone quit?

"Otherwise you'd be late, right?"

I rubbed my eyes and ended our chat quickly. I needed coffee. Vinnie sat on the threshold, switching his tail, anxious for his first cup o'cookies, too. Marie peeped in agreement as I shuffled past her door.

I revved up our morning routine, then peered outside. It was dark and wet and dreary. But at least I didn't have to worry about shoveling myself up or down the driveway. This was evidenced by the dark green Crown Victoria sliding out of my driveway with ease. It had been parked just behind my van. Now it peeled into the road and screeched out of sight. Odd. Lost newspaper delivery person? Don't they use GPS now?

I tossed on my service wear and winter gear, and headed out the door. Vito stood on his front porch, waiting for me.

"Kinda early, huh, Toots?"

"You're telling me."

"You headed to the mall? This early?"

"Squirrel Run. Last minute." I yawned.

"Geez, I hope they don't want you to use your van for deliveries."

"Does it still smell bad?"

"I guess. I was going to take a look at it for you, remember?"

"Sorry. I've got to go."

He shrugged. "You gotta do what you gotta do. But I'd leave the windows open, if you know what I mean."

I opened the door and immediately understood.

I rolled down the front windows and sang loudly to a chorus of "Jingle Bells", hoping I could make up in volume what I was losing in warmth. At the first traffic light I pulled my scarf over my head, tying it under my chin. I caught my image in the rearview mirror. I looked ready to peddle apples.

I parked in the lot and launched myself into the kitchen in record time, more than glad for the warmth of the bubbling kettles and ovens. My glasses fogged up. Several stockpots went clattering to the floor as I bumped into them.

"Hey, what gives?"

"Sorry!" I took the glasses off and gave them a wiping.

"Keep your coat on. You've gotta go," Hilda hollered, fussing over a large tray.

"Where are the orders?"

"There," she tilted her chin toward the board.

"They aren't taped to the trays?"

Hilda shook her head. "Not taking any chances. We need you back this morning."

I removed the orders and read them. "There's just two deliveries?"

She nodded. "Chef will fill you in."

"I need your help in the kitchen, after the deliveries, okay?" he asked.

My help in the kitchen? Oh boy!

"Sure! That'd be great!"

"Thanks. Arnie's out sick. I'm short a dishwasher."

Okay, maybe not so great. My pride suffered some instant deflation. But in comparison to the other part time job, it was a definite boost.

I pulled out of the parking lot, and sat waiting at a traffic light, waiting to make the left turn onto Stoney Battery Road. The car waiting on the opposite side of the traffic light put on his right blinker, and made a right on red. The light turned green. I turned and noticed a dark green sedan idling on the side of the road. Odd.

My first delivery was downtown, to what appeared to be some kind of social club. I thought this because the sign read, "Gusto's Club." Because of the hour I got curbside parking. I hopped out with their fruit and muffin trays.

I quickly found out that actually it was Gusto's Boxing Club – they forgot a small detail in their sign. I placed the tray on a reception desk and looked around. There were lots of folks working out, male and female, young and old, mostly beating a bag. "Hello?" I called out.

A buff black guy walked toward the counter. "Hi. Are you interested in a membership?"

"Nope. Just interested in delivering your breakfast."

He looked me up and down. "That's too bad. You look too young to be so out of shape."

"Oh, well. Ha, ha." Thank you? At least I got credit for looking young, right?

"Here's our flyer. You should read it. New members get the first month free."

"Wow. That's great. But everyone here just boxes, right?"

He looked at me funny. "It's a boxing club."

"Oh."

"You interested?"

"Could you teach me how to protect my shins?"

He raised an eyebrow. "You fighting midgets?"

He signed for the tray and carried it away toward a table set up around the corner with coffee, teas and juices.

"Hey, what do you have there, Cal?"

"Your official member appreciation breakfast."

"Breakfast? Where's the eggs? And the donuts?" another guy joshed.

I exited the door on a wave of good-natured laughter. I started the van, and leaned out the open window to check traffic.

A couple walking their boxer passed by. "Pew! Did you close up the bag?"

"Yes!"

My last option was to breathe through my mouth. I checked the directions on the clipboard and signaled to pull out onto the one-way street.

A car pulled behind me and signaled for my spot. I waved "thank you" in the rear view. A man with a ski cap and large scarf over his face waved back. He was driving a dark green Crown Vic.

What a coincidence. How many dark green Crown Victoria's could there be in Lancaster? That said, it is a Grandpa kind of car. And this certainly is the land of the Grandpas. They probably have a union.

I made my way toward Leola, and an outfit located somewhere off of New Holland Pike.

As I pulled up to a crossroad, I read the directions again. "This can't be right." The only buildings around me were a farmhouse, a barn, and some kind of warehouse distribution center.

I pulled up the long driveway to the farmhouse, hopeful to find someone home and ask for directions. A Mennonite family looked like they were getting ready to leave for market.

"You delivering manure?" the man asked.

"No."

I asked for directions. He gave them.

"Happy to help," the man waved me off. I noticed he kept waving his hand in front of his face after I drove off.

It looked like I was going to the warehouse, after all. I got ready to make a left back onto the road, and had to wait for a green Crown Vic to pass.

WTH? Was there a sale?

I pulled into the warehouse parking lot, up close to the front entrance. A plump, middle-aged woman poked her head out the door. "They're here!" she hollered back inside the front door.

I pulled out the sandwich trays pronto, and stacked the brownie and cookie tray on top. I wanted to make sure I got clear of the van's aroma with food ASAP, for the customer's sake.

"Oh! You need a hand!" the lady grabbed the cookie tray, while a tall, older man helped with the other. We went into a makeshift lobby area, complete with a card table, chips, punch and a mini fiber optic Christmas tree.

I looked around while the woman put down the tray. There wasn't a logo or piece of marketing material to be seen.

"So, umm… what do you do here?"

"We rent space."

"For what?"

"For just about anything. You name it. So long as it fits through those doors, we can store it."

I looked to where she pointed at a large window that looked out onto a huge, aircraft-style warehouse, complete with a huge sliding door. A herd of elephants could have strolled through, no problem.

"But we're not self-storage. Let's not confuse folks," the older man chided.

I glanced at the warehouse. "Sure would be a lot of boxes."

He chuckled. "You got that right. No, what we do is mostly commercial storage. Extra equipment, merchandise, forklifts and such. Sometimes containers of retail product."

"But not if they're perishable! Remember that?"

"Sure was a stinker of a problem."

I wasn't sure I wanted to hear what perished, so I grabbed a signature for the delivery sheet and boogied.

Outside it was drizzling freezing rain. Driving with the window wide open wasn't going to be a warm and fuzzy experience. I stopped at a traffic signal, and glanced at the rearview mirror. Behind me sat a Crown Vic with the same bundled driver I'd seen downtown. I wasn't sure I liked the coincidence, especially after being recently kidnapped for tape. After the light turned green, I pulled over and pretended to look for something in the glove compartment. The car sped past me, sending a shower of dirty, slushy water through the open window. Really?

I wove my way back to Squirrel Run. Back in the kitchen, it was a cozy 98 degrees and trolleys and people and bus pans careened across the floor. Life was good.

"Here, next to me!" Hilda shouted across the kitchen.

I dashed to hang up my coat, and quickly stood by her, scrubbing pots and pans like nobody's business.

She looked at my wet hair. "What happened to you?"

"A puddle."

"What did you do, swim in it?" She shook her head, then checked her watch and got behind a cart full of continental breakfasts and pushed it into a banquet room.

"Mina, here!"

I whirled around to see Chef waving me over toward the line. My palms got sweaty, and my feet felt tingly. This didn't look like dishwashing to me!

"Stir this constantly, like this," Chef showed me, stirring a pot of creamy sauce. I took the spoon and paid full attention to the Sacred Sauce. Chef jumped to some burners at the end, and began flipping omelets, working his way down the line across a half dozen or so pans.

The sauce was reaching a nice velvety consistency. "Do you want me to…?"

"Shit!"

"Huh?"

Flames spewed from underneath one burner, and quickly spread to the next.

"Oh my God!"

Chef quickly plated an omelet, then poured salt on the burner. "Mina, shove the sauce to the back! Come here!"

He continued to cook another omelet at the next burner. I followed his lead and poured salt over the burner to put out the successive fire. We did this in rotation until the fires were completely out.

"I need omelets yesterday!" Hilda hurried back in. "Where are they? Oh, here they… what's the matter with you two?"

Chef was leaning over the counter. I felt like all the blood had drained from my face.

"You better get a move on. Next party's coming up."

Chef nodded and dashed to the sauce. "Crap."

"What's wrong? Did I botch it?"

"Nothing you did. I mean, that I didn't tell you to do."

"Is it ruined?"

"Maybe not." He grabbed some plastic wrap, and laid it over the top of the sauce, then carefully pulled it away. He looked at me. "If I had stirred, I would have mixed in the skin. That would have ruined it."

"Gotcha. What happened with the stove?"

"Don't know. There was probably extra grease on the linings. Maybe they didn't get changed out."

"Yikes."

"Yikes is right. We're both lucky we still have eyebrows."

"Do you want me to change them?"

"Wait until they cool off. Right now, I need you to grab some fresh basil from the walk-in."

"Sure."

The walk-in was jam-packed. After peering around a bit, I found the herbs up high. I noticed a bucket full of stock on the floor. I stepped over the bucket, and reached for the basil. Stepping back carefully, I successfully landed my right foot smack dab in the middle of the bucket.

Shit.

I carried the basil and the bucket of unusable stock to Chef.

"Thanks. But I don't need any stock."

"That's a good thing."

"Why?"

"You don't have any." I put the bucket down, and tossed my soggy sock in the garbage.

Chef stared at the pot and shrugged. "Stock happens."

"Sorry."

"It's okay. In about a half hour, we'll have a window to make sure we idiot proof the walk-in and the burners, so we don't wind up in the weeds."

"Thanks for being nice about it."

He went back to his sauce. "It's not the end of the world."

"It would be to me."

"Nope. I've done that. This is nothing."

I stared at him, but he just kept stirring. I tossed the stock down the drain. It was a shame. It smelled wonderful. "On the upside, my foot smells really great."

"I never noticed you not smelling great."

"Huh?"

"Hurry up with that, or we'll be late."

"Oh."

He stirred.

By about noon we'd finished up with the morning's events, and got the kitchen back under control.

Hilda caught up with me as I pulled on my jacket in the locker area. "We're really slammed today. Stop by tomorrow sometime, and I'll have your check for you."

"Sure. No biggie."

Hilda sniffed. "Do you smell soup?"

"No."

I got back home relatively painlessly (thank you, "Ave Maria") and pulled up the driveway to find a geriatric chain gang stretching from my front door to Vito's.

The seniors were lined up shoulder-to-shoulder, passing cardboard boxes from my house and into his.

Oh no. Oh so very, very no.

"Vito!"

Miriam and Vito whirled around as did Evelyn DiSantos and Ed and a majority of the St. Bart's crowd.

Vito held up his hands toward me. "It's not what it looks like, honest!"

"It's for church!" Miriam spluttered.

I looked at my own, wide-open front door and his, then rubbed at the migraine growing behind my eyes. "Where's Vinnie?"

"We got him all tucked up comfy in your room," Ed said.

Well, that was nice.

Ed sniffed and made a face. "Hey, didn't you get your van cleaned last summer?"

"I did."

"Phew!"

Evelyn walked toward me, and sniffed. "I don't smell anything. No wait. I smell soup."

I flapped my arms and went inside.

"We're almost done. And I remembered to turn your heat down, so we didn't waste your electricity," she said.

"Peachy." I looked at the thermostat. My home had cooled to a crisp 58 degrees. How long had they been at this?

I made my way past their assembly line and into the kitchen. The phone rang.

"Mina Kitchen?"

I sighed. "Speaking."

"Hi. This is Tory from the HR Department at Countryside Mall."

My heart fell to the floor. Were they seriously going to fire me before I worked off the new vest?

"Yes?"

"I'm sorry to bother you. But I work for Jane Brubaker. She asked me to call you, to see if you can fill in for Barry at Santa's Station."

"What's wrong with Barry?"

"He called in sick. Honestly, he sounds awful."

I fidgeted. "Isn't there anybody else?" While I could use the extra dough, I could have used a day off. Any more bruises and I'd be direct depositing my paycheck at the doctor's.

"Sort of. But he's a rookie; it's his first shift."

"Great."

"Super!"

"Huh?"

"Can you be here for the one o'clock shift? We need you for the lunchtime crush."

I looked at the clock. It was almost twelve-thirty.

"I guess."

"Thanks! And Mina, make sure you have your vest with you, okay?"

I agreed and hung up the phone soundly, wondering how I could camouflage the birdie accident and avoid the purchase of another vest.

The phone rang again.

"I'm leaving as soon as I can, really!"

"Mina, that is not a proper salutation." It was Auntie. Super.

"Sorry. I'm in kind of a rush. I picked up another shift."

"That's wonderful! With James?"

"No."

"The chef?"

"Nope."

There was a long pause. "You're not still trick-or-treating as an elf, are you?"

"That's Halloween. And I'm not an elf. I'm a Sidekick." I thought hard for a moment about the "kick" part.

"Well, at least you're working."

"Thanks."

"So, do you want to hear our news?"

OMG! "Did Ethel have the twins?"

"Not yet! She's going to be induced!"

"Wow! Do they have a date yet?"

"No, they're supposed to find out Wednesday."

"Great! Call me then, okay? I gotta run."

We said our good-byes and off I dashed away into the non-fallen snow.

Vito was wrestling around in the back of my van while Miriam and the crowd of seniors looked on, holding their noses.

"Got it!" Vito yelped triumphantly, pulling out several bags filled with litter, and the stuff the litter's for, from the wheel well.

"Yuck! I thought your guy got rid of those last summer?" I covered my face with my scarf.

170

Vito nodded. "He did, Toots. This here's a different vintage."

"What the heck?"

"That's what I think. I'm gonna take these off your hands, and see if I can get them analyzed."

"Geez, honey – it doesn't take much to figure out what's in there!" Miriam coughed into her glove.

Vito shook his head. "Whoever did this, was probably the mook who done it before. Just with a different spin."

I stared at Vito, feeling the blood draining from my face. "You mean this time, there were no explosives set up under my van?"

"Under the van might be the least of your problems."

I tried not to shudder. "I better go or I'll be late."

"Where are you working now?"

"The mall."

Vito shook his head. "Maybe you want to borrow a car? Driving the Doo-doo may not be so healthy for you. If you know what I mean."

"Well, of course!" Miriam yelped, springing toward the back of the van. "Here!" She whipped out a vial of perfume from her purse and sprayed the inside of the van for all she was worth.

We took a collective step backward.

"You like it? I'll get you some!"

"What is it?" I coughed.

"Rosé Femanique! Smells just like fresh roses, don't it?"

I nodded, clambering in and opening the windows. I started the ignition. It sputtered and died.

"Oh! You forgot, didn't you?"

I pounded my head gently on the wheel. "Yes, Miriam, I did."

"Well, that's no problem! C'mon gang!"

I launched down the driveway as Miriam conducted the gang's serenading my exit with, "There's No Place Like Home for the Holidays."

The mall was packed. I waited in line to claim a parking space – even the employee ones at the way back were filling up. A dark navy blue Lincoln Towncar sped past me, leaving the mall. I looked up just in time to see Myron Stumpfs behind the wheel. Wasn't that Buddy's new Towncar? Or did they buy matching ones, for Mail-It-2? Weird idea for branding, if you asked me.

I pushed through the crowds towards Santa's stand. It was empty, except for Santa sitting on his throne, eating a seven-dollar cookie.

I threw off my jacket and donned my Sidekick wear like a whirling dervish.

"What's with the cookie?"

Santa pointed. "The 'Cookie Break' sign is up."

"That was from the last shift."

"You want the kids should think Santa fibs?"

I rolled my eyes back toward the North Pole. The line of kids waiting to sit on Santa's lap was slightly less than one to sit on Justin Bieber's.

I looked around, then stared at Santa. "Where's the other Sidekick?"

"Got me. I'm not HR. I just make toys."

"Very funny."

I got ready to switch gears and launch into solo mode – ugh – when a high school kid climbed over the rope and stood in front of me. He continued to text.

"Can I help you?"

"Sure."

"If you want your picture taken with Santa, you'll need to wait at the end of the line."

The kid actually broke eye contact with his phone. "I'm not having my picture taken with Santa!"

I shrugged. "Well, you do seem a little old for that."

"I'm here to be a Sidekick! I'm supposed to report to the other Sidekick, Mina Kitchen." He pulled on his Sidekick vest with as much disdain as a seasoned veteran.

"Really? Oh. Well, that's me."

"You're a Sidekick?"

"Yep."

"Aren't you a little old for that?"

"My checkbook doesn't think so."

Several lifetimes later, we approached the end of our shift. As usual, my knees had been knocked, my shins smashed and for a little added variety, I stubbed my foot against a step and was pretty sure I'd broken a toe.

Text-boy did nada regarding crowd control. Zippo. He was the black hole of social interactions. Except online. He was instrumental at making sure the line stayed strong and linear via Facebook, Twitter, and God only knows what other social media. On the upside, he was good with the computer – so for once I didn't have to call Nelson.

Jane came up behind us. "So, how did Stevie do?"

I whirled around. "Oh! Ah, great! Hey, can I…"

"Star."

Jane turned to him. "You're interrupting."

"Mom, how many times to I have to tell you? It's Star now, you know?"

Mom?

Jane rolled her eyes heavenward, and back to me. "So?"

Realizing that dissing the boss' progeny might be unwise, I retro'd back to my Jersey roots: I lied like a cheap rug. "Terrific! He's some kid!"

Jane smiled. "That's wonderful."

"Don't mention it."

"Oh, and Kitchen, here." Jane handed me a brand new vest. "I noticed the back of your vest is somewhat… soiled."

"Another vest?"

"It's all right, Kitchen. Just get yours cleaned and return the new one, and we'll call it even."

"Oh. Okay."

"But just this once."

The mall was open until midnight, so there were still throngs of shoppers packed inside. As I passed the Mail-It-2 kiosk on my way out, I noticed a closed sign. A huddle of disappointed gift-givers stood around grumbling.

"Crap."

"Now what am I supposed to do?"

"UPS, here I come."

"With that kind of delivery cost, I might just as well take it myself and visit them after all. Rats."

I wondered why the kiosk would be closed with Christmas around the corner – less than two weeks away. It seemed funny that all three of them-- Bernie, Myron and Dexter-- would be off at the same time. Then again, they didn't strike me as rocket doctors. They probably got their wires crossed and were going to have a fit and fall in it once they realized they gave themselves the same shift off, and their stand stood closed.

I drove home, muttering to myself about vests. I couldn't take it to Lickety-Split – especially while Mrs. Phang was AWOL. And I really didn't want to fork over another thirty bucks. I pondered the idea of calling K. and asking about his dry cleaning network, when suddenly I looked up and realized the car in front of me was at a complete stop and I was not.

My van banged nose to bumper with a dark green Crown Vic.

The driver got out and walked steadily toward me.

"Hey, Mina. I figured we'd run into each other again."

"Ha, ha. 'Run into each other.' Good one. Wow, really sorry, Dexter. Complete accident on my part." Dexter! OMG WTF?

"No it wasn't. I made sure to slam my brakes hard. But the cops will figure it was an accident."

"You're calling the cops?"

He shook his head. "No need to. They'll figure it out after they find your van."

"Huh?"

He opened the door and grabbed my arm. "Why don't you step inside my office and I'll explain it to you?" He dragged me out of the van toward the Crown Vic.

I responded reasonably by slamming him upside the head with my clipboard.

"Youch!"

"Hey, how come the Doodoo's pulled over? Your radio on the fritz?" Trixie pulled up in her Jeep. Mike was with her.

Dexter threw me down on the ground hard. Before I could look up, there was a squeal of tires and he was gone.

Mike helped me up. "Should I call that in?"

"No. I don't know. We had an accident."

Mike checked out the bumper, while Trixie checked my bumps. "Yeah, I know about these kind of accidents. Usually these guys wait by a traffic light. Then, when the light turns and the victim accelerates, they ram into him, creating an 'accident'. The victim gets out of his vehicle, ready to trade papers, and then he gets jumped."

"But I hit him."

"Really?"

"Actually, he said he hit his brakes hard on purpose."

Mike looked at me. "You know this guy?"

176

I gave him the thumb-nail sketch of our unhealthy mall employee relationship as well as Dexter's psychopathic tendencies.

"You'd be better off staying clear of this guy."

"You think?" I was about to tell Mike about feeling followed, and all the Crown Vic sightings I'd had. But something held me back. It was probably my humiliation-alarm warning me I was about to sound like a whacko.

"I just called Vito. He's expecting you in fifteen minutes." Trixie clapped her phone shut and shoved a piece of gum in her mouth.

"Vito? You sic'd Vito on me?"

Trixie shrugged. "You won't get a cell phone. And we've got tickets. So I can't follow you home."

I pretended to kick a rock. "I can drive myself home. I don't need a babysitter."

Trixie shook her head. "If that looney's this hostile toward you about some stupid mall job, he could be waiting for you at home."

Well. That was a sobering thought. Maybe Vito and Miriam weren't so bad after all. At least, as long as they didn't make me eat their food.

"Actually, he might be sore about the bird repeating his conversation in the men's room."

"You were in the men's room?"

"Just outside it."

"A the bird was in the men's room?"

"No. The bird was with me. After I rescued Walter from it."

"Walter was with a bird? He hates birds."

"I know. That's why Ida Rose had me take the bird."

"Ida Rose?"

"She was helping Walter with his book signing."

"Damn! I knew there was something I forgot! So whose bird was it?"

"No one's. It was up for adoption at the mall, and kind of got out. Along with the mastiff."

"Mastiff?"

"Yeah. I was walking the mastiff and the bird back, when we overheard Dexter and Myron arguing something about boats and vacations and Buddy Bergers."

"The fast food chain?"

I shook my head. "It's an unfortunate coincidence. Apparently Buddy's an old pal of Vito's."

"This smells like trouble. You better keep your left up. You might want to fill Mike in later. Or Appletree." She unwrapped another piece of gum, and popped it in her mouth.

"Didn't you just put a piece of gum in your mouth?"

Trixie shook her head. "Anti-smoking gum. Smoke-Done. Right now I could use double strength."

Trixie and Mike waited to make sure I drove off okay (thank you, "Grandma Got Run Over By a Reindeer") and they took off for the Yankee Music Theater. Dusk was falling, and the rosy pink sky grew dark quickly. I made my way home with nary a Crown Vic in sight.

CHAPTER 8
Monday

I said it before, and I'll say it again: I hate
Mondays. I shuffled downstairs and into the kitchen
with all the enthusiasm of a minimum wage laborer.

"I guess I got a little carried away."

Vinnie agreed. He thwacked his tail against a pot
on the floor. I sighed and wiped some sauce off of it.
His tail. Not the pot.

As promised, last night Vito stood waiting for
me on the front porch, looking as anxious as a dad on
his daughter's first date. Miriam compounded the
mix by insisting on inviting me over, and producing
cocktails. That's when I discovered Miriam's
mixology skills keep an even pace with her recipe
replacements. How the heck can you screw up a
Bloody Mary? Oh, I remember: substituting rum for
vodka (they were all out) and cramming burnt bacon
strips for stirrers into it (they were also out of celery).

179

After insisting I was fine dining solo ("Gosh! I almost forgot! I already ordered a pie to be delivered! Sorry!") I was finally released. It was my second virtual kidnapping for the week and I was feeling a bit nervy. As soon as I got inside the front door, I got cooking. I had to-- otherwise I'd break out in hives.

Yesterday had been an off-putting day, at best. Especially with visions of Dexter dancing through my head. Quicker than I could put a finger to the side of my nose, I'd whipped up several pans of roasted vegetables, a creamy cauliflower casserole, home-made pickled red cabbage and a pork tenderloin with reduced balsamic vinegar and raspberry gastrique. It took a while to make and by nine o'clock I was feeling hungry. Luckily I had last night's lasagna at the ready.

But as quickly as I'd become possessed by the culinary crazies, I crashed. I'd wimped out big time in the clean-up department and now there were dirty pots and pans karma to pay.

I set to washing until Vinnie stood up, patted my hip and sauntered over to the pet food cabinet. He sat in front of it, gave me his silent meow, and nodded his chin toward the cupboard.

"Oh, geez."

Marie piped up in agreement from upstairs. Another county heard from.

I made the rounds and got them happy, then decided to make myself happy with some gourmet coffee I'd been saving. This morning might not be a special occasion but it sure needed something to get the lead out.

I no sooner got my hands submerged in the sink, when the phone rang. I glanced at the clock and muttered an oath. It was just past eight o'clock. I really, really hoped Barry wasn't calling in sick again.

"Mina Kitchen?"

"Speaking."

"This is Lori, from the Kinzers Employment Agency."

My heart did a flip-flop. Could a normal job actually be on the horizon? "Yes?"

"You interviewed with us several months ago. Are you still available for temporary assignments?"

Oh. Temporary. Well. But, maybe it would lead to something? "Yes, unfortunately, I am; ha, ha."

The joke fell flat. I heard papers being rustled. "Wonderful. Do you do transcription?"

I assured her I could, and she quizzed me about the technical details.

"Now, the rate for this assignment is eighteen dollars an hour. It's marked as an ongoing assignment, so it could be through the end of the week, the end of the month, or longer. Are you okay with that?"

Eighteen bucks an hour! After what I'd been getting paid at my part time jobs, I felt like I'd moved into the next tax bracket. Hey, maybe I could quit the Sidekick job – woot! "That would be acceptable." Jersey girls never let you see them sweat.

"Now the law firm is located on Lime Street, just before you get to Orange." She gave me the address of the firm.

"Oh, yes. I know where you mean. When do I start?"

"Actually, this morning. They open at nine. Can you be there?"

I stared at the clock, wishing it were in a time warp. "Wow, this is cutting it close."

"I understand. If you'd rather decline the assignment…"

"No! I definitely want it. Can you let them know I'll be there as soon as I can?"

We hung up, and all Vinnie saw of me was my dust as I flew upstairs.

I raced downtown and parked at the Duke Street garage. My high-heels clicked along the pavement, and I felt a little ill at ease. It'd been a long time since I'd worn heels, or worked in an office. I hadn't really missed it – but my creditors had. Luckily, I had tons of nine-to-five outfits that still looked cute. Even though I berated myself for wearing the heels. They're not appropriate footwear if I seriously thought I was being followed by a psycho like Dexter. But it was daylight, and besides, vanity won out. What kind of a psycho attacks first thing in the morning?

I stepped out of the elevator and into a large reception area. I walked toward the receptionist to introduce myself.

The gal at the front desk was hissing into the phone. "I told you I mailed them! Two weeks ago! What do you mean, they're not there?"

"Excuse me?"

"I can't track them. I don't have the stupid number. They sent it."

"Pardon?"

"Look, I am not going to buy those Xbox games again! They cost a fortune!"

"I'm here to see…"

"Fine! Go ahead and tell them I'm the meanest Auntie in the world!" She slammed the phone down and clasped her forehead.

"I'm here to see Mr. Hamilton?"

She looked up and noticed me for the first time.

"We don't accept solicitations."

I sighed. "I'm not selling anything. I'm here to work for Mr. Hamilton."

"Oh. You're the temp. Just a minute."

She buzzed the inner sanctum. "Madeline, our office manager, will be out in a minute. Have a seat."

I sat my temp butt down in a temp wing chair and waited. Temp. Feh. But I reminded myself it was a way to get my foot in the door. You never know. Although I was not digging the office vibe.

Madeline Craybill came out and introduced herself. She escorted me past a series of cubicles and offices with uptown furniture and downtown views. She stopped in front of a secretary's station. "This is where you'll be working. There's a coat closet, just there," she pointed.

I hung up my coat.

Then she walked me over to the nearest office door. "Mr. Hamilton, your temporary assistant, Mina, has arrived."

"About time. We start work here promptly at nine, miss."

I stared at them both. "I'm sorry. I thought the agency told you…"

"They did. Mr. Hamilton, Mina was contacted just this morning."

"I see. Well, see that you're here on time tomorrow. You do transcription?"

"Yes."

"Here." He handed me several micro tapes - the old fashioned kind. I took a deep breath. It was going to be a long day. Week. Month. Yes.

"Thanks." I plastered on a smile and turned to leave.

"Oh, and while you're at it, take this and get me some coffee."

Get him *coffee*? Was he joking? What did he think this was, 1964?

"I'll show you to the break room, Mina." Madeline walked out and waited.

Well. I stood corrected. I wondered where to buy my pill-box hat. As well as what they'd make of the internet and Priuses if they ever ventured outside the office doors.

I took the coffee mug, dumped the cassettes on my desk and followed. Madeline gave me the run-down of the office schedule and made the usual small talk. Was I from Lancaster? How long have I lived here? Cold winter this year, yes?

"This is regular, and this is the decaf," she pointed toward the pots. "We have extra mugs in this cabinet, in case Mr. Hamilton has a visitor. He usually doesn't."

"Thanks."

"Oh, and feel free to help yourself to coffee."

"Oh! Thank you." Huh. I guessed I'd been a tad judgmental.

"Certainly. The donation box for staff is just there, to the left of the creamers."

I stood corrected -- again. A certain lyric from bygone days of "The Music Man" sprang to mind, from the song "Iowa Stubborn." Musical theatre buffs take note. 'Nuff said.

Madeline left as I went to toss the leftover coffee into the sink, but found it wouldn't budge. That's because it was held back by a giant green stopper. This, in fact, was a thick, round layer of mold. It had taken apparently taken residence inside Hamilton's mug since dinosaurs roamed the Earth. Yick!

For a moment, I considered pouring the new coffee on top of the putrid growth. I took a breath, counted to ten, and decided to make eighteen-bucks-an-hour my new mantra.

I scrubbed out the gunk, poured Hamilton's coffee, and grabbed some creamers and sugars and stirrers for him. Just to be on the right side of karma.

Outside Hamilton's office door, I heard him yelling into the phone. I placed his beverage and fixings on the desk and fled. I sat at my new desk and started transcribing. After several false starts, mostly because I couldn't hear the tape above his ranting, I got up and quietly closed his door.

Lunchtime came, and I'd finally finished the first drafts. I bundled them up and went to his office and found the door still closed. I knocked. No answer. I went back to my desk, and saw his line was still busy. Was he still on the same call? Couldn't be.

It was almost one o'clock and I fretted about fitting into Madeline's lunchtime parameters. I walked back and knocked timidly on the door. "Mr. Hamilton? I've got your drafts."

Silence.

"I thought I'd go to lunch, if that's all right?"

Not a peep.

Well, this was a conundrum. I couldn't just leave. I had to give him his drafts. Otherwise he'd think I hadn't done my job, right?

I thought for a moment and figured the best bet would be to leave a note on top of the stack letting him know I was leaving for lunch and when I'd return.

I finished the note and walked back to his door. I knocked once again – for luck? No response.

I was a bit nervous about getting HA'd (hollered at) for interrupting a private conversation, but there wasn't much choice.

I turned the door handle and stepped inside. Hamilton sat in his chair, with his back to me. I walked over and quietly put the papers down on the desk. His head leaned forward, slack on his chest. This made sense, given the fact that his 23-inch monitor was blinking full tilt with a gambling site that flashed a 54 font sized message: he'd just lost $96,000. That, and he appeared to be dead.

I flew out of his office and slammed the door shut. I leaned against the door, panting.

"Hey, are you all right?"

I whipped around to find a woman walking briskly toward me.

"Uh, yes."

She shook her head, and lowered her voice. "You don't want to be slamming doors around here. Especially Mr. Hamilton's."

I nodded.

"You're his new temp, right?"

I nodded again.

She motioned me to follow her. "I'm Amber. I started out as a temp here, too. It's not so bad."

"It's just that Mr. Hamilton, he's umm…"

She rolled her eyes. "Let me guess. Told you to get him coffee, screamed on the phone at his wife for an hour, and then locked the door."

"He didn't lock the door."

"Holy crap! You walked in on him?"

"I didn't mean to."

Amber looked around a little furtively. "What was he doing in there?"

"Not much."

"What did he say?"

"Nothing."

"Really?"

"Really."

"Why?"

"He's dead."

"What?"

Amber ran into Hamilton's office, with me hot on her heels. "Oh. My. God."

"I know! I know! Who starts a job and her boss croaks on the first day?"

Amber put a hand to her forehead. "C'mon, let's get out of here. We better call Madeline ASAP."

I glanced at what remained of Hamilton and his coffee. I had an uneasy feeling that maybe the last coffee maid had ignored the mold.

We walked over to Amber's desk and she dialed Madeline's extension. "Yes, *dead!* Really!" There were a few more uh-huh's and she hung up. "Madeline wants us to meet her." We walked back and waited outside his office.

She looked at me. "We all knew he was doing something personal in there, especially after the daily fight with the wife. We figured it was porn. But gambling? Who knew?"

"It sure looked like he lost a bundle."

"Really? How much?"

"The screen was blinking $96,000."

"Holy crap. You're right. Do you think he had a stroke?"

"I would have."

Madeline whisked around the corner and faced us. She pointed toward Hamilton's door.

We nodded.

She opened the door and looked inside. We peered in behind her.

Yep, he was still there. Dead as a doornail.

188

Madeline walked over to the computer, maneuvered the mouse from beneath Hamilton's death clasp, and closed the web page.

"Umm… isn't that some kind of tampering?"

Madeline whirled around and glared at me. "The reputation of this firm will not be compromised by a momentary lapse in judgment. Nor would this be respectful of Mr. Hamilton's legacy with this office."

Amber elbowed me hard in the ribs. I coughed and nodded.

"Amber, I trust you will treat this with the utmost delicacy?"

"Of course!"

"You must have had quite a shock. I'll understand if you would like to take some compensatory time for the rest of the day."

"Great! I mean, sure, thanks."

"It will be understandable if you wish to remain at home tomorrow."

"Gee!"

"I'll need to call HR to find out what to do next. I mean, about him."

We nodded in tandem.

Madeline made her way past us – and the corpse.

"Sorry to bother you," I began, "but I was wondering if you don't mind if I take my lunch now? I could be back a little after two?"

Madeline swung around. "Two?"

"Well, it's after one now, I got kind of delayed on account of…" I nodded toward Hamilton.

"Oh yes, of course. Never mind."

"Thanks."

"No, really, never mind. There's no need for you to return now."

"Huh?"

"Just fill in your time sheet for up to well... I'll be generous because of the shock. Let's say one-fifteen. Then you're free to leave."

"Oh. Great. Thanks."

Madeline's shoes clicked away.

"Too bad you're not full time," Amber said. "I bet you she would have comp'd you the rest of the day, and tomorrow, too."

I stared at her.

"Well, better luck next time. Maybe I'll see you around? I've got to dash – wow, maybe I can finish up my Christmas shopping!"

Clearly, Hamilton's life had made a lasting impression upon the staff.

Amber skipped away while I dug around for a timesheet to fill out and retrieved my coat. I wandered around and eventually found Madeline on the phone.

She motioned for the time sheet and signed it, and pulled away her carbon copy as she hung up the phone. "You understand that you are not to say a word about Mr. Hamilton's internet activities, yes? This is a law firm – we could sue you *substantially* for defamation of character."

I gaped at her. I hadn't deformed his character. He had. But I didn't want to test the waters, either. "Gotcha."

I walked into the lobby and noticed a conversation at the receptionist's desk growing loud. I looked. Myron was shouting at her.

"Nice try. I know Hamilton's in his office. He called me and told me to meet him here. You tell him I need to see him *now*."

The receptionist rolled her eyes. "I told you – our office manager said he's been taken ill, and he's gone!"

"Did you see him leave?"

"No…"

"Precisely. I'll wait right here. I'll probably catch him on the way out to lunch." Myron made himself at home in a leather club chair. The receptionist seethed.

Then he spotted me. "You! What are *you* doing here?"

"I…"

The receptionist piped up. "She's just a temp."

"Who are you temping for?"

I sighed. "This firm. Mr. Hamilton."

"See?" Myron pointed at the receptionist. "I told you he's here!"

"In a manner of speaking." I leaned against the wall. Wait for it.

"You see? He hasn't left."

"Nope. He's gone. But not like on a trip."

"Not like on a trip?"

The elevator doors opened, and an EMT unit – not in very much of a hurry – rolled in with a gurney.

"Oh my gosh! Is someone sick? I better call Madeline!" The phone buzzed and she picked it up. There was a lot of uh-huhing.

I looked at Myron. "I think that gurney's for Hamilton."

"You're kidding, right? Well, he gets points for being creative. But he's not getting out of this one."

"I think he kind of did."

"What do you mean?"

The gurney slammed back out, with a sheet draped over the corpse.

Myron stared as they wheeled the body out. He looked at me. "Hamilton?"

"Yep."

He drummed his feet on the floor and had a fit. "You killed him!"

"No I didn't! I just transcribed for him!"

"You probably gave him a stroke!"

I thought for a moment and considered an honest answer. "I think he did have a stroke. But it wasn't me."

Myron shot into the next elevator, shouting loudly at the voices in his head. I pondered if he might be another stroke victim in the making.

I made my way back to the garage, realizing that cute high heels were not ideal footwear for psychopaths or driving sleet. I found the van, wove my way down toward the pay booth, and waited in line, hoping my ticket wouldn't stretch into the next hour. I was bobbing my head to, "All I Want for Christmas is My Two Front Teeth," when I heard shouting. I looked up to see Myron and Dexter in full rant out on the sidewalk. Then Dexter sped off on his motorcycle. I shrugged. I guessed they'd figured out the hard way that somebody has to mind the store at all times and that they'd given themselves the same shift off again. Not too bright. But given my last encounter with Dexter, I locked my doors to be on the safe side.

I got home and found an equally chilly reception. The garage door wouldn't open. I walked around and unlocked the front door. The thermostat read sixty-five. I played with it. Nothing. I raced upstairs to Marie's room to make sure she wasn't frostbitten. Thankfully, her room has the southern exposure, so it's the warmest room in the house. No worries for the moment.

I noticed the light was off so I flipped the switch. Nothing. I closed the door and peeked into my room and saw the alarm clock was also off. "Great. A power outage." I dug out the phone book and called the electric company to report the outage. I still can't figure out how your phone works when your electricity doesn't. Eventually, I got an actual person.

"Hold on, let me check for you. What's the address?"

I repeated my address and waited.

"That's strange. We have no power outages reported in your neighborhood."

"Well, you do now."

"Can I put you on hold, please?"

I sighed. "Sure."

An eon later he returned. "I'm sorry to keep you waiting."

"No problem."

"There is a teensy weensy bit of a problem, actually."

"Oh?"

"It appears that you are delinquent in your bill."

"What? I just mailed it!"

"You might have, but we never received it."

"Can you turn the power back on?"

"After you make your payment, yes."

"It's in the mail! Are you telling me you stop services if a check is just late?"

He sighed. "It's a new company policy. We don't wait for three months anymore. We mailed you a copy last July."

"Who reads electric company junk mail?"

"I know, I know. It's becoming very problematic." He sighed again.

"So what do I do now?"

"If you want the power back on quickly, I suggest you put the delinquent amount on a credit card. Or pay cash."

I gulped. Cash was not an option. "What happens when you get my payment?"

"We'll credit your account toward next month's bill."

Great. I got to pay my back rent and next month's rent the same month. Fabulous. The VISA guys would be flipping cartwheels. "I guess I don't have much choice."

"No, I'm sorry. You don't. Just a minute while I get your information." He took down my credit card vitals and we concluded.

"So when will the power come back on?"

"I think we can get this on by the end of the day. This is a residence, and not a business, correct?"

"Yes. I live here."

"In that case, you should be fine."

We finished the closing banalities and I hung up firmly. I began to consider alternative venues for Marie for the evening. Vinnie and I would be okay, but frosted feathers wouldn't be a good option for a cockatiel.

I dug around and found a seven-day candle, lit it and said a prayer to the electricity gods to get us back up to speed, pronto. Then I looked around in the fridge, quickly, for lunch. I was starving. A half day of office work had done me in. I settled on a hunk of cold lasagna.

As I stood eating over the sink, I heard a key in the front door, and whirled around with my mouth full. Vito lumbered in.

"Whoops! Sorry, Toots. Guess I should have knocked."

"Stranger things have happened."

"What?"

"Never mind."

Vito stepped cautiously inside the kitchen, and stared at the lit candle. "Wow, I didn't realize you had a romantical date and all." He glanced around furtively. "Where is he?"

I finished swallowing. "There's no one here but me."

"Mweee Ooo!" Vinnie amended this factoid with a direct editorial comment.

Vito scratched his head and shrugged. "Whatever."

I gave Vito the ground work re: tardy electric bill.

"The bums! Well, hey, I guess that explains it."

"What?"

"Your mail." He plunked an assortment of bills on the counter.

I felt my blood pressure hit the ceiling. I hadn't realized I had this many overdue bills. This was clearly becoming an unhealthy habit. I forced myself to peer at them. "What the?"

These were not new bills. Oh, no. These were notices for the old bills I had already mailed. All returned with the word, "Counterfeit" stamped across the postage. I groaned at the thought of repeating the electricity hassle in triplicate – if not more.

"Wazzup?"

"I mailed these bills. Cripes they were already old. Now they're returned, and I'm going to have to contact each one separately to make sure nothing else gets shut off."

"You need cash?"

"Yes."

Vito pulled out a roll of greenbacks that could choke a hippo.

"No!"

"I thought you said yes?"

"Yes, I need cash. No, I don't need yours. At least not yet. I don't think."

"You want a ride to the bank?"

I shook my head. "No. I better get to Squirrel Run and get my pay from Hilda, and then get to the bank."

"That makes good sense."

I considered the time, made some mental departure notes to myself, and then got a bit panicked. "Hey, are you going to be home for a while?"

"Actually, we are."

"Miriam's over?"

"Natch."

"Can you keep Marie over at your place? Until they turn my heat back on?"

"No problemo."

I swaddled Marie's cage with a blanket and schlepped her across our adjoined porches, much to her protest.

Miriam gushed and got Marie comfy in a corner, away from Stanley's reach. Then she turned feral after Vito explained my dilemma.

"The bums! You should sue!"

Vito shrugged. "It's an option."

"It's pretty much straightened out. Sort of."

Miriam looked doubtful. "You're not staying at your place with no heat, are you?"

"Vinnie and I will be okay for one night. But it probably won't come to that."

"It sure won't! You're staying here!"

Vito brightened. "Hey, that's a great idea!"

"Well, actually…"

"Sure! And you could help us win!"

"Win?"

Vito gaped a toothy smile brilliantly at me. At least, most of a toothy smile. "We're practicing for the Manischewitz Cook-Off Contest! We're entered!"

"Oh. Wow." Frostbite was sounding better and better.

"Yeah! We got just three weeks to practice! See?" Miriam waved the contest literature in front of me.

"So, it's a kosher contest?"

"Of course!"

"Do you have an entry dish?" I know, I know. But someone has to ask, right?

"Several. We're still making up our minds. So we're starting with the first one tonight. You can help taste it!"

"What are you making?" Look, you want me to ask. Besides, you don't risk digestive surprises where Vito and Miriam are concerned.

Miriam pumped a wooden spoon in the air. "Concord glazed bacon wraps with shrimp!"

I considered a hasty Plan B involving a bald faced lie about visiting the preggo sister in Northern VA. Or having shingles. Something.

I looked again at the contest information, noticing the word *kosher* used about every other sentence, highlighted and in italics. Even though I'm goy, I get it about bacon not being kosher. But somewhere in the back of my head thumped the memory that shellfish wouldn't be a welcome ingredient, either. "That's pretty fancy."

"Well sure!"

"Maybe you might try for something a little more…rustic?"

"You mean not washed?"

"No, Miriam. She means like big chunks. Don'tcha Toots?"

I swallowed hard. "It's very in now," I fibbed.

"You see, Vito? That's why we need Mina's help! I knew it!"

I made a point of looking at a watch I wasn't wearing. "Sure. Hey, I got to get going if I'm going to make the bank."

"We'll take good care of Marie!"

I fled out the door and into the van, racing toward Squirrel Run Acres. It hiccupped a little down the drive, but all was fine after I hummed a chorus of, "O Come All Ye Faithful."

I pulled into the lot and sped through the icy air and into the kitchen. Everything was black. Well, that is, everything was black except for the candles and flashlights dotted around the counters and on the range hoods. "What the?"

Hilda came bustling out of her office with her coat on, her hat pulled down firmly to her eyebrows. Hector followed behind, waving his arms and shouting a lot of stuff with exclamation points.

"I know! I know! I'm going!"

"Why you not pay bill?"

"For the two-hundredth time – I did! They say they never got it."

"Why they no get?"

"How do I know? Do I run the post office?" Hilda spied me hovering near the stove. "Mina! Didn't you and Chef mail the electric bill?"

Chef held up a hand. "I did. It probably just got held up, somehow."

"How late we behind with this bill?" Hector's face was turning a nice, warm shade of fuchsia.

"We've never been behind. Until now. That's why I don't get it."

I sighed. "It's their new policy."

Everyone stared at me.

"They shut off my electric, too. Said they hadn't received my payment."

"For a first time being late?"

"Yes. The guy I talked to said they started the new policy last summer."

"Sounds like a publicity snafu in the making." Chef shook his head, held a flashlight in his left hand and tossed greens and scallions sautéing in a pan with the other.

"Yeah. I can't wait to see what else of mine gets shut off."

"What?" Hilda's cheeks glowed a nice bright pink.

"My bills were returned to me with 'counterfeit' stamped across the postage."

"Well, that's just peachy."

"Huh?"

"Thanks for giving me the stamp, Mina."

"Oh my gosh! I totally forgot! Geez, I'm sorry!"

"I'm off. The gal there said if I pay cash right away, we'll get the lights back on in an hour."

Hector threw his hands up in the air and stomped toward his office. I was pretty sure he was also stomping toward an emergency bottle of Sambuca, but that was only a guess because his breath smelled a lot like licorice. Unless of course he had a secret stash of Good 'N Plenty candies under his desk.

I started after Hilda, but she was gone. "Crap."

"What's wrong?" Chef asked.

"Same thing as here. I was hoping to get my pay from Hilda, so I can get to the bank before they close."

"You need to pay cash too?"

I shook my head. "They took my credit card. But I need to make sure I've got the cash to pay the credit card." Well, at least this portion of it anyway, I thought.

"Watch this," Chef said, and handed me the tongs.

I half-heartedly poked at the greens.

Chef returned and thrust an envelope in front of me.

"Oh, wow, thanks!"

He took the tongs back from me and began plating. "Not a problem. There's extra there, too. The client left a nice tip."

"Thanks!"

He stirred the pan some more. "We could use you Wednesday. That is, if you haven't got anything else going."

"Nope."

"Great. We've got an early breakfast scheduled. Five o'clock."

"You want me to be here at *five*?"

"No, the breakfast starts at five. I need you here by four at the latest. Are you game?"

I shook my head. "Okay. Sure. Geez, what are they, farmers?"

"Yep."

"I might need a wakeup call."

He grinned. "Because of the hour?"

I wasn't sure I could ask anyone for a pre-dawn wakeup call, except for Trixie. And I had no idea about her crazy calendar. "Pretty much."

Chef looked sideways at me. In the glow of the flashlight he looked a bit flushed. "Okay, not a problem. Hey, what are your plans tonight?"

"You want me to work tonight, too?"

"No. I was wondering what your plans are?"

"Huh?"

Chef sighed. "You have no electricity. You're not staying in your house with no heat, right? Do you have someplace to go?"

"Oh, right. We'll be fine." Of course he wasn't asking me out. What was wrong with me?

"We?"

"Vinnie and me. Marie's already at Vito's."

"Smart thinking."

"Well, you know me. Always planning ahead, ha, ha…" I began my awkward retreat and backed smack into a bus trolley chockfull of dirty dishes. A tsunami of dishwater sailed up over me. Splatters of water sizzled on the stove top.

"Hey, watch the greens!"

"Watch your back!" Arnie ran behind me, just barely catching the tower of cascading plates.

"Thanks," I mumbled.

"It's pretty dark in here. You better be careful. Or Hector will take it out of your pay!"

Arnie was right about that one. If I continued like this, I'd be paying Hector for the privilege of working here.

I slunk out of the kitchen, relieved for the anonymity of the parking lot. I drove along to the bank, absent-mindedly singing something about five gold rings.

After a mild scuffle at the drive-up ATM, I headed home. I hit the remote. Zippo. The power was still off. Great.

I headed to the front door, racking my brains to think of where I might have stashed a flashlight. That is, if I had one. Hmm.

As I fumbled for my key, I saw that only the storm door was on. The inside door was open. Great. Vito must have returned to my place for a secret ingredient. Like water. Well, at least the storm door was closed and Vinnie wasn't on the outside of it. Vinnie? Why wasn't he waiting for me as usual? "Vinnie?"

A groan sounded from the basement. A human groan.

I rushed to the basement door, convinced Vito had taken another tumble. I grabbed the candle in the kitchen, lit it, and headed downstairs.

There, at the bottom of the steps, sat Vinnie on top of a prone form. "Vito?"

"Feh. You know his real name's Vladimir, right?"

I stared at Buddy as he struggled to sit up. Vinnie continued to conquer his basement lair invader. Buddy swatted him away. "Keep it up, and I'll turn you into a pair of mittens."

Vinnie chose to save the battle another day, and dashed upstairs between my feet.

"What are you doing in my basement?"

"What are my boxes doing out of your basement?"

"Huh?"

"Look!"

I did as directed and held out the candle and looked –the maze of Vito's questionable boxes were gone. But I wasn't about to let on to Buddy. My Jersey came back on. "I don't know what you're talking about."

"Oh, yes you do, girlie!" Buddy lurched toward me, then fell back, holding his head.

I held my candle higher. He had quite a nasty gash on his forehead and it was bleeding all over the place. Him, the floor, everywhere.

"Look, I don't know why you're here. Or why you're bleeding all over my basement. But I'm going for help." I hurried back up the steps and locked the door.

"You're going to leave here me alone? Bleeding in the dark?"

"You were bleeding in the dark before I got here. Deal with it."

I hustled out the front door and clambered over Vito's porch rail, tout de suite.

"Oh, I knew you would come home soon! How's the electricity? Do you want a sample? We decided for rustic bacon with peanut butter on soft pretzels with concord glaze. It's amazing!" Miriam held forth a platter.

My stomach did a somersault and I really, really wished I didn't have Vito for a neighbor/roommate. However, at this particular juncture, I did want him to eliminate his old-time chum from my basement. And my life.

"Actually, I really need Vito's help for a second. Is he around?"

Miriam turned to summon him, just as Vito stuck his head out from the kitchen. "Need help?"

"Yes."

"Got it."

For once Miriam didn't toddle along – she was probably contemplating the rustic aspects of diced gumdrops – while Vito stepped out with surprising alacrity. I filled him in.

"Okay, got it. Hold on a minute." He went to his car trunk, and returned with what looked like a small briefcase.

I stared at the briefcase. "Are you going to make him an offer?"

"Not exactly."

When we got back inside my house, we heard Buddy beating the band out of the basement door. *"You'll never get away with this! I'll have you for lunch!"*

I turned to Vito for some help with the situation, when I noticed he had unpacked his briefcase and assembled what looked like a gun. With a silencer.

I gave into the moment. "If you shoot him in my basement, we'll never get him out. He's not exactly a light weight."

Buddy pounded some more. "I heard that!"

Vito waved his hand and made shushing motions at me. "You got Vinnie locked up?"

"Dunno. I'll check." Exit stage left. Didn't have to tell me twice.

I found the frowning feline in the middle of my bed staring reproachfully at me. "Look, it's not my fault, okay? Hang in there." I shut the door and raced back downstairs. Vito stood waiting. "All clear. He's in my bedroom."

"Good. Why don't you go over and help Miriam with the shrimp?"

"But I thought you did the bacon thing?"

"We did. But we already defrosted the shrimp, you see?"

It was as clear as mud to me.

I exited my front door with every trepidation known to man tap-dancing across the back of my brain. I'd left Vinnie with Uncle Vito and his silencer. Not to mention Buddy and his selves.

Miriam stood waiting at the door. "Come in, get out of the cold. Here, you need this." She thrust a glass of what appeared to be mulled wine in my hand.

"Why, thanks."

"Sure. It's quite a thing to be involved with a former Moil. I know."

There was scuffling and shouting from my house. Personal note to self: if I ever have a boyfriend again, make sure all arguments are held someplace other than within my very thin walls.

"You ripped me off!"

"You're hallucinating!"

"Blood! I need blood!"

"You don't even have a scratch!"

Miriam pushed the glass at me. "Mina, drink. You're better off. It will be over soon."

Then there was a thud.

Miriam stared at her wrist watch. "Three, two, one…"

Vito walked calmly through the front door, like he was ready to unload groceries. No panic, no sweat, nothing. Wow. I guess this was what being a professional was about, after all.

"Is he dead?" I had to ask, right? I probably had a big bleed to clean up.

"Who, Vinnie? I thought you said he was in your room?"

"Buddy! Bernie! Whoever he is!"

"What, you think I'm going to prison for him? Nah."

Miriam and I exchanged glances.

Miriam cleared her throat. "Sweetie Pie, what was the thud we heard?"

"Oh, that was just Bernie after I tasered him."

A taser? When was that unpacked?

I fretted. "So what do we do now?"

"We wait for his ride."

"Ride?" Miriam and I sang in unison.

"What kind of a heist has a ride?" Miriam tsked.

"The kind who has his driver's license revoked."

"What? He just bought that beaut of a car!"

"I know snookems. But he got pulled over since he bought the car. Seems like he got the car just before his license expired."

"And?"

"And, PennDOT insisted on his taking an eye exam. And he failed."

I shook my head. "Geez, no wonder he fell."

"Actually, Vinnie tripped him."

"Really?" Good cat!

Vito cleared his throat. " Bernie said Vinnie was real friendly-like, especially after he gave him some kitty treats."

"I have kitty treats?"

"Don't you? Like Stanley's Tweetsie Wheatsies?"

"Tweetsie Wheatsies?"

"Oh my yes! You don't have to say that twice!" Miriam winced.

Stanley bounded into the room and gnawed Vito's trouser cuff with fervor.

"Does my good boy want his Tweetsie Wheatsies?" Vito dragged Stanley by his ankle into the kitchen in search of puppy treats.

"Umm… I don't mean to be a stick in the mud, but when do we think Bernie's ride will get him?"

Miriam nodded. "That's a good question. We'll find out after Vito takes care of Stanley. Have a sip. How do you like it?"

I sipped the mulled wine gingerly. It looked like red wine. And it felt warm. With some sort of spices. And sugar. And something that tasted like a bit of a Worcestershire sauce back kick. But worse.

"My."

"Warms you up inside, don't it? Bet you can't figure out my secret ingredient!"

With every fiber of my being – and wanting Vito to rid my house of his long lost pal – I concurred.

"Ha! I knew it! It's Manischewitz with ginger – and a little Chinese fish sauce! It's international!"

Oh boy.

Vito strode in solo and looked out the window. "Looks like I'll need to get Bernie ready for his ride."

"How do you know?"

"He told me he was getting picked up at four."

"That seems a little early for a heist, honey." Miriam took a long pull at her mulled Manischewitz.

Vito shrugged. "He said he didn't want to miss the early bird special."

He lumbered out and into my house. A few moments later, they both came out, with Bernie a bit worse for the wear. Getting tasered can't be comfy. Miriam and I watched a car pull up. Vito left him in the middle of the lawn, and waited. The sun poked out for a moment. Bernie immediately pulled his coat over his head.

Dexter drove up in Bernie's new car. He stepped out and tried to negotiate him into the car.

"I can't be out in the light! I'll burn!"

Dexter shoved him forward. "You're not in sunlight, you old coot. Get in the car!"

"I had a hat! And an umbrella! And a scarf!"

Who did he think he was, the Invisible Man?

Vito dashed in and out of my house more nimbly than was conceivable. He handed Bernie's props to him.

"Thank you."

"No problemo. Not a big deal for an old pal."

"You're not my old pal anymore, you thief!"

Well, Mr. Pot, meet Mr. Kettle.

It got a little chilly outside watching the boys bickering in the snow, especially with Dexter leering at me in front of a running car with an open door. I started to shiver and it wasn't from not wearing a coat.

"Well, I'll leave you boys to it then." I whirled around and raced back to the front porch.

"I'll be seeing you, Mina. We got a lot to catch up on," Dexter shouted after me.

I returned a fake smile, shot inside my house, and flipped Dexter the bird from the safety of my closed door.

I no sooner stood inside, when the smoke alarm chirped, and was chorused by every other appliance in the house. The electric was on – huzzah!

I cranked up the heat, checked the fridge settings and dashed upstairs to release Vinnie. Vinnie responded by yawning and settling down for the remainder of his nap on top of my pillow.

The doorbell rang. I dashed back downstairs and found Miriam. "You should come back over. You shouldn't sit around in the dark and the cold. You'll get depressed."

"The electric's back on, see?"

Miriam peered around and smiled. "That's a relief!"

Agreed.

"We're going to be trying the other recipe tonight, the one with the shrimp. Would you like to come over and help us?"

Bless their hearts.

"Actually, I think I better check my fridge to see what might have defrosted and needs taking care of."

"Then maybe we could bring a sample over later?"

I pulled the throttle loose on concocting lies. "I'm pretty sure I'm going to need to prepare for another party."

"Oh! Those massage parties! They sound like a great idea! Say, what kind of food do you make for people to eat lying down? Something with skewers, huh?"

I fumbled desperately at the back of my empty gray matter for another lie when Vito walked over. "C'mon sweetie, Mina's got to check her house and all."

"Oh, I wasn't even thinking! You'll be resetting clocks and timers for hours, I bet."

I looked gratefully at Vito.

"Well, we'll leave you to it. All's well that ends well!"

"I'll be right with you, Miriam. I left something of mine in Mina's basement."

"See you in a few!" Miriam exited and I exhaled.

Vito walked toward me. "I made a kind of a fib, just now."

"Oh?"

"I already put my business case away, if you know what I mean."

I nodded and pretended I did.

"I didn't like the way that Dexter guy was looking at you. You know him?"

I sighed and gave Vito the condensed version of mall workers gone postal. As well as his being in business with Vito's old pal. And my ex-coworker, once removed. From jail, that is.

"You make sure you walk to your car with a buddy after your shifts, you got it?"

"You want me to walk with Buddy?"

Vito flapped his arms. "That wouldn't be my first choice."

"Oh. Got it."

"I don't know who that guy is, but if he's hooked up with Bernie, and that guy Myron, he can't be up to anything good."

"Am I going to find anything else in my basement that I should know about? I mean, besides blood?"

Vito shook his head. "Nope. You're good."

"So no more unexpected visitors, right?"

"Exactly." Vito headed toward the door. "You want I should bring Marie back?"

"Oh, yes! Almost forgot!" I hurried after him, and while Vito distracted Miriam in the kitchen, I covered her up. Soon we were lugging her into the front hallway.

"I can take her upstairs from here, Vito. Thanks. And I'll play it safe and lock the door as soon as I get back down."

"No problemo, Toots. I'll lock your door with my key." And he did.

I spent the rest of the evening resetting clocks and alarms. Even though things had returned to normal, I felt a bit unsettled. I found a Chinese recipe that called for air drying a duck to give it crispy skin. Since the one I had on hand was frozen, I defrosted it in the microwave and used my blow dryer.

CHAPTER 9
Tuesday

I have to stop sleep cooking. It's just not working for me. Once again, my kitchen was a disaster area. Although the roast duck with Pomegranate-Hoisin glaze looked superb. I wondered idly if I could give it to Trixie and Mike, as an early Christmas present.

I didn't have anything on my calendar until the evening. The only up to this side was that my limbs wouldn't be inflicted with another pediatric beating, even though the income ledger would suffer. The rest of the day should be dedicated to soy sauce mitigation. I figured a good seven hours of scrubbing might return the kitchen to its proper self. Note to self: liberally applying soy sauce across counter-tops has severe repercussions. I was glad I hadn't re-painted since I'd obviously aided and abetted the Disney-puked walls.

Vinnie and I had rolled through our morning

routine and I was deciding how much longer I could procrastinate doing the first shift of dishes when the phone rang to the rescue.

"Whatcha doing?"

"Scraping soy sauce from underneath my fingernails."

"Haven't you heard of a manicure?"

"They wouldn't take me."

"You're kidding!" K. was horrified.

"Maybe not. But it's a good guess."

"I'll have to give you *volcanic soap* for a stocking stuffer!"

"Do you think it will work?"

"Let's find out. Do you want to play shopping?"

I sighed. "The mall?"

"Of course!"

"I'm a bit malled out…"

"But you'd be going as a *civilian*. Sans Sparkle."

"My jammies are already sans Sparkle."

"Don't you have *any* more Christmas shopping to do?"

"No. But I have a duck."

"Pardon?"

"Never mind. Actually, I do have one errand to run there."

"Oh. This sounds like a return." He sounded sad.

"Just stamps."

"Are they damaged?"

"Definitely."

"That settles it. Come pick me up and a mall-ing

we will go."

"What's wrong with your ride?" I frowned at
the taxi service implication. Besides, the soy sauce
stains had me irked.

"Nothing. Just the annual check-up."

"Check-up?"

"Inspection. Can't get it back until tomorrow."

I sighed. We made our plans and I dashed
around like a maniac.

K. all but leapt out his front door and into the
van. "Secret Savers!"

"Huh?"

K. tapped his phone. "Just texted me three
minutes ago!"

"What is it?"

K. stared at me. "Super secret sales."

"On what?"

"Don't know. It's a secret. See?"

I shrugged. I really didn't.

We hummed our way along to "Good King
Wenceslas" and parked at a ridiculously long
distance from the mall entrance. It was almost as far
away as the employee parking.

"My! It must be a super sale!" K. hastened his
stride.

I hurried to keep up. "Well, it's sure not a
secret."

We dove inside the mall panting, glad to be out
of the cold. We were both flushed.

"Back for more abuse from the kiddies?"

I whirled around and saw Myron standing
behind me, sipping a jumbo-sized soda.

I took a breath. "Actually, I think a little's come your way, finally."

"Flies…honey…" K. crooned.

I waved him off, and dug around my purse. "Here. I want a refund."

Myron looked at the book of stamps, and smiled nastily. "I'm sorry, we can't refund *used* stamps."

"No? Maybe you can refund *counterfeit* stamps?" I waved the "counterfeit" stamped envelopes at him.

Myron's face went pale.

"Counterfeit? Really? What a nuisance. Why don't we just return them at the post office?" K. asked.

"*No!* We'll take care of that right away. It must be some error on their part. The post office has hired so many part-time helpers for the holidays, nobody knows a thing. I'm sure it was a mistake. Follow me." Myron all but raced to the Mail-It-2! Kiosk currently dubiously manned, by Dexter.

"Please be careful with that! It's bone china. I marked it fragile especially," the plump woman on the other side of the counter instructed him.

"No problem." Dexter took the package, went behind a screened area, and tossed it soundly into a bin. So much for fragile.

Myron leaped behind the counter and opened the register. "Here, now give me the stamps."

I handed him the remainder of the booklet and he gave me fifteen dollars.

"This is too much. I can't make change."

"That's all right. Consider it a reward for

bringing this to our attention."

Was he actually being nice to me?

Dexter shot me a sideways look, and hastily finished his transaction with the woman whose China he'd smashed.

"Well, look who we have here. Very convenient of you, Kitchen. You left me in the cold yesterday."

"Now, now Dexter. Mina's done us a considerable service by making us aware of some odd stamps in our inventory."

"Odd, huh?"

Odd is right. "They're not odd, " I said. "They're counterfeit."

Dexter grinned. "You don't say."

Myron glared at him. "It's hard to believe, but one never knows. Why don't you re-check our inventory, Dexter?"

Dexter smiled creepily. "I might have other plans. Mina might need some help out to her car."

"But we just got here!" K. cried.

"That's too bad. Maybe later."

I turned around to see Myron making slashing motions at his throat. Dexter was nodding and smiling. I didn't like it. I grabbed K.'s elbow.

"Well, thanks for the refund."

We hurried away from the kiosk, just as an elderly woman in a wheelchair approached them tentatively. "I don't suppose you could sell me just one stamp? I don't need a whole book. I've just got to mail this check to my daughter."

Dexter and Myron exchanged wicked smiles. "Why, of course we can."

K. and I skittered into the middle of the mall and flopped down on a bench.

"I don't like him," he said.

"Who?"

"Myron."

"I thought you were going to say Dexter."

"Him either."

"Ditto."

We retreated inside a jewelry shop for some much needed bling therapy. Which bought me time to fill K. in on Dexter's back-story.

A few dozen stores later, K. was laden down with shopping bags while I chomped on a soft pretzel with mustard.

"I can't believe you didn't buy a thing!"

"I bought a pretzel."

"It's almost gone. And it doesn't count." He spotted a Starbucks. "I need a boost. C'mon. My treat."

We got our Christmas-oomphed lattes and found a table outside the store. K. took a sip, then coughed.

"Too hot?"

He shook his head violently.

"Are you choking?"

He nodded. I slapped his back a bit. He grabbed me by the shoulder, and pulled my ear toward his mouth. "*Look over there. Dexter!*"

I carefully looked up to see Dexter leaning against a store window advertising maternity wear, staring at me with a wild grin. I wondered idly about Dexter's mother, and how Dexter got to be

Dexter. That was, if she hadn't left him swaddled at the entrance to a prison.

"I think it's time to go."

"Done."

After loading the van with K.'s shopping, we hopped inside and shivered. The radio blared and we zipped off. I glanced up at the rearview and noticed the car behind us. I made a left out of the mall, then a right onto Harrisburg Pike. It did, too.

"What's the matter?" K. asked.

"I think we're being followed."

"Really?" K. turned around for a better look.

I made the left onto Good Drive, but the car continued past us up Harrisburg Pike. It was a green Crown Vic.

After depositing K. and his treasure, I trundled on home. It was getting dark and a fine, icy mist came swirling down. The windshield wipers slipped in and out of time with the radio, the driver's side wiper smearing a big icy blotch over my side of the windshield. Great, another thing to buy/replace. Feh. I was thinking a night home with Vinnie sounded a lot cozier than meeting James at the Darn Boor.

I pulled into the garage. Vinnie was waiting for me inside the front hall, as usual. "Anyone interesting call?"

"Mgaw-ooomph."

"Really?" I checked the voicemail and found nothing. I could have sworn he said Ma called. Also, no word from James, so I figured we were still 'on'.

I changed sweaters for something that could double as date-worthy, without being too obvious: a semi-scoop-neck red cashmere pullover. I threw on a grey blazer at the last minute; so I wouldn't look too much like a date (in case this wasn't) and more like a business meeting (which it probably was.)

I fed and petted Marie, went back downstairs and did the dinner thing for Vinnie. While I waited for him to finish, I indulged in a sip of mug o'Merlot.

"You be good. I'll see you later." I patted Vinnie on the head, and went back out into the tundra.

I found the Barn Door after passing it by and re-circling several hundred times. No wonder it was a local watering hole. You couldn't find it unless you were a cow.

But inside it was cozy and warm and had a good share of patrons. I looked around for James.

I found him sitting at a table by himself, with a newspaper. "Well, there you are, Kitchen."

Kitchen? Hmm. Definitely not a date. "Sorry to be late. Wow, it was tough finding this place!"

James folded his paper. "Yes, I forgot the first time can be somewhat geographically challenging. My bad. Beer?" He poured me a glass of beer from a pitcher that sat on the table.

"Thanks." Well, beer was a nice change, right? I noticed that at least it wasn't Krumpthfs.

A petite blonde with red and green streaked bangs bounced up to our table. "Hello? My name is Heather, and I'll be your server tonight. Would you like to hear our specials?"

"Please," James answered.

And so on. The specials consisted of a lot of items I suspected were headed toward a dumpster. I stuck with standard fare: cheeseburger and fries. James ventured on the adventuresome side and chose the Chef's plate: a thick-cut pork chop stuffed with chicken liver, mushrooms and kale.

"So, how are the new clients coming?" I asked, attempting at some business-like small talk.

"Swimmingly! I never dreamed holiday stress could be so profitable."

"That's great."

"And the catered gift cards are selling like hotcakes. You'd better be prepared to be very busy after the first of the year."

"That's wonderful!"

James nodded. "It seems like we've found quite the niche."

Heather came back with our orders. "Anything else?"

James looked at me. I shook my head.

"Great. Enjoy your meal!"

I looked at my dish. It was completely pedestrian: an overcooked frozen burger with a side of soggy fries. I looked at James' plate: his pork chop looked fried.

We ate our meal somewhat awkwardly, amidst the usual pleasantries about the weather and more talk about his clients, yada, yada. And of course, with James continuing to outline the coming months' calendar of events. Which, while not date-worthy, provided more than a glimmer of hope work-wise.

Heather returned. "Anything else?"

James nodded. "Just the checks."

Checks?

"Sure. Two?"

"Yes, please."

Well. Decidedly not a date.

After some more awkward banter, Heather returned with our checks. "Gee, it's too bad you didn't come tomorrow night."

"Why's that?" asked James.

"Wednesdays are BOGO nights. Buy one entrée, get the other free."

James raised his eyebrows. "Well, we certainly will take that under consideration, won't we Mina?"

"Umm… sure." I wondered how many times I could wash my hair on Wednesday nights.

We paid for our meals, with James insisting he leave the tip. I have no idea what that was all about. Then we walked out to the parking lot.

He held the van door open for me. "Well, goodnight. Thank you for meeting me for dinner."

"Oh, sure. Thanks for inviting me."

And that's when James leaned over and kissed me on the forehead.

I'm so confused. It wasn't a date, was it? We talked only business, right? And we split the bill, no? Yeeshkabiddle.

I sang at the top of my lungs and hot-footed it home, determined to make it all the way without incident. My wake-up call from Chef was going to roll around pretty quickly, it was already close to seven-thirty.

At home, I opened and closed the fridge a half dozen times searching for a beverage. I'd had enough beer and didn't want any wine. And considering the evening's fare, was seriously considering going to the store for Tums. I settled on distracting myself with the news. Vinnie settled on snuggling next to me on the sofa.

An extremely flustered post office manager squinted at the camera lights shining on him.

"So, you're saying, that the counterfeit stamps did not originate from the post office?"

"No, sir. That's why they're counterfeit."

The reporter looked like he wanted to palm slap himself and/or the post office manager.

"What should people do, if they find they've purchased bogus stamps?"

"Well, the first thing, is you should always buy your stamps from the post office. Or online at usps.com."

The reporter rolled his eyeballs. "That's true. But if someone is unlucky enough to have purchased them elsewhere, then what?"

"Report it. The first thing you should do is report it to your local post office."

"What will you do then?"

"We'll ask the person where they bought the stamps, if they have any left, and still have the returned mail bearing the counterfeit stamp."

"What happens to the shop owners who sold the counterfeit stamps?"

The man shook his head. "Nine times out of ten, these guys think they're buying discounted stamps they can turn around for a profit. They have no idea."

"But the stamps help you to track down the counterfeit operation?"

"Eventually. Sometimes. It's a steady problem. It sure does give us a lickin'."

The reporter stared at the manager. He nodded back energetically.

He turned and faced the camera. "And that, my friends, is how counterfeit stamps are giving the post office a licking."

Vinnie and I exchanged groans, and the phone rang.

"You're finally home! Didn't you get my message?" It was Ma. I frowned at Vinnie, wondering if he'd figured out how to erase my voicemails. Then again, maybe he just forgot to write down the message. Ha, ha.

"Sorry. No, I didn't. How's Ethel? And Ike? And Aunty?"

"I don't know and I don't care. I'm hiding."

"Huh?"

Ma sighed. "It's getting a bit chaotic. I'm holed up at *Wired Coffees*."

"Internet coffee house?"

"Yep."

"Well, at least you can work a little while you're away. You won't be so bogged down when you get back to the office, right?"

"I suppose. Right now it feels like those little

brats are never going to see the light of day."

"But she's not due for another week or so, right?"

"Week. Year. Whatever."

"Is Ethel getting a little emotional?"

"Ethel's fine. It's Ike. He cries at the drop of a hat. And your Aunt has OCD. She's re-folded and re-sorted the baby clothes and toys a thousand times. And every time, she says the same thing over every blessed one of them. 'Isn't that sweet?' 'Wasn't that thoughtful?' 'Why in the hell did someone buy this?' You know, the usual."

I took a breath, and wished I'd eaten some Tums. A bottle of them. "Well, it won't last forever."

"Thank goodness for that."

I opted for a change of subject. "How's the coffee shop?"

"Café. And it's actually rather sweet. Even if it is work. Speaking of, how's your work going?"

Insert frozen-deer-in-headlights stare here. "Oh, great."

"Please don't tell me your still doing Santa's Sidekick shifts?"

"Umm... a few. But I met with James and it sounds like he'll have some catering jobs for me. And I had a temp job."

"A temp job, really? In an office?"

"Yes."

"That's wonderful. How did it go?"

I counted a beat. "It was kind of a dead end."

"Well, that's too bad. How about Squirrel Run?

Don't they have any work for you?"

"Oh, yes. Actually, tomorrow morning. I'm helping with breakfast."

"Breakfast? Goodness that sounds early. I suppose you'll have to be there before eight."

"Actually, more like four-thirty."

"*In the morning?*"

"Yep."

"Well. I better let you go then. I'll call you tomorrow. What time do you think you'll be home?"

"Hmm. The breakfast is at five so I'm not sure."

"Good grief, what are they, farmers?"

"Yes."

"I'll call you around nine. Not before."

"Okay."

"And Mina?"

"Yes?"

"Your Aunt's going to quiz you about some paint swatches she sent you."

"Thanks for the heads up."

"You're welcome. Besides which, I sent you some I'm sure you'll like much better."

I pounded my noggin gently against the kitchen cabinet. Then we said our bye-byes and hung up.

I went upstairs, tucked Marie in, washed up and headed for my jammies. The phone rang again. I considered not paying that bill just to shut the darn thing up.

"Sorry, Toots. Miriam and me's got a question for you."

"Shoot." Well, at least Vito had called and not

invited himself over to ask my advice dans le boudoir, ha ha. Sheesh. I've got to start cutting back on reading French cookbooks…

"The thing is, Miriam and me realized we can't enter the peanut butter, pretzel and bacon thing, on account of bacon's not so kosher."

"You don't say?"

"Yeah, it should've been second nature for us. We got too caught up in the moment, getting excited about the Concord glaze and all."

"At least you realized it now, before you entered."

"Are you kidding? Boy, would that have been humiliating."

"I'm not so sure about humiliating, but you definitely would have been disqualified."

"We figured hanging around with the St. Bart's gang got us immune to bacon, what with all the breakfasts and all."

"I can understand that." And I could. I once worked my way through "The Joy of Butter" and eventually became so accustomed to using copious amounts of the stuff that cooking with a couple of sticks butter became *de rigueur*. That was, until Auntie's eyebrows flew off her head once she understood how much I'd infused in a béchamel. I was then instructed to keep the butter to my brioche and not much else, as far as her consumption was concerned.

"So, the thing is, we're trying to figure out something else. Keeping the kosher food in mind, of course."

"Of course."

"But the other thing is, Miriam's got the Concord glaze thing down. And it goes great with ham, bacon, shellfish – all the food that's not kosher!"

"That's a problem."

"I'll say! We were hoping you could suggest some substitutes?"

"Hang on." I headed downstairs to quickly check my cookbooks. I cringed at the idea of assisting, but winced more at the thought infusing lifelong repentance onto some unsuspecting orthodox judges, through no fault of their own.

After discussing the pros and cons of turkey bacon, imitation crab and the like, we decided the safest route would be for Vito to purchase his supplies at Kosher City, a retail grocer in Lebanon.

"That's great, Mina! It's a swell idea! Miriam will love it! We can even buy some Lebanon baloney while we're there!"

I'm pretty sure the Lebanon baloney Central PA knows and loves is not prepared in a kosher fashion. But who knows? I was impressed that Vito was becoming a one-stop shopper.

I headed back upstairs, jumped into my jammies, and settled into bed with Vinnie and my "Dictionary of Culinary Substitutions" book, now that my interest was piqued. I set the alarm clock, flipped the pages toward, "bacon" and hunkered down for a good read.

Someone sneezed.

"Bless you."

Another sneeze. I looked at Vinnie but he was sound asleep with his paw over his nose.

A third sneeze.

I leaped out of bed and a hand grabbed my ankle, hard. I went crashing down.

"*Ow!*"

"*Quiet!* I'll hurt you a lot worse if you don't shut up!" Dexter struggled out from under my bed, pulling at my ankle with one hand, and holding a gun in the other.

I stared at the gun and feared I would tinkle. "What are you doing here?"

"What am *I* doing here? When the hell were *you* going to be here? Does your phone ever stop ringing? I've been lying under your bed rolling around in cat fluff since five-thirty, waiting for you to get home."

"Right. Sorry. I mean, *huh*?"

"Shut up and stand up. Careful like."

I did as I was told. "How did you get in here?"

Dexter gave me a dirty smile. It was dirty. It looked like he hadn't brushed his teeth in a month. Yick. "Through the garage, of course."

"But I didn't leave it open!"

"You didn't need to. I have my own garage door opener."

"But I never had another opener…"

He waved me off with his pistol. "Let's just say I got a universal remote. After I watched you drive off and close your garage door a few times, I finally got the entry code. All wireless. Sometimes it takes a few tries. But eventually I get in and out of anywhere I want."

Vinnie came up behind him on top of the bed, and head-butted Dexter's side affectionately. Just my luck to have a cat who likes psychos.

"What the?" he swung around and slapped Vinnie soundly across the jaw. Vinnie went flying to the other side of the room.

"Stop it! He was only being friendly!"

"I hate cats." Dexter took aim at Vinnie, while Vinnie shook his noggin and tried to get his bearings.

"Don't shoot him!"

He pointed the gun at me. "You scream one more time, the kitty will get it, understand?"

I nodded and gulped and tried to keep from crying. I'd comply. But I doubted Dexter was a man of his word. I prayed Vinnie would get back to his normal self and scram.

"That's better." Dexter took aim again at Vinnie.

"NO!"

"You scream again, and he gets it, got it?" Dexter kept his gun on Vinnie. Vinnie, in his usual style, sat in the corner and began grooming his whiskers.

"What do you want from me?"

Dexter grinned. "You're real excitable like. That's fun. It's a shame I can't off your cat in front of you, it would be fun to watch. But you'd make too much noise. We're going to make this look like an accident."

"Accident?"

"You'll see."

I felt a little faint and leaned on the dresser.

"Oh, no you don't. Downstairs, sister."

I headed down the stairs in my bare feet. Marie shrieked from her bedroom.

"What's that? Not another one that talks, right?" Dexter demanded.

"No, she's just a cockatiel. She doesn't talk. She just lays eggs. Sometimes. But that was a long time ago. Mostly she just watches musicals."

"You're nuts, you know that?"

"I don't dictate viewing preferences."

We got to the landing and he pointed the gun in my face again. "Get your coat and shoes on, slowly. Don't get cute."

I shoved my feet in my loafers and pulled on my coat.

"Now, allow me." Dexter pushed the gun in my back, and me into the garage ahead of him. He shoved me out of the garage and into my driveway. Then he reached into his car – the dark green Crown Vic – and remoted my garage door closed. He opened his trunk.

"Hop in."

"You want me to ride in the trunk?"

"It's easier this way. Trust me."

"Look, I won't say a word. Promise. I could ride in the back?" I stalled. Being locked inside the trunk wouldn't exactly help a last minute get away. Besides which, trunks aren't heated and it felt like it was about five degrees. All right, it was probably thirty; but I was in my jammies, you know?

"Nice try. Get in."

I reluctantly climbed in, and crawled into a fetal position toward the back. The trunk door slammed shut. Then I heard Dexter start the ignition and pull away.

A cell phone rang. "Yeah, I got her. Finally. Looks like we're on our way."

The conversation on the other end must have relayed something he didn't like. "I understand you. We're coming."

Even after a short distance, I couldn't tell where we were. Except that Dexter was obviously finding every bump in Lancaster County to God knows where. I tried very hard not to cry. Getting upset wouldn't help me get out of this jam. Besides, my nose would only get stuffed up, and frozen boogers are the worst.

I had to think of something – but what? I racked my brain as to how to smooth talk Dexter into letting me inside the car. Maybe that way, I could make a break for it later. I was pondering my somewhat limited options when suddenly, the car veered onto what felt like a dirt road, and rolled to a stop.

The motor hummed steadily. Dexter hadn't stopped the car. I heard him get out and slam the door.

I fumbled around frantically for a release to let me inside the cab of the car and drive away. Nothing. My luck. They sure didn't made Crown Vics the way they used to. Which I suppose is why they don't make them anymore.

The car door opened and shut again. Dexter put the car into drive, slowly. We pulled into some type of building. He got out again, and I heard another large door close. It sounded like a metal door. Then the trunk lid popped open.

"Get out."

I blinked at the bright lights shining in my face. I climbed out, shivering.

"Get in here." He held open what looked like a door to a large dog kennel.

I crouched down and stepped in. He padlocked the door.

"What are you going to do?" I was hesitant about adding the "with me" part of that statement. I didn't want to give him any more ideas. I didn't know if there were any cats around.

"Shut up." He walked off to the back of the building.

I looked around at what looked like a large airplane hangar, or warehouse. It was a huge metal structure, with a domed roof. But it had lots of fenced-in enclosures and enormous shelving units. One level of shelves held plastic-wrapped sofas and desks. Another held huge storage boxes. I wondered if this was all stolen loot? How much of a market was there for hot sofas? Or desks?

There was a large picture window at one end of a far wall. I peered toward it and made out the outline of a desktop Christmas tree. Holy moly! If I wasn't mistaken, I'd been brought back to the storage facility in Leola, where I'd made a delivery.

I heard a motor turn over. Suddenly, a large

truck came straight at me. Its cargo bed was not a typical freight carrier, but looked like some kind of shrink-wrapped plastic. Dexter stepped out of the cab, and came toward me swinging handcuffs.

"Wanna play?"

"No."

"Too bad. But we're running out of time. Turn around."

I turned around inside the kennel, my back toward Dexter. I heard him unlock the door.

"Now put your hands behind your back."

I had been fretting about this kind of a moment. "Look, do you really think this is necessary? You can just leave me in the trunk, right?"

He clanked the cuffs on my wrists. "You're coming with me. Now get out nice and slow."

Since I had to crawl out backward on my knees, that was the only option.

He grabbed me under the arm and hauled me to my feet.

"Ouch!"

"No talking, got me?"

"Okay! Okay!"

"Let me make this easy for you – I got the garage opener to your house. And I don't like cats. Am I clear?"

"Crystal."

"Good. You gotta ride in the cab with me for a while. And don't get cute."

"Fine, I'll get ugly. Enough already!"

"Shut up! No talking!" He held the gun up as if to hit me with it. I winced, expecting the blow.

Dexter laughed. "Good. Now I know you're taking me serious."

He pushed me in the passenger's side, and went around the truck to open the hangar door. Then he hopped behind the wheel, drove the big rig out, put it in park and manually closed the door again. Back inside, he shifted gears and quickly we headed off down the dirt road, onto Route 23 and then Route 30 East. I tried to keep track so I could figure out where I'd been killed, later on.

As we drove past the outlets, Dexter turned on the radio. A talk show came on, something about people going back to school for training, after they'd been laid off.

"Losers."

"Well, at least they're trying."

He shot me a look. I rolled my eyes.

"The only reason I didn't gag you was because I didn't want some snoop calling a cop, you see? It's not because I'm a nice guy."

"Agreed."

"Besides, what you need to make it in this world is talent. Those losers are like a bunch of sheep. Punch in, punch out. All they want is a paycheck."

I cleared my throat but kept quiet.

"Yeah, I know. Go ahead, say it – 'what's wrong with that?' I'll tell you what's wrong. *Talented* people like me wind up paying for all the losers who can't get off their lazy butts."

I nodded. What else could I do?

He looked at me. "I know what you're thinking. I'm driving a truck, and worked a retail stand for

Myron. You're wondering how come I think I'm talented, right?"

I nodded again. This was a little like a Ouija board but backward.

"I'm gonna make it big – big! I'm a real artist. I'm the real deal. You'll see. Everyone will see."

I slapped a fake smile on and turned to stare out the window. It was dark. There was almost no one else on the road, and soon he was making turning onto 896.

I looked at the clock on the dashboard, it was almost ten. I thought about my former life: Chef giving me a wake-up call. In that life, I'd be to work at dawn and Ma would have called me later. I wondered idly how long it would take anyone to realize I'd run into foul play. I also wondered how long I'd be kept alive. Which made me start to cry.

"What the hell?" Dexter screamed so loudly it made me jump.

"What's the matter?"

"Are you bawling?"

"Allergies."

"To what?"

"Kidnapping."

"Nice one. Get over it. Here; blow." He tossed a box of tissues at me. They landed at my feet.

I looked at him.

"Whatever. That's what sleeves are for, right?"

We drove on in darkness. Eventually I saw signs welcoming us to Delaware.

Delaware? Great. I'm in Delaware.

A long while later Dexter took us from main

roads to back roads whose trees barely skimmed the top of the cargo. After what felt like a decade I saw signs for Port Delaware. I dimly recalled it might be near Lewes but wasn't sure.

We pulled onto an exit ramp, and headed toward what appeared to be an industrial area. Dexter drove down a service road, headed toward a locked gate. He flashed his lights twice, and the gate opened. We drove in. We headed toward a large warehouse, but he passed it, driving the truck slowly around the building, down another long service road. Soon I heard waves and saw a commercial dock. He stopped the truck, and I heard another vehicle come to a stop beside us.

"Looks like your luck's holding out. You got good weather tonight."

"What's the wind?"

"Ten knots from the south. You'll have the wind at your back."

"Good. Might help with the time."

"You bet."

Then there was a lot of ripping sounds from the back. I spun around but there was no back window. I turned around, and could see Dexter and another guy tearing off the plastic wrap surrounding his load – whatever it was—in the side view mirror. After a while, I heard metal crashing as it was pulled from the back. More metallic clanking, then the other guy's vehicle starting up.

Then I watched as some kind of mammoth pickup truck on steroids hauled a motorboat toward the water.

I hunched down in the cab, which was becoming cold with the motor shut off, and tried very hard not to think about a watery death.

The pickup came back up the road much sooner than I'd expected. I had absolutely no Plan B. Dexter stepped out of passenger's side of the truck.

"Thanks again for the help."

"No problem. I owed you one, right?"

"Yes, you did."

"Well, sorry about doing time for it. Nobody's perfect, right?"

"Sure."

"Say, you taking your girlfriend along with you? Far out."

I pulled my face back from the window.

"You saw, her, huh?"

"Yeah. Cute kid."

"Too bad." And then I heard a silencer. Well, at least I guessed it was. It sounded a lot like the ones you hear in the movies. And then a horn blared.

I shot up and saw Dexter's buddy's carcass leaning across the steering wheel. There was a dark spot beside his eyebrow just starting to ooze. Dexter reached over and tossed him aside like a sack of potatoes.

I slapped myself against the back of the seat and tried not to hyperventilate or puke.

Dexter opened the truck door.

"Get out."

I hopped out and didn't utter a syllable. If he'd just murdered someone who'd just done him a favor, no telling what he'd do to me. I was playing for time and running out of cards.

He put the gun in the small of my back. "Walk."

We walked silently toward the water. I heard the lapping of waves and saw the boat bobbing on the water, tethered to the dock. The motor was running.

"Get in." Dexter pushed the gun hard against me.

"How?" I croaked.

He pushed me and I found out – I landed hard on my knees. I heard him jump down after me. "You really are a klutz, aren't you?"

"You didn't have to push me!"

"Sure I did. Now, get down there." He opened a door and I saw a small staircase. And that was all I remember seeing, after I got tossed down the steps and locked inside.

CHAPTER 10

Wednesday, late morning

I woke up cradling my forehead and a big headache. I looked around and saw that I was sitting on a very wet concrete floor. Raw lumber framing leaned against some not-so-secure cinder block walls. There were no windows. Some light shone through a crack under a door at the top of a short flight of stairs. A figure sat on an upturned bucket underneath the steps in darkness.

"Where am I? What do you want?" I sat straight up, but the throbbing in my head forced me back down.

"Be quiet. He's not gone yet," a female voice hissed at me.

I rubbed my forehead. I was getting a little tired of being told to be quiet, and getting konked on the noggin. Then I noticed I *could* rub my forehead – the handcuffs were gone. I began to stand up, but the female waved me back down. I sat still.

"I want to come back with you! It'll be lunchtime soon and I haven't fed yet."

"Myron told you, he needs you to watch the girls. Check the fridge."

"Pooh. There's nothing I can eat in the fridge. Besides, I'm the head of this outfit. Those broads are locked up. And you've already got one handcuffed."

"It's too bright outside, remember? You're better off here."

"What if I forget myself?"

"Have fun."

"Who's minding the store?"

"Myron."

"You tell him to get here *now*. It's his turn to babysit. This was all his big idea, anyway."

"He'll be back. And so will I. Don't worry."

"I don't like it that you're taking the car."

"I'll be back soon."

"I don't like being without a vehicle."

"You've got the boat."

"Ha, ha. You know any mermaids selling raw burgers?"

"Okay, I'll bring you back a burger."

"Raw, remember?"

"Got it."

"You'll be back soon, right?"

"Yes."

"Not too, latc, okay? I'm so hungry, I got a bellyache, and a headache."

The sounds of a screen door closing resounded,

followed by a car starting. We heard a man's voice swear, not-so-softly. Then footsteps above us meandered around, and shuffled off in the distance. The creaking of stairs suggested our babysitter had gone up to a second floor. A door slammed closed.

"That's a relief. He finally hit the can. Here, let me take a look at you." The figure came toward me, lighting a vintage butane lighter in my face.

"Mrs. Phang!"

"Shhh!"

"What are *you* doing here?"

"I could ask you the same question."

"Where are we?"

"Mantoloking."

"New Jersey?"

"Yes."

"I thought I was in Delaware?"

Mrs. Phang lit the end of a cigarette and puffed at it. "You probably were. It's not likely Dexter could take a boat from PA to here."

"Why didn't he just drive all the way?"

"Some of the roads here still have checkpoints.

"Checkpoints?"

"Ever since Sandy. This area's still in recovery, so there's a lot of security."

I thought about it. "Dexter's not so dumb. He could have faked some kind of pass."

Mrs. Phang took another drag from her cigarette. "He has. But he probably didn't want to risk having you seen. Handcuffs don't look too friendly."

"When did he take them off?"

"He didn't. I did. We better make sure to put them back on when they pay us a visit. I can take them off again."

"How'd you do that?"

Mrs. Phang smiled. "Buddies with Vito, remember?"

I was grateful for friends in low places. Even if the places were apparently wet basements.

"How long have you been here?"

Mrs. Phang crunched the stub in the remnants of a puddle. "Ever since I was dumb enough to confront Myron about my counterfeit postage."

"Me too!"

She shook her head. "I thought he was just another retail slob trying to make a buck. I bought stamps from him for our Christmas mailing. Had over 4,000 cards returned."

"So did my bills."

"Yeah, and we don't know the half of it."

"What do you think?"

"I know these guys are into counterfeit stamps. And enough got released that returned letters and packages were becoming a problem."

"So?"

"So that's when I heard them talking about selling mail services, about mailing letters and packages directly."

"But if they're still using fake postage, the mail would still get returned to sender, right?"

"That's just it. *If* they sent the packages."

"You think they just dumped them?"

"Pretty much."

"And meanwhile they pocketed the money for selling the stamps and the services?"

"Along with any money or gifts being sent. I wouldn't put forging signatures on checks past them, since they're already fair postal forgers."

"Wow. That's pretty Grinchy."

The sounds of water gurgling through the pipes made us jump.

"He just flushed. Scoot. Lean back against that beam where he had you."

I hustled back. "Who's he?" I whispered.

"Bernie." Mrs. Phang snapped the cuffs back on me.

"Bernie? You mean Buddy?"

"Yes," Mrs. Phang hissed. She jumped back under the stairs just in time.

The door to the basement banged open. "The one, and the same, Cookie." Bernie closed the door, turned the lock, and came downstairs. A flashlight's beam shone down on us.

"How many times do I gotta tell you, not to smoke down here!"

"Sorry."

"I told you I'd let you smoke out back, when the coast is clear, remember?"

"I forgot."

"Geez, you must have a head like a sieve. No wonder your business is floundering."

"I thought you quit?" I asked.

I heard Mrs. Phang exhale, and figured she must be counting to a thousand.

"How's the kid doing?" Bernie ventured down a

few steps, shining the beam directly in my eyes.

"I could be better."

"No doubt. That's some konk on your noggin."

This was fast becoming an unwelcome trademark.

"You think you can let her out of the cuffs, Bernie?"

He shook his head. "No can do."

"I'll keep tabs on her."

"I'm sure you will, Tina. But Dexter took the key with him. Wouldn't leave it with me."

"How's she supposed to tinkle?"

Tinkle? Yikes I hadn't even thought about that.

Bernie came down and looked around, and picked up the bucket Mrs. Phang had been sitting on. "Here. Use this."

We shot him looks of revulsion.

"Hey, you're both gals, right? Guys see each other at urinals all the time."

"But they don't help each other pull their pants down, Bernie."

He shrugged. "What are you gonna do? Dexter's POed I didn't keep *you* in handcuffs. I explained to him about Auld Lang Syne, but he wasn't having none of it."

"You two know each other?" I all but shrieked.

"Tina was friends with Vladimir. Vito. Whatever. Him and me used to be good business buds, if you know what I mean."

Good grief.

"Luckily Tina complained about the phony stamps within my earshot, before she had a chance to blab to Vlad. Or the police."

"That was before I knew you were in on the act," Mrs. Phang spat.

Bernie shot the flashlight on her. "Temper, temper. You always were a hothead."

"So you kidnapped her?"

"No. Myron did. I had to explain about our previous circumstances and all."

"That's terrible!"

"No, no. It's only temporary until we shut down the stand, after we collect the rest of the money. Dexter's done some tweaking to his template, so we've sold thousands of rolls of stamps, and they've all passed muster. We're good to go."

"Dexter?"

"He's the talent. Friend of Myron's."

Mrs. Phang stared at me. "Myron and Bernie met in prison, waiting for their bail bonds to get posted."

I stared back.

"A lottery strike for us! We're gonna retire and live on islands. Except for Myron." Bernie rocked happily back and forth on his heels.

"Myron's not retiring?" I asked.

"Sure he is. It's just that he wants to go to Iceland. Imagine that! Iceland! Brrr – too cold for my blood."

What could we do? We nodded in agreement. Iceland is cold.

"Speaking of blood, I'm hungry. But I promised to keep you in one piece. Damn. I better go back in my box. Later." Bernie started back up the steps.

Mrs. Phang shot up. "You know, we're hungry, too. You want me to help you find something in the fridge?"

"Oh, no you don't! The last time you did that, you caused a lot of monkey business."

"It wasn't what you think! I wanted a smoke. And the door was locked."

"You were climbing out the window!"

"Bernie…"

"Besides, you know how much flack I'll get if those bozos know I'm even giving you smoke breaks?"

"I know, I know. It's very nice of you. Very civil."

"You're darn right it's civil! I may be a vampire, but I've still got some social skills, you know?"

"Vampire?" I croaked.

She shot me a look. "Bernie's succumbed to some kind of protein deficiency."

"Protein, schmotein. I tell you, I need blood. And now I gotta wait hours before I can even think of feeding again. I'm going back upstairs and lie down in my box."

"Hey, Bernie, why don't we order take-out?"

Bernie stopped in his tracks. "That didn't work out so good for me last time."

"I know, I know, my bad. They just misunderstood *raw* for *rare*."

"Well…"

I sat up and shook my head. What kind of looney tunes kidnapping was this?

"And this time you can use my credit card, okay? My treat."

"You better make sure you tell them. NO GARLIC this time. Vampires don't like garlic."

"Absolutely."

"I had indigestion for days."

"My apologies. I'll make sure. Why don't you circle what you want from the menu, and I'll make sure to tell them exactly, especially no garlic and raw."

"Well, the menus are all upstairs. I have no clue where a pen is…"

Bernie ambled up the steps, and left us. The lock on the door clicked firmly behind him.

"What the hell? Your treat?" I hissed.

"Yes, you fool! My credit card number will be traced."

"Assuming you're being looked for."

"Of course I'm being looked for! Hasn't anyone reported me missing?"

"Actually, I suggested that to your sister-in-law."

"You suggested it? Ugh, she always was a little slow."

"She said you had an argument. It was an honest mistake."

"I know, I know. She's too nice. She's lived in Lancaster too long."

I nodded in agreement.

"What the hell happened?"

She sighed. "They kidnapped me. I thought I found a way out when I recognized the delivery kid.

He's my second-cousin's youngest. I tried to have him deliver a note to the police. But he went wombat on me, afraid he'd get deported. So I told him to hide a note inside a fortune cookie, and deliver it to Vito."

"That was smart."

"That's what I thought. Besides, getting rescued by Vito will be safer. I think they're up to something very bad." She uncuffed me and led me to a chink in the cement wall. "Look."

It took a few seconds for my eyes to adjust to the daylight, but eventually I saw a small shed, with its door ajar. It was loaded with gasoline cans. Dozens more were piled outside.

"He's sailing to Iceland?"

She put her hand to her forehead. "No, fool! He's stockpiling fuel a little at a time, sneaky like. You see?"

"But why?"

"Probably to get rid of any evidence."

"Like?"

"Us."

"You mean, if he thinks the cops are going to rescue us, he'll blow up the house?"

"Sky high."

"Won't that be a tad unusual?"

"In this neighborhood? It's unusual that this house is standing. It'll probably be considered a gas leak, until forensics gets through with it."

"And us."

"Precisely."

"So Vito's getting to us first would be lots

safer?"

"A silent Towncar versus a three-alarm fire. You pick."

"I guess this would be bad time to tell you about the fortune cookie I got telling me someone was being held prisoner in Mantoloking?"

"YOU got the fortune? What did it say?"

"Help – prisoner 1465 Conch Avenue, Mantoloking, NJ!"

"Well, that's almost what I told him to say, with the exception of my name. How did *you* get the fortune?"

"Norman took us to lunch at Lucky Palace."

"Lucky Palace? Oh, the little twit."

"Huh?"

"Lucky Palace is a franchise, the one down here where the kid works. He probably set the damn thing down in a box of fortunes getting shipped to PA instead of taking by hand to Vito like I told him to."

"I guess your instructions got lost in the translation."

Mrs. Phang flapped her arms. "Well, what's done is done. At least now I know why it's taken so long."

The basement door flapped open and Bernie thumped downstairs. I dove back to the pole and put my hands behind my back.

"Okay girls, what'll it be? You've got lots of choices but I'm not so sure I'm gonna like any of them."

"Sure, you will. It will be fun," Mrs. Phang

walked toward Bernie and his menu. Bernie held up a gun.

"Sorry, Tina. Nothing personal. Just business."

Mrs. Phang took a step back. "I just wanted to see the menu, Bernie. Honest. I'm trying to help you."

"Sure. Understood. Here's the menu, and a pen." He tossed the menu and a ballpoint on the floor.

Mrs. Phang picked up the menu, trying to see. I noticed it was trembling in her hands. Bernie hadn't put the gun down.

"So, let's see. It's Asian Fusion so we have lots of choices."

"What do they got for appetizers?"

"I guess fried is definitely out for you, right Bernie?"

"You betcha. Terrible for my cholesterol."

"How do you feel about sushi?"

"You mean raw fish?"

"Yes."

He thought a moment. "Does it have any blood?"

"It probably did at one time."

"Okay. I'll try it. But I don't want no wasabi mustard. It ruins my sinuses."

I banged the back of my head calmly against the pole.

"And for your entrée?"

" I'll try the pepper steak again. And they can cook the peppers. But NO onions. And I want the steak RAW. And no rice."

"Got it. Now let's see, Mina – would you like some dumplings?"

I rolled my eyes. This was a bizarre last meal. "Sure."

"Do you like General Tso's chicken?"

"Yes."

"Spicy? Extra spicy? Mild?"

"Spicy."

"Great. Now, I think I'll have the vegetable spring rolls, and veggie lo mein."

Bernie winced. "What are you, some kind of vegetarian?"

"Actually, I've been one for some time now."

I raised my eyebrows. "You don't say?"

Mrs. Phang nodded.

"I've got to look into that. I don't know that much about vegetarian cooking per se; and almost nothing about vegan recipes."

"I understand there's a lot to prepping and technique."

"That's what I thought. You see, James is going to have a lot of catering clients for me at the beginning of the year, and…"

"LADIES, please! Tina, you got your orders?"

"Sorry. Sure, here." She handed over the marked-up menu.

"Fine. I'll place the call. I already got your credit card, Tina. Thanks a mil."

Tina smiled. "Anything for an old friend. Just one thing before you call though, okay?"

Bernie huffed with impatience. "What?"

"Well, I mean. I know I gave you the go ahead

to use my card."

"Yeah."

"And you know it's okay."

"Yeah?"

"But the kid taking the order might wonder why a middle-aged white guy is placing a credit card order under the name of Tina Phang."

"Huh."

"Besides, you want to make sure you get your meat umm… the right way, this time, right?"

"Yeah?"

"So how's your Vietnamese?"

"Huh?"

Mrs. Phang rubbed her forehead. "Remember, the kid taking your order last time mentioned the owner is Vietnamese?"

"So?"

"Bernie, listen: I speak the language. Like as in, special order?"

Bernie brightened. "Oh, yeah, right! You got an inside track on the gook thing."

Mrs. Phang and I winced.

She smiled tightly. "Yes, it's a special club."

"Okay, here. But no monkey business this time, you got it?"

"Enough with the monkeys!"

Bernie dialed and handed the phone over to Mrs. Phang, pointing the gun at her head. To her credit, she appeared to calmly commence ordering. She smiled and nodded her head a lot, with a lot of uh-huh's.

"How's your handcuffs, kid?"

I sat up, wide-eyed. "Okay."

"You know, if they're rubbing you the wrong way, I got some powder upstairs."

"That's great. But I'm fine, thanks."

"You sure? Here, let me take a look…"

Mrs. Phang leaped in front of him. "Here you go, Bernie! Said they'd be here in twenty minutes!" She shoved the menu at him.

"Hey, how's that for service? Last time I called it took over an hour."

"Glad I could help."

"Sure. Thanks." Bernie started upstairs. Then, he turned back around.

"And Tina?"

"Yes?"

"Put the cell phone on the steps, where I can see it, okay?" He held the gun resolutely by his side.

Mrs. Phang's face went pale. "Oh, right! Ha, ha, almost forgot."

"Sure, it's an easy mistake. Wouldn't want to go using up my minutes now, would you?"

"Ha, ha."

"Ha, ha."

He took the phone and went back up the stairs, locking the door.

Mrs. Phang fell to her knees, shaking and crying. I sprang up and hugged her.

"You did great! You're really brave!"

She shook her head. "We'll see."

"How did they take the part about the raw meat order?"

She wiped her eyes. "Dunno."

"Huh? You were on the phone with them for over five minutes. And I saw you give them a credit card number."

"I asked for a manager right away. I was afraid a kid would think it was a prank call."

"Our order would be a prank call?"

"No. Our escape."

"That was smart!"

"Maybe."

"What'd the manager say?"

"He yelled at me for taking up their business line playing games. I told him to take our order and check my card number with the police."

"Did he take the order?"

"I think so. Don't know. I'm not too hopeful."

"Why?"

"He said he was going to call back to verify it. And that pranking about kidnapping wasn't funny."

Upstairs we heard Bernie's cell phone ring. "Why, yes, my uh, wife just placed an order with your outfit a few minutes ago. Yeah, she ordered that. Uh, huh. Yep. Great. Thanks."

The minutes ticked away. I felt like Dorothy in the Wizard of Oz – the wicked Chinese take-out manager had upturned our hour-glass timer. We heard a siren wail and we scrambled toward the chink in the wall to see. Then it faded into the distance. So did our hopes. We were scared. We used the bucket.

"I guess they've been treating you okay?"

"Mostly. But mostly it's been just Bernie and me. Myron and Dexter have only made guest appearances. " She shivered. "They had me locked upstairs in a bedroom. At least it had a toilet."

The heat exchange kicked in. "And you had to have been warmer there."

"I know. I should have thought of that. Maybe we should have played for more time." She rubbed her arms.

"I don't know. Not if Myron and Dexter are both coming back tonight."

"That's exactly what I'm afraid of. This isn't the norm."

Awhile later we heard a car pull up to the house, and footsteps spring up to the front door. The doorbell rang. A chair scraped against the kitchen floor. The front door opened.

"Delivery for Tina Phang?"

"Yes, thank you."

"Sign here please."

"Where do I sign for your tip?"

"Tip? Oh, *thank you*! Here!"

Mrs. Phang spewed a deluge of whispered expletives that I'm sure would choke someone later. Particularly Bernie, since he was over-tipping on her dime.

The front door banged shut and we heard the tumbler lock. Steps were heard going into the kitchen. A bag rustled. We smelled food.

"Insane bastard's gonna eat it all. Raw my ass," Mrs. Phang whispered.

"Then he'll get a belly ache. Then maybe we could sneak away?"

She shot me a look. I guessed I was a little too

Nancy Drew for her Ellery Queen.

The door to the basement opened. "All right ladies, come and get it."

I started to get up when Mrs. Phang shoved me back down, kicking some boxes over on purpose, while she slammed the cuffs back on me.

"Hey, Bernie, love to oblige. But Mina, you know?"

Bernie ambled down the steps. "Oh, right. Sorry. Forgot. I'll give you her food, and you can feed her, after you eat with me, okay?"

Mrs. Phang closed her eyes, and crossed her fingers. "The atmosphere down here might not be conducive to eating."

"Huh? Whaddaya mean? If this anymore of your monkey business…" Bernie lumbered down and stood at the base of the steps. "Phew! It smells like piss down here!"

Mrs. Phang stood with her hands on her hips. "You know?"

"Geez! I was only kidding about the bucket!"

"Why you not say?"

"All right, all right, don't go getting all Asian on me."

"Do you have a key or don't you?"

"Of course not. I wasn't kidding about Dexter. But I got this." He opened up a small, sharp instrument from a keychain in his wallet – the kind your grandpa wore.

Bernie leaned over and picked open my handcuffs.

"This is great! Thanks!" I pretended, rubbing

imaginary numb wrists.

"Don't mention it. And I mean, don't mention it. We're gonna eat, you girls take a pit stop, then back down here you go. I don't wanna piss off the boys."

Mrs. Phang cleared her throat.

"Yeah, seriously. Let's get out of here." Bernie led the way up the steps, standing at the top with his gun trained on us. "Just to make sure there's no monkey business."

"What monkey business? Would you forget about the monkeys already?" Mrs. Phang fumed.

" Look, you're cranky because you're hungry. It's all set. Let's eat."

We stared in disbelief at the domestic arrangement before us: a kitchen table laid with placemats, napkins and water bottles.

"Dinner is served, ladies."

Mrs. Phang and I exchanged glances.

"Actually Bernie, I'd like to wash up a little first, please."

"Use the kitchen sink, Tina. You get one trip to the bathroom after we eat."

Wow. He was mean. I figured she was faking. But who makes someone try to eat when she has to tinkle?

"Wow, would you look at this? They finally got the order right. Here girls, dig in." Bernie energetically arranged the take-out boxes on the table.

"Now." He waved the gun at us. We sat down.

"This is more like it!" He dove into the sushi

enthusiastically.

Mrs. Phang and I exchanged more glances and put pieces of dumplings and spring rolls on our plates. We picked them up and looked at them. Bernie chewed heavily. Eventually, we took some bites. This was just as Bernie chose to spit out his sushi out in front of us.

"Pwah! Ugh! This ain't raw!"

Mrs. Phang stared at the remains on his plate. "It should be. Sushi is raw fish."

"I know what sushi is! This is pickled! Here, you try!" He shoved the remainder of the uneaten sushi in the center of the table.

I looked at it. "Actually, I think what you think is pickled is the pickled ginger. It's a garnish that comes with the sushi."

"Really? Well, I don't want no garnish."

"You probably picked up a piece of ginger by mistake. Try this." I picked up a piece of the fish, removing it from its rice bed, and put it on his plate.

Bernie plopped it in his mouth, and chewed tentatively. He smiled, shook his head and swallowed. "Well, I'll give you this. It's raw. But I ain't no seal." He dove for his entrée and tossed it on his plate. Blood poured forth, along with thinly sliced raw beef.

Mrs. Phang looked down. I stared in disbelief.

"This is great! I owe you one, Tina!" Bernie proceeded to suck and slurp his way through his portion of dead, bloody cow.

I silently vowed to consider the vegetarian thing.

He looked up. We stared at him. "Whatsa matter? Ain't you hungry no more?"

"Umm… it's just that umm…" Mrs. Phang looked him directly in the face, specifically where some bloody spittle was drooling down his chin. She dabbed pointedly at her face with her napkin.

"Oh, jeez. You mean my choppers! I don't need them to feed like this. I feed on the liquid."

"Beg pardon?"

"I only use my choppers to hunt. I don't need them to eat stuff like this, just humans. I only have to suck the blood out of this." He proceeded to demonstrate.

I stifled the urge to wretch. "That's pretty creative."

He nodded and pointed to his temple with his forefinger. "I got it all going on up here. Never sleeps."

"Neither does rust," Mrs. Phang murmured.

"Say what?"

The doorbell rang.

Bernie swallowed his blood, and reached for his gun. "Of all the nerve. Just when we were getting all friendly like. You girls keep eating. I'll see this through."

I stared at Mrs. Phang. "What do you think?"

"Now or never."

We crept toward the doorway to watch Bernie, just as he was about to open the front door. Mrs. Phang hand-signaled me the 1-2-3 drill, with her giving the 'go' signal. She held up her hand for me to wait.

Bernie opened the door a crack. It was another delivery kid.

"Hey, Mr. Phang. My buddy forgot your fortune cookies. So I'm helping him out. But I got to tell you, after I told my manager, he just started laughing and laughing. 'Help, I'm being held prisoner in a Chinese Fortune Cookie Factory'. Ha! Ha! Wow, that's a classic. Your wife sure does have a good sense of humor."

"You don't say?"

"Yeah. Wow, it's great to deliver to folks like you. Hey, it's great to deliver to anyone these days. Anyway, my manager wants me to give you this." He handed Bernie a piece of paper.

"A gift certificate?"

"For an order of free fried rice. My manager really appreciates a good sense of humor."

"Uh, thanks, umm…"

"Leon. Leon Martini."

"Martini?"

"Martini, like the drink, get it?"

"Yeah, I got it."

Mrs. Phang gave the three-finger and we dived toward the door.

She threw it open. "Help!!! We're being kidnapped!"

Leon Martini spun around but never saw what was coming. Bernie pulled the trigger from behind her and down he went.

"*No!*" Mrs. Phang cried. She spun around, face-to-face with Bernie. He calmly pointed the pistol at me.

"Your call, Tina. It's not any harder to hide two bodies than one."

"Maybe he's not dead?" I asked cautiously. "It was an accident, right? You just over-reacted?"

"Why don't you find out, Cookie? Tina and I will wait for you here." He waved the gun at me, pointing toward the door. Then he held the gun to Mrs. Phang's forehead.

"Sure," I lied. Geez. This was the second dead guy in a week. It was a surreal adjustment to see someone dead, just moments after you'd met them alive. I walked out slowly, and stared at the prone body. Leon Martini's eyes were wide open, staring into infinity. There was a small hole in the center of his down vest. I bent down and touched his throat for a pulse, just in case. My hands were shaking and I wasn't sure. I turned around and faced Bernie and Mrs. Phang standing inside the doorway. I shook my head.

"Bring him in here," Bernie shouted.

I looked at him. "You're kidding, right? I can't lift him by myself!" Truth was, I couldn't. And even if I could, I'd probably puke. I was also stalling for time. A car had to drive by sometime, right? We couldn't be the only inhabitants on the block, right?

Bernie shoved Mrs. Phang hard and she fell out the front door. "Drag him in here. And no monkey business."

Mrs. Phang walked toward me, muttering. "Monkeys! He got monkeys on the brain..." She sighed, looked at me and closed Leon's eyes.

"C'mon. We'll get him into a sitting position, and put both his arms around us."

I did as I was told.

"All right, on three: one, two…" We got the corpse to his feet and dragged him by his toes into the living room and laid him down. Bernie slammed the door behind us.

"Not here, you dummies. He'll ooze all over the floor."

The thought of oozing made me feel sick to my stomach.

"Move him to the basement."

We stood there, dumbstruck. Was he really going to make us share our basement prison with a dead guy?

"Now!"

We repeated the one-two-three thing and dragged him through the dining room, kitchen, and down the short flight of stairs. Bernie shone the flashlight down the steps. We lay him near the bottom, trying to keep him away from any puddles, for God knows what reason. Mrs. Phang felt around, and found a canvas drop cloth. She laid it over Leon's body, and pulled it up over his face.

"Nice touch, Tina. Very respectful like."

Mrs. Phang whirled around. "He was just a delivery guy! Why'd you have to kill him?"

Bernie came down a step, shining the light in her eyes. "I didn't kill him, you did. Remember, *help-we're-being-kidnapped*?"

"You can't blame a gal for trying."

"Didn't say that I did. But you gotta understand

something, Tina. Soon – very soon – I'm spending the rest of my life on an island. Sipping cocktails in the sand. And no one's going to ruin that for me. *No one*."

"How are you going to do that?" I asked.

He waved the gun at me. "It's all paid for; lock, stock and barrel."

"I'm sure. But how are you going to sip cocktails in the sand? Unless of course, I mean, are you only going to do that by moonlight?"

"Huh?"

I waved my arms in frustration. "You just made an elaborate order for a bloody meal, and you forgot you're a vampire? I don't know too many vampires who sunbathe on the beach."

Bernie stared at me. A smile twitched at the corners of his mouth. "You're right, Cookie. That's *exactly* what I need. An elaborate meal." He shut the door to the basement and turned the deadbolt with his key. He pointed the gun at me. "Go get the handcuffs. Now!"

I backed up and tripped on some bags of concrete mix. I fell back onto the handcuffs.

Bernie rolled his eyes. "You're a real klutz, you know that?"

I nodded, wide-eyed, staring at the gun.

Then he came down the steps, pointing the gun at Mrs. Phang's head. "Go ahead, have a seat." He pushed her down hard on the floor, next to the beam where I'd been handcuffed earlier. "Put the handcuffs on her."

Mrs. Phang looked at me, and I sat up against

the post, waiting.

"No, not you. Her. Mina, handcuff Tina like a good girl, won't you?"

We exchanged glances, and held our breaths. There weren't a lot of options. I put a handcuff on Mrs. Phang's left wrist, and started to repeat the same with the other.

Bernie stepped over. "Oh, no you don't. Wrap her arms behind the pole."

"You want me to handcuff her to the pole?"

"Is there an echo in here?"

Mrs. Phang hung her head. I tried to keep from crying. Somewhere on Bernie there was that thing he used to pick the lock. And the key to the deadbolt. How could I get them off him?

"Good. Now stand up, nice and easy like. Away from Tina." He pointed the gun directly at me. I backed up away from her.

"Great." He rested the gun on top of a high shelf, full of old baby jars filled with nails, bolts, and other odds and ends. "Let's start with the first course!" Bernie lunged toward me.

I screamed.

Mrs. Phang screamed.

Bernie screamed.

"What the fuck? You gonna rape her? You old enough to be her grandpa! You senile!" Mrs. Phang slipped back into broken English.

I slipped into a panic and ran around the basement like my hair was on fire. I stubbed my toe and fell onto a workhorse, throwing planks and hardware everywhere.

Bernie stood with his hands on his hips, shaking his head. "I'm a vampire, Tina, we don't do sex. Truth is, we can't."

"Fabulous. Dolores must be thrilled."

"It's not my fault!"

"Of course not. It happens to a lot of men your age."

"You don't understand. We're separated!"

"Sorry."

"I'm not sorry! I did it on purpose! To save her! In case I forgot myself."

"Forgot yourself?" I asked, immediately wishing I'd kept my big mouth shut.

"I couldn't suck the life blood out of my better half, could I? It's not her fault I turned into a vampire. We've been married for fifty-three years!"

"Congrats."

"Congratulate me in the afterlife, you stupid blood-pumping piece of flesh!" Bernie lunged at me, and we went tumbling. My head narrowly missed a pile of broken cinderblock, and connected with the cement floor instead.

I blinked a few times as I came to, dimly realizing that Bernie was sucking on my neck.

"Yecch!" I pushed him off and shoved him away. "What the hell are you doing?"

"I'm feeding!"

"You have no teeth!"

"Crap. You're right. I left them upstairs in the glass. Be right back." He hustled away for his gun and leaped up the steps, locking the door behind him.

I rubbed my neck and wiped away his spit. "Pretty spry for an old guy."

"Quick! Can you barricade the door?" Tina asked.

I grabbed the flashlight and looked around. "There's a bunch of cinderblocks, but I don't think I have time to lift enough of them. Besides I can barely see."

Tina thumped her head against the pole. "My luck, I gonna die with a stiff and a piss bucket while you get gummed to death."

"I know, I know. This is pretty bad."

Tina stopped thumping and sat up a bit. "The delivery place is going to be looking for that guy, sooner or later. What we need to do is guarantee us being here later."

"Yeah?"

"So this is what you're gonna do…"

CHAPTER 11

Wednesday afternoon

Bernie came thundering back through the door, locking it behind him. I switched the flashlight off.

"Very funny. You think you can hide from me in the dark? Vampires *live* in the dark. I can see everything in the dark."

Mrs. Phang and I waited.

Bernie thumped down a few steps. "This will make things more interesting, anyway." We heard him creak down another step.

I patted the chunks of cinderblock next to me, making sure they were within reach. Then I clutched the handle of the bucket.

"Olly, olly, oxenfree… C'mon Mina, Bernie needs a nosh."

I heard him come down another two steps. Mrs. Phang had me count them before, to make sure. Just four more steps to go.

My blood was pounding in my ears. I couldn't believe he didn't hear it even if he didn't have preternatural powers.

Another step. "*I can smell you...*"

Two more steps.

Mrs. Phang pretended to cough.

"Ah-ha!" Bernie leaped toward her, directly in front of me.

I tossed the bucket of piss in his face.

"*Ughh!*"

"Quick, Mina! Now!" Mrs. Phang screamed.

I grabbed a chunk of cinderblock and tossed it in the direction of Bernie's screams.

"Ow!" Bernie grabbed his forehead.

"Another one! Knock him out!"

I grabbed another piece, instantly feeling guilty I was hurting a person on purpose, even if he was a deranged vampire. But I didn't have a lot of options. I turned the flashlight on him, then hurled the next chunk. There was a squishy thud as Bernie crumbled to his knees.

"Now, Mina! Hurry!"

Mrs. Phang's voice brought me back to the moment. His head was bleeding. I pushed him down on his belly with my foot and quickly took the gun.

Bernie lay still, breathing hard. It looked like I'd knocked him out. At least for the moment.

"Get the keys!" She hissed.

I felt around his back pocket and found his key holder thingy. I brought it over to Mrs. Phang. She walked me through lock picking 101. After what felt like a decade, we had her free.

Bernie groaned.

"Hurry!"

We leaped up the stairs, fumbling with the keys. After a half dozen tries, we found the right one and opened the lock and threw the door open.

Myron stood waiting for us.

"Thank you, Kitchen. I certainly wouldn't have been able to open the deadbolt without the key."

Mrs. Phang grabbed the gun from me. "Back off! I'll shoot!"

"As will I." Myron pointed a very high tech gun at me. There was a trail of a red laser beam aimed at my face. "Put the gun down. Here, by my foot."

She leaned past me and slid the gun onto the kitchen floor.

"Now, put your hands up, behind your heads, and walk up here slowly, where I can see you."

We trudged reluctantly up the stairs and into the kitchen.

"It appears the mice have played, while Dexter was away." Myron nodded toward the take-out spread on the table.

"We got hungry," I answered simply.

"It appears Bernard did, too, yes?" Myron gave a disgusted look toward Bernie's plate.

A loud groan sounded from the basement.

"Yes, well I suppose that answers that. Come upstairs, Bernard."

"Oh, my head! Oh, my Gawd!"

Myron shook his head resignedly and shouted down the steps, "Let's postpone the histrionics, shall we?"

"My teeth! She broke my friggin' teeth!" Bernie stumbled upstairs. While his being a geriatric vampire was a bit terrifying, he now looked like something straight out of a horror movie. His face was covered in blood, and he was completely soaked from head to toe in urine. That, and he was waving his teeth at us in his left hand.

"You see what you done? You know how much these cost? You little brat!" Bernie took a few steps toward me. Myron waved at him to sit down.

He sat down at the table with a thud. "Ugh. I should have stuck with the beef blood. This stinks."

Myron waved a hand in front of his face. "You certainly do. Please get changed. Immediately!"

"All right, all right. I knew I should have stayed in my box."

"Agreed."

Bernie glowered at Myron a few moments. "You might want to be more careful around me, kid."

Myron grabbed the dentures from Bernie's hand. "Because you'll gum me to death?" He tossed the broken choppers in the sink. They fell with a clattering, cracking sound.

"That's gonna cost you."

"Terrific. Send me the bill."

Bernie stood up. "Don't forget who's the brains behind this outfit, huh? Your piece of the pie hasn't been wired to you yet."

Myron's face turned plum. "You said you were going to do that *yesterday*."

"I lied."

Myron's face went purple. "You're double-crossing me?"

Bernie held up a hand. "You're always such a hothead. No, I ain't no double-crosser. Just a little insurance. To make sure I don't leave any loose ends."

Myron stared malevolently at him. "Quite. Speaking of loose ends, you wouldn't want to tell me whose car is parked out front, would you?"

"Sure. It's the delivery guy's."

"Delivery?"

"For the Chinese food."

Myron closed his eyes and took a deep breath. "And where is the delivery guy now? Canvasing our whereabouts door to door?"

"Nope. He's in the basement."

"You took *another* hostage?"

"He didn't get that lucky."

Myron rolled his eyes. "You didn't try to suck his blood, did you? Did you cut him? What is he doing, bleeding to death down there?"

Bernie scratched his head. "Geez, I wished I'd thought of that. Nope. I shot him."

Myron blinked. "You shot the delivery man?"

"Leon."

"Leon?"

"Leon Martini. Like the drink."

"Well, what the bloody hell? Couldn't you have just given him a tip?"

"I did! This was the other one. He came back with the fortune cookies!"

"You shot him over fortune cookies?"

273

"No! I shot him because these two were crying 'help, we're being kidnapped' and the guy was gonna take off."

Myron thumped his gun down on the counter. "Well, this is a pickle! This is a pickle, Bernard! This is quite the mess!"

Bernie shrugged. "It's just one body in the basement. When Dexter gets comes back, he can take care of it."

"Precisely how do you propose he do so?"

Bernie shook his head. "We got a stiff in the basement, a motor boat, and a ton of loose cinderblock. We also got the Atlantic Ocean in our backyard. You need me to paint you a picture?"

Myron looked up, and smiled. "I misunderstood you Bernard. Yes, you really are the brains."

Bernie tapped his temple with his forefinger. "Always thinking."

"Yes, well. I do wish you'd have thought a bit further before you got doused in piss. Phew!"

"That was a miscalculation." Bernie glared at me and Mrs. Phang. We tried to shrink back into the woodwork.

"We've got to lose his car."

Bernie shrugged. "It's not like he's gonna report it stolen. All we gotta do is park it in the back. Besides, he's probably got a pretty good security pass, for deliveries. That'll give us an extra set of disposable wheels when we blow this joint."

Myron squinted in thought. "Yes. Quite. Let's move his car, immediately."

"Gotta get the keys."

"You didn't take them off him?"

"I got distracted." He smacked his chops in my direction. I felt my stomach lurch.

"Fine. Go get the keys off him, and let's move."

Bernie rubbed the back of his neck a bit. "Not so fast. I'm not going back down in the basement with a stiff. Besides, she konked me pretty good. The kid's not such good luck for me in the konked noggin department."

"Yes, I can see that. All right, move." Myron pointed the laser gun thingy at my middle.

"Me?" I croaked.

"Yes, you! Get downstairs and get the car keys off that guy."

"Off the *dead* guy?"

"Now!"

I crept down the steps, dreading the given chore.

"Go on, you can go faster than that!"

"I can't see!"

"Too bad."

Bernie stood behind Myron at the top of the steps. "You put him near the bottom, nice and peaceful like, remember? Pull the cover from over his head, and check his pockets."

Oh boy.

I reached the basement floor, and walked cautiously. I didn't want to step on the dead guy and squish him by accident. My shoe bumped into a sneaker. With a foot in it. I knelt down, and felt the canvas cover. I'd found him.

"I'm-sorry; I'm-sorry; I'm-sorry," I whispered, groping around the front pockets of his vest. I found the keys in the second pocket I tried.

I stood up holding the keys, and all but flew back up the steps.

Myron pointed the laser at me. "Do you have the keys, Kitchen?"

"Right here." I held the key chain up for him to see.

"Good. Now toss them up here like a good girl."

"Mina, don't!"

"I said DO IT!"

I threw the keys onto the kitchen floor. They landed with a clunk.

"Now, I think you girls need a little time out. Bernard, please escort Mrs. Phang back to her room. I'll move the car."

"What about the kid?"

"Oh, she'll be quite safe." Myron pushed me down the steps, closed the door, and locked it.

Luckily I fell on top of the dead guy, or I'd really have fallen hard. Dead guy? *Ugh!*

Mrs. Phang shouted a lot of unintelligible curses. I heard a smack, and then silence. Then I heard shuffling up the flight of stairs to the second floor. A few moments later, I heard the front door open and shut.

I kneeled on my knees and bowed my head. "Christ, I hope they didn't kill her."

"Don't worry, they didn't."

I whirled around and found myself face to face with the stiff. I opened my mouth to scream, and he clapped a very firm – and large – hand over it.

"Don't make a peep, whatever you do!" he

whispered. "We've only got a moment! I'm Agent Mitchell."

I nodded.

"We've been tailing Bernie since last summer."

I nodded again.

"There were two sets of steps up the stairs. Not one. You see? One had to be Tina's."

I relaxed a bit.

"Now, I'm gonna take my hand off you, and you're not going to scream, right?"

I nodded.

He took his hand away.

"You're not dead?"

"Not yet, anyway." He unzipped his vest. "Kevlar."

"Then why the hell were you playing dead?"

"My first time. It kind of knocked the wind out of me. And you gals also thunked my noggin pretty good on the floor."

"Sorry."

"I started to come to right as you raced up the steps into the other guy."

I shook my head. "We totally weren't expecting that."

"Anyone else here besides you and Tina Phang?"

I shook my head.

The front door banged open and shut.

Agent Mitchell put a finger to my lips, then ducked back down underneath the drop cloth to play dead.

I heard water rumbling through the pipes.

"Have you got her secured, Bernard?" Myron's voice trailed up the stairs.

"Of course I do."

"What are you doing, then?"

"I'm taking a shower and getting changed, natch."

"Right. Good thinking." Myron's steps paced overhead. "Disgusting old fool."

A few moments passed. "Yes, Dexter, it's me. Where are you? Why aren't you here yet?"

There was a brief silence while Myron apparently listened to Dexter's response. I could only imagine his smug look of impatience.

"Yes, he botched it. Although it's not entirely his fault."

Another silence.

"Let's not get into who's blaming whom. Let's just finish this and get rid of our baggage quickly, shall we?"

There was another brief pause, followed by Myron's ending the call and muttering a mocking, "*Whatever*."

Myron's steps came back into the kitchen. A chair scraped the floor, and paper bags rustled.

OMG was he actually *eating*?

The water stopped running through the basement pipes. Some more water came gushing down, Bernie must have flushed the toilet.

A little while later, Bernie thumped downstairs and into the kitchen.

"Hey, you're eating my food!"

"I wouldn't touch that bloody mess if you paid

me."

"Oh. Well that's all right then."

Another chair scraped against the floor. Some more bags rustled. There wasn't a lot of small talk between them, just chewing. And slurping.

A car pulled up the gravel driveway. It stopped and a door slammed. The door off the kitchen banged open.

"What the hell? You tell me to get here ASAP, and you're sitting around having coffee and pie?"

"Calm down, Dexter. You'll live longer."

"Thanks a lot, Bernie. Here's your stupid burger."

"I appreciate that."

"Sure."

"I do. This stuff's stale." Bags were crumpled and tossed. Onto the floor?

"Great."

"Have a seat, Dexter. We have a problem."

Another chair scraped against the floor.

"It appears that Bernard has not allocated our funds into our private accounts yesterday, as we previously agreed."

"What the fuck?"

"You eat with that mouth?"

"Look who's talking? You're drinking fucking blood."

"Gentlemen! Dexter, your iPad please."

"It's in the car."

"Retrieve it please."

The chair thumped back and the door slammed open and shut.

"What's your plan, Stan?"

"Clever, Bernard. I simply mean to put our original plans back into place."

"Which is?"

"That you arrange to have our separate accounts wired immediately. You're a day late."

"But not a dollar short. I have other plans."

Dexter's steps thumped back into the kitchen. "Here." He plunked his device onto the kitchen table. "And don't splash any blood on it this time!"

"You're a little sensitive, kid. First things, first."

"What is it this time, Bernard?"

"We got a few loose ends to wrap up. I want our arrangement clear, before I wire any cash."

"The reality is, Bernard, that after we dispose of our baggage, we will be separated for the rest of all time. And while you've been very democratic thus far, I don't trust you to wire the funds after the fact."

"That hurts, Myron."

"You'll get over it."

Hands slammed on the table. "Enough with this bullshit. Look old man, you wire half the funds now. *Now*. Then you set it up so the other half's wired after we quit this burg."

"What a perfectly acceptable arrangement, Dexter. I'm pleased to see you've learned a thing or two."

"Yeah. I learned I'm not gonna be the fall guy for you two cons. I'm outta here. Get tapping, Bernie."

There were several moments of silence,

punctuated by frustrated expletives – mostly at Bernie's lack of notepad savvy and forgetting his password. More silence.

"Bingo! You did it Bernie, we're done."

"By tomorrow morning, Dex."

"Fine."

"Agreed. And by tomorrow morning, we'll be off on our separate adventures, gentlemen."

"That sounds good. Too bad we don't have nothing to celebrate with."

"You mean like champagne? Us vampires don't drink alcohol. Besides, I never drank much as a human, even."

"Forget it, Bernie."

"Don't be so disappointed, Dexter. We might be able to celebrate without consuming anything."

"How'd you mean?"

"Do you like fireworks?"

"Sure."

"Then we might have the next best thing."

Agent Mitchell sat up next to me, and put his hand over my mouth again. I had a feeling neither one of us was going to have much to celebrate very soon.

"What are you going to do?"

"Not me, you Dexter. I'd like you to go out to the shed, and start bringing in all the containers of gasoline."

"In here?"

"Just put them in the basement."

"What about the stiff? And the girl?"

"Yeah, Myron. First we gotta sink the stiff in

the Atlantic, you know?"

"I've reconsidered that, Bernard. Now that we're about to retire, and are no longer in need of our baggage, it seems a waste of effort."

"Huh?"

Myron sighed. "We're leaving now. We don't need this house anymore. Or Phang, or Kitchen. We'll just tidy up all the loose ends with the stroke of a match."

"Hey, that's some stroke of luck. Good thinking, Myron."

"Sure beats cleaning up the dishes," Dexter added. Myron and Bernie guffawed at their good fortune.

"Beats cleaning up the dishes! Good one, Dex!" Bernie coughed a bit.

"You ought to be careful about that cold, Bernard."

"Vampires don't catch colds, idiot. I'm the undead, you know?"

The back door banged open and shut.

I tugged at Mitchell's shroud and hissed. "What are we going to do?"

He put a hand over my mouth.

"Don't open the basement door without me, all right Bernard? We don't want to underestimate that misfit."

"Gotcha. Where you headed?"

"To use the facilities."

"Oh. Sure."

We listened to Myron going upstairs. Bernie's chair scraped away from the table, and we heard him walk to the front of the house.

Mitchell pulled his hand away. "Can you feel these sacks of cement?" he whispered.

"Yes."

"Help me pile them underneath the ground cloth."

"Then what?"

"Then we hide underneath the steps and hope the cavalry is on the way."

"That's a hell of a plan."

"It's all I got. Besides this."

"What?"

He reached for my hand and pulled it toward him. At first I thought he was trying to pull some last minute whoops-we're-gonna-die-what-the-hell deviant shit on me, until my hand felt something cold and hard. His gun. We crawled underneath the steps and waited.

Dexter banged back through the back door. "Open the door to the basement, Bernie."

"No can do."

"What the fuck?"

Bernie sighed. "Myron's in the can, he wants us to wait. Besides, he still has my keys."

"Oh. So what do I do now?"

"Line 'em up."

"Why don't you help me? There's gotta be a hundred cans out there."

"Rank has its privileges, kid. Besides, it's broad daylight."

"Great. Batty old fuck…" the door banged open and shut.

Water sloshed through the pipes again. Any moment now, we'd hear Myron coming back downstairs. I wished I remembered where the piss bucket was.

"Bernard, I require your assistance upstairs, please."

"What's the matter? You can't flush?"

"How vulgar. No, I'd like some backup checking on Phang. She's been suspiciously silent."

"So what? We're gonna off her anyway."

"Is there a window in her room?"

"Yeah."

"Do you remember locking it?"

"Sure."

Silence.

"I mean, I think I'm sure. You know?"

"Precisely."

"Shit."

Footsteps thundered overhead.

The back door banged open and shut. "Stupid fucks. I should have been forging Picasso's. That's what I'm gonna do next time, that's what. Stupid stamps." More cans got set on the floor. The door banged shut.

A whoosh of two pings sounded faintly from upstairs.

A single set of steps came back downstairs.

The back door banged open. "Say, I'm running out of room here. You gonna open the basement door, or what?"

"Certainly. Let's just make sure our guest isn't on the ready, shall we?"

"Huh?"

"Let's make sure Kitchen doesn't make a break for it."

"Yeah, right."

"Here's the key. Open the door."

"Hey, don't point that gun at me, man!"

"It's not at you, you fool! It's in case she runs away."

"Right. Hey, you got a light? I can't see for shit down here."

"Here."

We heard Dexter catch something. A flashlight shone down the steps. "What do you want me to do with the gas?"

"Pour it down the steps."

"*Pour* it down?"

"Yes."

"You gonna light it, while that chick's still alive?"

"Yes."

"Man, that's cold. Bernie okay with this?"

"I have it on the best authority."

"Okay, dude. Your karma." Gasoline splashed down the steps, pooling at the bottom where Mitchell's faux stiff lay. He tossed the can in after.

"That's very good thinking, Dexter. You're very efficient."

"Whatever." More gasoline came splashing down. Another can was tossed down.

Mitchell led me silently away from under the steps, to a far corner away from the pooling gasoline.

Dexter's gasoline dousing repeated itself. The fumes were noxious. I stifled a cough.

"My apologies about the stench, Kitchen. But it will soon be over."

I coughed again.

Dexter coughed, too. "Hey man, open a window, would you?"

"What a brilliant idea."

"What?"

"Oxygen, Dexter. A fire can't burn properly, or quickly, without oxygen."

"Yeah, right. Where the hell is Bernie? Why can't he fling a can?"

"He's indisposed."

"Great. You mean he's in the can."

"Actually, he's in the bag."

"Huh?"

"Goodbye, Dexter."

One ping sounded and Dexter hurtled down the steps like a sack of bricks. His fall was broken at the bottom by the cement wall, followed by a sickening snap of his neck.

"The very best parties all have fireworks." Myron tossed a lit match and basement steps were ablaze. The door to the basement shut and locked for a final time.

Steps were heard treading rapidly upstairs, toward Mrs. Phang.

"We've got to get out of here now! He's going to kill Mrs. Phang!"

"I can shoot the lock open, but the stairs are already on fire. We're gonna get burned."

"I know! Our shoes will get soaked."

"When we reach the top, do you know how to tuck and roll?"

"Do you know how to play dead?"

Mitchell fired a round at the lock and the door blasted free. We raced up the steps with the flames of hell literally at our heels.

I tucked and rolled on the kitchen floor for all I was worth – my shoes and jeans were on fire. Suddenly I felt a cloth thrown on me, and got tackled. We rolled then abruptly stopped. Mitchell got off me, and stood leaning on the kitchen sink, like a smoking gun. Which he really was. His jeans were smoldering and he was holding a gun.

We heard crashing down the steps. Myron came into view, holding Mrs. Phang with his gun to her head.

"Forget something, Kitchen?" But his eyes opened wide seeing Agent Mitchell, aka dead Leon Martini.

"Nope," Mitchell answered, just after he blasted a bullet straight through Myron's forehead.

Myron fell. A small explosion sounded beneath us.

"C'mon! Let's get out of here!" Mrs. Phang screamed, grabbing my hand. Mitchell followed.

Myron, Bernie and Dexter did not.

CHAPTER 12

Sunday

"You almost ready, Toots?"

I surveyed the mitigated damage in the mirror. Trixie shrugged. "It's hair. It'll grow."

Thanks to Agent Mitchell, I'd been spared the severe burns I might have had. But my pony tail suffered a casualty so a good three inches of singed hair got hacked a day after the hospital declared us A-OK, at the Godmother's insistence, and on her tab. I now sported a kind of layered bowl cut. It wasn't completely unflattering. But it wasn't me. I looked like me in someone else's hair. Luckily, I didn't cave at the stylist's suggestion (insert grappling of wills here) to have my hair tipped ala Ombre. Right now, I wished I could press my belly button and make it grow like my childhood doll had.

"Almost," I called back to Vito.

He and Miriam spent a couple days in a panic about my disappearance, as I found out. Which is why they've been acting a little clingy. That, and Ma and Aunt Muriel told them to. They want to make sure I stay safe and sound, until I go visit them in Virginia since the twins were born earlier than expected. Although their arrival might not have been premature, considering my sister thinks she swallowed a button instead of a birth control pill.

So there was an upside to Vito holding onto the spare key to my place: Vinnie and Marie were well fed and petted in my absence. The downside was Vito's past life and associated thinking. After he found my van and not me, and after a ton of phone calls from Ma wondering where the hell I was, he checked in with Trixie. She blabbed to him about to my non-date with James. Since James was the last person to see me before Dexter kidnapped me, Trixie and Vito assumed the worst and dragged Mike into the picture. Lucky for James that K. wandered into the mix, otherwise we'd still be bailing him out. Mike isn't big on kidnapping, even if it was just me.

Hence, Agent Mitchell. Sort of. Mike wasn't convinced it was as dire as Ma and Trixie made out. But after he chatted up Bauser and Norman, and they told him about the non-fortune cookie, he had a buddy investigate. Thank goodness Mitchell took his undercover work seriously, and made sure there was a backup plan in place. When he hadn't called his partner soon after the fake fortune cookie delivery, the rest of his plan fell like dominos. The game, not the pizza. So right after Mrs. Phang, Mitchell and I busted out of Dodge, the house exploded and the cops showed up. Pretty much in that order.

Eventually the firemen came out to play. What was left of Myron, Dexter and Bernie wasn't pretty, but was identifiable.

"Girls, really! We're going to be *late!*" For all of K.'s wonky creative tendencies, he does harbor a sincere work ethic. Which I guess is why he's so successful. As well as becoming increasingly compulsive about *never* being late.

"Coming! Coming!" Trixie clopped down the stairs.

"Brrr-wuf?"

"Yep, I'll be back soon, sugar bear." I hugged Vinnie hard. In fact, since I got released from the hospital, I hadn't ventured about the house without him tagging alongside. And vice versa.

Mike Green stood at the bottom of the steps, his arm around Trixie's shoulders. "You be good. Don't spend too much. And nothing…fancy, right?"

"You're so boring."

"That's why you love me." He kissed her softly on her forehead.

"Are you sure you're okay staying here, Mike? It's not necessary," I began.

"*Yes it is!*" chorused everyone else. Marie piped up from her room.

Yeeshkabiddle.

Mike pretended to clear his throat. "I'm better off here. I'm not big on craft sales."

"Besides which, your pets are on the nervy side. They didn't know what happened to you!" Miriam bobbed her head up and down emphatically.

Vito flapped his arms. "Sure they did! They smelled burnt hair, right?"

"What's that supposed to tell them? Their mother stuck her head in the oven?"

He frowned. "The oven's electric."

"You see?"

I considered it. Unless my pets thought I was about to commit suicide with an electric oven, this made sense. That, and Vinnie's trip to the vet – thanks to Miriam, after she noticed him walking funny – probably did mean they were on the nervy side with my taking off for a bit. Even if it was just for a couple hours at the Christmas Bazaar.

"I don't really need to buy anything. Maybe I shouldn't go."

K. rolled his eyes. "Of course you should go! You shouldn't shop because you *need* something!"

"But my Christmas shopping's done."

"No it isn't. I saw that stash of chicken stock in your freezer and I refuse to accept it as a gift."

"It's useful."

"So is toilet paper. But you don't give it as a present!"

I gave him the squinty eye. "Ha! So *you* dumped the Hoisin Duck!"

"Huh?"

"I made a glazed duck. I left it in the fridge."

Trixie leaned in. "That sounds yummy!"

"I hoped so. It was going to be your present."

Miriam cleared her throat. "You mean that big chicken?"

"Chicken?"

"In the middle of your fridge."

"It was a duck."

"Well, it was."

"Was what?"

"Delicious!"

"Huh?"

"We got a little side-tracked, what with looking for you and still working on the Manishewitz contest and all. And then we found the chicken – errm, duck - with the glaze on it. And we wondered if it tasted like our glaze."

Vito help up a hand. "You wondered."

"I did not!"

I rolled my eyes and shrugged at Trixie. "So much for your present."

Trixie smiled. "You can make us another."

"Or maybe actually buy something normalish, at the bazaar?" K. asked pointedly.

"Whatever."

Trixie and I hopped into her Jeep and waited to tag behind Vito and Miriam to St. Bart's.

K. took off in his loaner Mini. Staring after the matchbox size car, I hoped it was a phase.

"Thanks for cleaning up all the blood in the basement."

She shrugged. "No biggie. I do it all the time." She pulled out a cigarette and puffed.

"I thought you quit?"

"I did. This is an e-cigarette."

"Oh. Mike's okay with that?"

She exhaled. "I can't keep snappin' gum all the time. My jaw hurts."

We followed Vito's new Towncar into the parking lot and parked side by side. Vito popped open his trunk and pulled out a gigantic cardboard box loaded with cartons of tape.

I stared at it. "I thought there was a shortage?"

Vito shook his head. "I wondered what everyone was making such a fuss about. I knew I smelled a rat."

"Or in this case, a vampire!" Miriam wiggled her eyebrows.

Vito stared at Miriam. "I told you, that wasn't no such case."

"I know, I know. But it sounds lots more interesting."

"I told you I had the whole thing figured out. Especially after finding the pickle."

"Pickle?" I asked.

He nodded. "It was Bernie's signature. I figured he was behind blowing up my car. Especially after I out-bidded him at the auction."

"Auction?"

"A wholesale auction for tape and giftwrapping and such. I was bargaining for the bizarre."

"Bazaar."

"Whatever. Anyway, Bernie had a fit after he saw me there, bidding on a bunch of office supplies, which included a ton of tape."

"Naturally."

"It seemed to me he was acting like a complete

whack job. Especially after he bit me on the neck and all."

"Natch."

"But I didn't figure out how involved Myron was with you getting kidnapped, until after I got your ride dusted."

"Dusted?"

"For fingerprints!" Miriam was really enjoying this. "You see, Vito was worried about the Doo-doo getting blown up, after finding more doo-doo again, see? And especially since he knew Bernie blowed up his car. He thought we'd find Bernie's prints."

I rubbed my forehead.

Vito waved at her. "A friend owed me a favor."

"What do you mean?" I had to ask. I needed closure to the poopy thing.

He tapped the side of his nose. "Myron got fingerprinted, after he got arrested for the Världen Vänder caper, right?"

"So?"

"So before that, there was no record of his fingerprints. Afterward, there was."

"And?"

Miriam hopped up and down, giddy with excitement. "His paws were all over your van! Especially in the wheel well, where he hid the poop!"

I rubbed my head some more.

Trixie unwrapped some more gum. "What I'd like to know is where he got all that poop from? And how he got it inside your van? It's parked inside your garage every night."

"But not while she worked as a Sidekick!" Miriam was fully in her element now.

"Huh?"

"Vito's pal tracked down the prints to Pets Galore! They were all over a whole bunch of crates used for pet grooming! One was even big enough for a mastiff!"

Huh. "Anything about a cursing parrot? Or a fat cat named Hamlet?"

Miriam looked at me funny. "Maybe you got hit on the head harder than we thought."

Vito tossed his arms in the air. "She'll be fine."

"She needs looked after!"

"She's all grown up!"

"But her mother's in Virginia!"

They walked off together, bickering their way toward the bazaar.

Trixie grabbed me by the elbow, and we followed.

"Buddy – Bernie – was on Mike's watch."

"He was in the program?"

"Barely. He wasn't much for laying low. But the department gave him a loose leash, to see what he was up to."

"The counterfeiting?"

Trixie nodded. "Apparently it's a widespread problem. Especially with the holiday crazies Bernie exploited."

"Huh?"

Trixie opened the door to the church. "Bernie had a hook into one of the producers at WPAL."

"What?"

"Blackmail. So the producer came up with the cockamamie scheme of creating local tabloid news about a tape shortage, right before the holidays."

"How was that supposed to work?"

"Easy. Anything that's on TV people take as gospel truth. Just like *War of the Worlds*."

"That was radio, not TV."

"Same difference."

"But it's so dumb! Just saying there's a tape shortage doesn't create one, right?"

"But it did. Because most shoppers believed there was a shortage, they created one by buying up all the tape."

"That sure was a long shot."

She shrugged. "For the kind of money wired into Bernie's account, Mike figured he thought it was worth the gamble."

"Really? How much?"

"Millions. Plural."

"Wow. From stamps?"

"Bernie sure would have been rolling in it, if he had lived."

"That's true. Except that as a vampire, he wasn't technically alive, anyway."

Trixie stopped in her tracks. "Bernie wasn't a vampire, you kook!"

"Yeah? What do you make of this?" I showed her the bruised spot where he'd gummed my neck.

She rolled her eyes. "Bernie wasn't one of the un-dead. He was one of the un-hinged."

"Huh?"

"After the house blew up, his cover was over.

296

His only next of kin was his wife, Dolores."

"They separated."

"Actually, they didn't."

"But he said…"

Trixie waved me to shush. "Yeah, they lived separately. Apparently he left it up to her to file papers, which she never did."

"Why?"

"Because she was worried about him. The guy was nuttier than a fruitcake. At least, that's what she told Mike, after he contacted her to give her the news."

"So you mean all the vampire stuff was because he was nuts?"

"Not exactly. Right before he moved out on her, Dolores said he was diagnosed with a bad case of UTI. Turns out it was listeria monocytogenes. Which makes perfect sense."

"Huh?"

"Causes headaches, cramps and *confusion*."

"Wow. So his complaining about his head hurting and a belly ache was legit, huh?

"Yes. Except that he thought those were symptoms of his being a vampire, not an infection."

"So the infection made him think he was a vampire?"

"Coupled with dehydration dementia. His doctor had him on the mend for a while, but he refused to keep up his fluids. His wife said he didn't like to pee so much at night. He was up and down all the time, what with his blood pressure meds and all. So he barely drank anything."

"Yikes."

"I'll say. Then she told Mike he'd been reading all these vampire novels. So on top of his starving his body of fluids, he was feeding his imagination with some pretty strange stories."

"So he imagined himself a vampire?"

She nodded.

"And folks around here got conned into imagining a tape shortage?"

She nodded again. "Let's hope they still think so."

"Why?"

"Vito's cornered the market for the bazaar. He's got tons of boxes of the stuff. And, he's targeting a 300% markup."

A virtual light bulb went on over my conked cranium. "Is *that* what he stashed in my basement?"

"Yep."

I rubbed my forehead. "Please tell me it's not hot tape."

Trixie shrugged. "Dunno."

"Good grief."

"That's nothing. Wait until you see the Lost and Found table he and Miriam have set up."

"What?"

"He told Mike he figured out where Dexter had been dumping the stuff that hadn't been mailed. With the exception of the presents the guy sold on eBay."

"He sold other people's Christmas presents?"

"Yep."

"Wow. That was mean."

"And stupid. It led Mike right to him. I mean, it would have, before he got charcoal broiled."

I winced.

"Anyway, so now Vito and Miriam get to make like Santy Claus. Look!"

Vito and Miriam stood behind a long table piled with packages, with signs labeled across the front A-E; F-L, and so on through the alphabet. Long lines of folks snaked in front of each set of letters. PennDOT would have been proud.

I rubbed my forehead. "Please tell me he's not reselling used Christmas prizes…"

"No! He's actually helping the police out. After Appletree got pulled into all this, he complained about the station not really have the staff or the room to deal with it. That's when Vito came up with the idea about returning the victim's things here."

"Without police staff?"

"Nope. Look." She waved at Appletree and several other officers.

"Ah, ha! So that's why you wanted Mike to hang back and babysit my pets!"

"Did you really want to see that much testosterone flying around?"

"No."

We ambled over toward the table. Trixie leaned in and proceeded to flirt shamelessly with Appletree, in a too-bad-so-sad kind of way.

Bauser tapped me on the shoulder.

"What are you doing here?"

"Getting your Christmas present."

"I thought you were giving six-packs?"

"I was."

"But?"

"I drank them."

I did a mental genuflect.

"Besides, Norman wanted to chip in. We got a little worried about you, what with your getting kidnapped a couple times and all."

Norman nodded silently next to him, sipping from a large Styrofoam cup.

"You're not drinking Krumpthf's *here*, are you?"

He held the cup out. I sniffed. "Earl Grey?"

"We're not a couple of alchies, you know?"

"At least not in church," Bauser added quickly.

"Here." Norman thrust a large, unadorned plastic grocery bag into my hands.

"What the?"

Jim stood up and pawed at the bag and my waist. He slid over. Norman caught him.

"Open it, okay?"

"You don't want me to wait until Christmas?"

They shook their heads adamantly.

I began to open the bag, feeling a bit sheepish. While I was able to pick up some cute things for them during my search-and-destroy coupon sale, I certainly didn't buy them anything extravagant. Knowing Norman's bottomless bank account, I figured this was something top notch.

I opened the bag. "A helmet?"

"Not just any helmet! A lacrosse helmet!"

Bauser chimed in. "Now you can get whacked

on the head with a ball *or* a stick – you won't even feel it!"

Norman shook his head. "No, no, no. Of course she'll feel it. The point is, you wouldn't get knocked out."

"Or more brain damage."

More brain damage?

"Umm. Thanks."

"Try it on!"

"Well, I..."

"See? It matches your crocs! You can even wear it to work!"

I sighed deeply and flopped the orange plastic insect looking helmet on my head. Judging by its wire cage, all I needed to complete my ensemble was a chain saw.

Bauser and Norman high-fived each other. Jim wagged and fell over.

"Thanks guys. I'll catch up with your presents later, okay?"

"No problem," Norman said.

Bauser sniffed. "I smell hotdogs."

And away they went. Mission accomplished.

I sniffed in the opposite direction, toward the aroma of funnel cake wafting my way. I turned around to find Chef standing behind me, munching on one.

"What are you doing here?"

"Lost and found."

"You lost presents to Mail-it-2?"

"No. I almost lost a particularly talented cook, and I was worried about her."

301

"Really?" Did he mean me? I whipped the armor off my head and hid it behind my back.

"I called your house. Mike answered and said you were here."

"You came here because of me?"

He nodded.

Trixie coughed a bit. "Oh. I forgot to tell you. Chef called asking about you, too." She returned to taunting Appletree.

Appletree stared at me with all the desperation a drowning man eyes a rope. "Actually, he called you lots. Then he called me, asking me to check your place. Which I did."

"Yeah, we sure did," Vito added.

"Smart thinking, letting Vito have a spare key to your place."

I closed my eyes and held my breath. Then I opened them. Nope, they were all still there.

Vito nodded behind the fake beard. "Sure. He could have been tangled up in red tape for weeks."

"I guess giving a *friend* a key to your place is a good idea, hmmm?" Miriam elbowed Vito in the side. He grimaced.

Appletree stood up from the table and continued – giving Trixie a wide berth. "That's right. If I hadn't seen all that blood on the basement floor, I wouldn't have thought very much about you being missing."

Trixie snorted. "That figures."

He ignored her. "Truth is, Chef was pretty upset about you're not showing up for work."

I stared at him "You were?"

Chef nodded. "I couldn't imagine you're skipping out on a shift, so I kept calling. After Vito answered and told me your van was still there, I called Appletree."

"Even after Trixie called Mike?"

Chef rubbed his chin. "I didn't know she'd called in the big guns."

"Hey, careful now," Appletree huffed.

Trixie rolled her eyes. "It was a two-pronged effort okay? Good grief."

Appletree pressed on. "It was damn lucky. Otherwise, the state police wouldn't have shown up when they did."

I stared wide-eyed. "Really?"

"Mitchell's partner was on the way. But he wasn't planning on calling for armed back up unless he thought something was really wrong."

"So he figured it out?"

"Eventually."

"When?"

"After the house blew up."

"That's a good clue."

"And it led Mike's outfit to another case."

"Really? What?"

"Hamilton."

"The dead guy?"

Trixie stared at me, open- mouthed. "You got another dead guy?"

Chef leaned against the wall, munching his funnel cake, smiling at me.

I waved my arms. "It wasn't my fault! He stroked out!"

Appletree nodded. "I'd have had a stroke too, if I'd lost all that money gambling, and my wife didn't know."

"I know! I know! $96,000!"

He shook his head. "Try closer to a million. The ninety-six was just the icing on the cake."

"So that's why he had a stroke?"

"That, and the pressure Myron was putting on him."

"About?"

"Gambling. He was blackmailing him against his marriage. And his job."

"That was rotten!"

"That was lucrative. Myron had connections to some top gambling sites. He got some names, and regularly hustled hush money out of some pretty high profile professionals."

"How high profile?"

"Let's just say, there are a few folks who won't be running for re-election."

"I won! I won!" K. came skittering into the mix.

"Won what?" I asked.

"The Mini Miracle!"

"Huh?"

"They just texted me!"

"Who did?"

"Don't you remember the 'enter to win' contest at the mall?"

"For a Mini Cooper?"

Chef joined in. "You won a Mini? Wow, that's great!"

"Well, I didn't exactly win a Mini, per se."

We looked at him.

"But I won a chance to buy one! At a discount!"

Clearly, not every crook hails from New Jersey.

K. pouted. "So, who's coming with me to claim my prize?"

Trixie pretended to help Appletree. Miriam adjusted Vito's beard.

"Oh, come on! It will be fun!"

"You want me to go to the mall?"

"Not shopping! To get my Mini discount!"

"Thanks. But I'm giving it a rest." And I have been. Given my PTSD over my near-death experience, I'd quit the Sidekick gig. I became faint at the thought of the mall. The other part of my therapy consisted of ordering a pasta maker. I was certain I'd feel lots safer once my windows were full of drying pasta.

"Pooh."

"You don't have to go right away, do you?"

K. bobbed with anticipation. "First come, first serve!"

Chef grinned. "You don't think this is a marketing ploy, do you?"

K. stared at him. "There are only so many cars!"

"And so few buyers?"

"Precisely."

Barnum was right.

"I'm off, Sweetie."

"Don't sign anything without me!"

"Never."

Trixie's cell phone rang. "No, I'm not buying anything weird."

Appletree rubbed his forehead. "She's helping me. That's weirder."

Trixie listened. "Yes, that was Appletree."

She listened some more. "No, that's not correct. Or fair."

Appletree began to whistle "It's Beginning to Look a Lot Like Christmas" under his breath, as he helped another victim sign their claim form.

Trixie whacked his shoulder. "All right, all right. I'll keep you company." She shut off the phone, looked at me and shrugged. "Anything you want to buy here, before I turn into a pumpkin?"

"When's that?"

"Now is good."

"We just got here!"

Chef stepped forward. "I just got here, too."

Trixie tossed on her jacket. "Okay, I leave you in capable hands." And off she went.

"So, anything in particular you want for Christmas?"

"Funnel cake is good."

He offered me his plate. "Anything else?"

I chewed on it. "Not really."

"Something tells me you've been a very good girl this year."

"Don't believe everything you hear."

He smiled. "I don't."

"Thanks a lot."

"There has to be something on your wish list."

"A job would be good."

"You have three."

I shook my head. "I'm down to two."

"I stand corrected. But you could use some time off."

"I guess."

"You'll have a blast with the twins over Christmas."

"I know. And you don't have to worry. I'll be back the day after, for the Hinkey party."

"I wasn't thinking about it."

"You weren't?"

"Nope."

I looked up into his deep blue eyes, which were sparkling at me intently. "Then what are you thinking about?"

"What are you doing New Year's, Mina?"

Dear Reader,

I hope you enjoyed *Christmas Bizarre*. Please spread the word, so others can have some fun, too. Please post a brief review on Amazon.com. Or recommend it to an online reader's group (like GoodReads.com), a book club, a Meetup.com group, etc.

I value your feedback – if you were kind enough to post a review, please let me know directly at lizzlund.author@gmail.com.

If this is your first Mina book, you might want to read how the story started with *Kitchen Addiction!* You can find both the ebook (Kindle) and paperback at Amazon.com. If you are local to Lancaster, "Pee-Ay", check out Aaron's Books in Lititz, PA for the paperback.

The sequel, *Confection Connection* is in the works, as is the fourth in the series, *Perfectly Pickled*.

Please stay in touch, and check out my website, http://www.LizzLund.com for updates and blog posts. And always feel free to email me directly – I do answer all emails: lizzlund.author@gmail.com.

For social media visits, on Facebook.com, I'm "Lizz Lund – Author." On Twitter.com, I'm @FunnyAuthor.

In the meantime, before you go, please continue on to the recipe section of this book. Enjoy!

--lizz

Lizz Lund

Christmas Bizarre – Recipes

309

CHrʲStMaS BɪZaɾɾe

Mina's Pot Roast

Mina's pot roast is based on my Ma's recipe. Her gravy uses crushed ginger snaps as a 'thickener' rather than flour or corn starch (pot roast purists – consider yourselves forewarned.)

3 lbs. bottom round beef roast ('rump roast'); approximately
2-3 tablespoons vegetable oil (not olive oil, as it burns)
1 medium onion
2 large carrots (or, 8 baby carrots)
1 tablespoon (about) whole allspice
3-5 large bay leaves
Ginger snaps
1-2 cups red wine (preferably, burgundy)
Salt, pepper

Heat the oil in a large pot with a lid (Dutch oven; medium stockpot). When the oil is hot, brown the meat, searing all sides (make sure to not turn the meat too quickly, or it will stick to the bottom of the pot.)

Chop the onion, and add to the pot after the meat has been browned on all sides. The object here is to get the onions soft/translucent, not browned.

Cut the carrots into bite-size pieces, and toss into the pot. These will be mashed later on, to provide added flavor to your gravy.

Add the allspice, and bay leaves (crinkling them as you add to the mix.)

310

Add 1 cup of wine, and some water so that the liquid rises to about two inches surrounding the roast. If this is not enough, add some more wine.

Simmer the roast for 2-3 hours, turning it on each side so that it cooks evenly throughout. If the liquid reduces too much, add a little more wine.

To serve: remove the meat from the pot and set aside on a cutting board. Strain/remove bay leaves with a slotted spoon.

Using a potato masher (or an electric hand blender, if you have one), blend the cooked carrots and onions into the liquid.

Mash the gingersnaps in a small Cuisinart (or blender) until you have about 2/3 C ground ginger snap crumbs. Add them a little at a time to the meat juices, mixing well, until you reach the gravy consistency you wish.

Serves 5-6 adults, approximately.

Suggested sides: cooked carrots, oven-roasted fresh brussel sprouts, mashed potatoes, pickled red cabbage.

Not-Vito's Choucroute Garnie

*I was horrified to discover that Vito's various means of
killing kielbasa are based (loosely) on fact, according to
my better half, the Chef. Apparently, there are as many
versions of Choucroute Garnie as there are Vito's best
intentions not to destroy it. Oy vey. The version below is
my take on this game; which personally I find well suited
as comfort food in the winter.*

1 large can of sauerkraut, rinsed
1 large onion, chopped
8 small red-skinned potatoes (or 4 large, halved)
1 lb. (small bag) baby carrots
1 apple; cored, peeled and chopped
3 bay leaves
1 heaping teaspoon caraway seeds
1-2 cups white wine (a good Chardonnay will do)
2 slices thick-cut bacon
1 lb. *smoked* Kielbasa
1 lb. Knockwurst
1 lb. pork chops

Preheat the oven to 350-degrees F.

Rinse and drain the sauerkraut well, and spread across
the bottom of a *large* roasting pan (I use glass/Pyrex).
Sprinkle the chopped apple and caraway seeds on top.

Cook the bacon in a skillet. Remove the cooked bacon
and set aside. Add the chopped onion to the bacon
grease (you may want to add a little butter.) Cook until
translucent. Combine with the sauerkraut/apple mixture
in the roasting pan.

Melt the butter in the skillet and combine with vegetable oil. Cook the pork chops to brown on each side; until about half-way cooked through. Add the pork chops to the center of the roasting pan, resting on top of the sauerkraut mixture. Crumble the bacon and sprinkle on top of the pork chops.

Prick the skins of the Knockwurst, then add to the roasting pan, to surround the pork chops. Add the carrots to the outside of the Knockwurst, to outline the meats with a carrot 'ring'.

Cut the kielbasa into 2-inch sections and add to the edges of the pan, alternating with the red potatoes.

Place the roasting pan on an oven rack, and add about 1 cup of the white wine. Bake until all meats are cooked, approximately 1 hour; times will vary. Also, you will want to look in on it every 20 minutes or so, to adjust adding more wine or not.

To serve: remove from oven and let 'set' for about 10-15 minutes. Serve with a slotted spoon, making sure a taste of each meat is included in each portion.

Serves 6 adults, approximately.

Suggested sides: green salad topped with sliced apple and a light champagne vinaigrette; French/Italian bread.

Christmas Party Cocktail Quiches

This is the type of hors d'oeuvres Chef Jacque could probably whip up in his sleep. He certainly would have served it (or something similar) at the catered Christmas party featuring Tipsy Town Gal. This is an easy take on making mini quiches for a crowd.

Mini-muffin tins (more than 1 is better here…)
Pam or other non-stick baking spray
2 packages refrigerated biscuit dough
6 oz. grated Swiss cheese
5 oz. diced ham (can be found pre-cooked/prepared)
1 ½ cups heavy cream
Small onion, minced
2-3 tablespoons butter
3 eggs
Dashes to taste: salt, pepper, cayenne, nutmeg
2 good shots of brandy (other 'spirit' substitutions can be made here if brandy is not on hand; blended whiskey; sherry, etc.)
Small can crushed pineapple
~ ½ cup white granulated sugar

Preheat the oven to 350-degrees F. Spray the mini-muffin tins with the baking spray.

In a small skillet, sauté the minced onion in butter (make sure the onion is minced *very* finely; I used my mini-Cuisinart for this one.) Transfer to a mixing bowl when translucent.

Mince the ham a little at a time in the Cuisinart (or, dice finely on a cutting board). Add to the mixing bowl with the onion.

Add the 3 eggs to the mixing bowl and stir well. Combine the cheese and heavy cream; mix well. Add salt, pepper, cayenne and nutmeg to suit. Set aside.

Break apart the dinner rolls, cutting each roll into quarters. Roll the quarters out until they can be manipulated to line each mini-muffin cut-out. (I'm not a huge fan of rolling pins; for this recipe I used a heavy old-fashioned glass and rolled *carefully* to avoid getting broken glass in the mix. It doesn't take much effort.) NOTE: open up 1 package of biscuits at a time, and keep refrigerated to roll as you go. If you are re-using the same muffin tins, wait until they cool before repeating this step. Otherwise, your dough will get very sticky and cling to everything – including rolling pins or rolling pin substitutes.

Divide the ham/cheese/cream mixture into the shells (I used a small gravy ladle which I found useful.) Bake for 10-12 minutes or until golden (everyone's oven varies; and the mini-sizes cook more quickly.) When done, remove to a platter to serve immediately, or to a cookie sheet if guest are to arrive later (these warm up well in the oven, on a 200-250 F setting).

To make the pineapple dipping sauce: strain the crushed pineapple and combine with about half a cup of sugar in a small saucepan and heat until simmering. Cook until the liquid reduces, and add a small amount of cayenne to taste, if you wish.

This recipe makes 60 mini-quiches; it can serve up to 20 adults if it is serve with other appetizers. This is also a recipe that freezes well; including the pineapple glaze. To freeze any extras; put the quiches in an air-tight freezer bag. Freeze the pineapple glaze in a separate bag (to avoid freezer burn.)

Not-Miriam's Bloody Mary

My husband and I had the dubious adventure of flying from Harrisburg to Tampa, during a period in which Chef Husband sported a full fiber glass foot cast on his right foot. We can vouch for the efficiency and compassion of the airport "train shuttles" in Charlotte, NC, as much as we can the Bloody Mary in the Tampa airport. The fun part of this beverage was it being served in a pub-style beer glass, edged in chili salt. Here ye be.

1 small can tomato juice
Tabasco sauce
Worcestershire sauce
Prepared horseradish
Chili powder
Cayenne powder (optional)
Salt
Fresh lime
Celery stalks (optional)
Vodka

In a small pitcher (or other container), combine: 2 shot vodka, dashes of Tabasco, Worcestershire, horseradish and chili powder to taste, along with some cayenne if you really like a zing. Add a good amount of ice, stir, and set aside.

For the glass to be served: combine about 1 teaspoon chili powder and ½ teaspoon salt onto a small saucer or salad plate. Quarter the lime. Rub the lime quarter on the rim of the glass, then 'dip' the glass into the chili/salt mixture to rim the glass. Fill the glass the ice, and pour the Bloody Mary mixture, straining the old ice. Squeeze the quartered lime onto the top of the beverage. Garnish with a clean celery stalk as a "stirrer" if desired. (Or, you might opt for a bamboo shish kabob skewer stacked with tomalives.)

Pork Tenderloin with Balsamic Raspberry Gastrique

An easy dish that looks like you fussed. Enjoy a good read while you wait.

1 pork tenderloin (averages 1lb. to 1 ¼ lbs.)
Salt and pepper, to taste
Olive oil
Crushed rosemary leaves, about 1 teaspoon
4 tablespoons balsamic vinegar
4 tablespoons sugar
1 heaping teaspoon raspberry jam

Preheat the oven to 425-degrees F. Spray the roasting pan with the baking spray.

Place the pork tenderloin in the roasting pan, and liberally rub with olive oil. Sprinkle the rosemary leaves over the top and sides, as well as salt and pepper. Add a small amount of water to the bottom of the pan (2-3 tablespoons) to avoid sticking.

Place in oven and cook until the top appears brown. When brown, remove the meat from the oven (it will not be cooked at this point). Lower the temperature to 350-degrees F. Once the new setting is reached, return the meat to the oven (if you keep the meat in the oven while waiting for the temperature to adjust, you will risk overcooking/drying the meat as these are usually very small/lean cuts of meat.)

In a small saucepan, heat the balsamic vinegar and sugar together and stir until completely blended, much like a simple syrup. Add the raspberry jam a little at a time, to taste. Heat until ingredients are completely dissolved, and the sauce reaches a thick consistency.

To serve: let the tenderloin rest for 5-10 minutes before slicing. Arrange slices on a platter, with the gastrique in a separate container for individual serving.

Serves 4 adults, approximately.

Suggested sides: roasted vegetables; red potatoes, onions, carrots, little parsnip, baby beets. Other sides: sautéed zucchini; cauliflower; baby carrots.

Roast Cornish Game Hens with Pomegranate-Hoisin Glaze

Mina used a duck for her version; but I'm averse to blow-drying in the kitchen. Also, the hens are pretty to serve whole on a platter (if they are small). If they are large enough for 2 adult portions, prepare by cutting in half prior to baking, then arranging the cooked halves on a serving platter.

4 small Cornish game hens (or, 2 larger hens)
4 tablespoons butter
½ teaspoon smoked paprika
Salt and pepper, to taste
½ cup pomegranate juice
1 cup Hoisin sauce
1 tablespoon brown sugar
Baking spray

Let the butter become soft, at room temperature. Preheat the oven to 350-degrees F. Spray the roasting pan with baking spray.

Rinse and clean the hens, discarding any enclosed giblets, etc. (If you are using larger birds and wish to half them, cut them in half at this point.) Place in roasting ban and pat dry.

In a small bowl, combine the softened butter with the smoked paprika. Liberally rub the butter mixture over the skin. Add salt and pepper to taste. Place into the oven and bake, uncovered, until the birds are almost cooked, about 45 minutes – 1 hours (depending on size).

Christmas Bizarre

While the hens are baking: in a small saucepan, mix together and heat the pomegranate juice, Hoisin sauce and brown sugar until everything is blended, and the consistency is similar to barbeque sauce, but a bit thinner.

Remove hens from oven, and coat them with the pomegranate-hoisin sauce mixture. Return to oven, lowering the temperature to 300-degress F (to avoid burning the sugar in the sauce; if your oven runs hot, you might want to lower more but adjust your cooking time, it will take longer to finish baking the birds.)

To serve: allow the birds to rest for 5-10 minutes before placing on servicing platter.

Serves 4 adults, approximately.

Suggested sides: wild rice, asparagus (baked or grilled), creamed onions, spring salad.

Made in the USA
Middletown, DE
05 December 2014